my
silver
LINING

ROSEWOOD RIVER

my silver LINING

ROSEWOOD RIVER

USA Today Bestselling Author

Laura Pavlov

Entangled Publishing, LLC
644 Shrewsbury Commons Ave., STE 181
Shrewsbury, PA 17361
rights@entangledpublishing.com

Amara is an imprint of Entangled Publishing, LLC.

Visit our website at www.entangledpublishing.com.

Edited by Sue Grimshaw
Cover design by Hang Le
Stock art by firina/iStock, tomograf/iStock, and Md Ashik Sarker/Shutterstock
Interior design by Britt Marczak

ISBN 978-1-64937-943-6

Manufactured in the United States of America

First Edition March 2025

10 9 8 7 6 5 4 3 2 1

ALSO BY LAURA PAVLOV

ROSEWOOD RIVER

Steal My Heart
My Silver Lining

HONEY MOUNTAIN

Always Mine
Ever Mine
Make You Mine
Simply Mine
Only Mine

MAGNOLIA FALLS

Loving Romeo
Wild River
Forbidden King
Beating Heart
Finding Hayes

COTTONWOOD COVE

Into the Tide
Under the Stars
On the Shore
Before the Sunset
After the Storm

*To every woman who already knows how to ride a white horse
and isn't looking for a man to rescue them...*

You haven't met Rafe Chadwick yet.

1

Rafe

"I think we could totally make a volcano," I said, scratching the back of my neck. My nephew, Cutler, was in town for the holidays, and they'd be heading home tomorrow. I'd taken him sledding earlier and wanted to spend a few more hours with him before I returned him to my sister, Emerson, and Nash.

"It's so cool, Uncle Rafe. We made one in school, and you've got to see this," he said.

Cutler Heart was seven years old and the coolest little dude around. My sister was engaged to his dad, Nash, and they were getting married here in Rosewood River in a few months. She was in the process of adopting Cutler, and our whole family was crazy about this kid.

I searched *DIY volcano* on my iPad, and it looked simple enough. "I've got a soda bottle we can empty and use, and I've got the dish soap. All we need is vinegar and baking soda."

"Oh, man, I hope we don't have to drive to the store. It's snowing outside," he said.

"I'm a resourceful guy, Beefcake," I said with a laugh. Cutler liked to be called by his handle, which was hilarious. Like I said, this kid was a cool cat. "I bet Uncle Easton has that stuff in his pantry in the main house."

I was temporarily staying in my brother's guesthouse, as my home was in the midst of a large renovation. He moved in with his girlfriend, Henley, whose house was up the street. Apparently, Henley's best friend was going to stay in the main house for a few months, and she'd be here at the end of the week.

All I brought with me was clothing, toiletries, and a few things from my home office. I'd be staying in the guesthouse for two to three months, or at least that's what my contractor had promised.

"I thought Henley's bestie was living in the big house?" Cutler asked, as he dropped my cowboy hat on his head and checked himself out in the mirror.

"Yeah, she had a bunch of boxes shipped here yesterday, but she won't be here until the end of the week. I've got the key, so let's go look in the pantry. I bet we'll find both of these things in there."

"Good idea. Can I wear your hat?" he asked.

"Of course. You look far too cool to take it off." I grabbed the key to the main house off my counter, and we made our way across the paved area leading to the back door.

When we stepped inside, there were a few boxes stacked against the wall. "Apparently, she's got a lot of clothes. I mean, she's only staying for three months."

I made my way through the kitchen, with Cutler right behind me.

"Yep. My mama has a lot of clothes, too, Uncle Rafe."

"She sure does." I pulled open the pantry door and immediately found a box of baking soda and shook it in front of him. "One down. Now to find the vinegar."

The sound of something falling from down the hallway had us both straightening.

"What was that?" Cutler whispered.

"I don't know. Maybe it's just the heater clicking on." I held up my hand for him to stay put. "Wait right here. Let me go check it out."

I came around the corner and saw the light from under the door in the bathroom. Did some teenager think he could crash here while no one was living here?

Are you fucking kidding me?

Was someone actually squatting in Easton's house?

This was Rosewood River. People didn't squat. Hell, people didn't break into homes here.

Before I could reach for the handle, the door pulled open, and honey-brown eyes locked with mine, just as a hard fist collided with my throat. The stunning blow had me falling back against the wall as I gasped for air.

What the actual fuck is happening?

"Who the hell are you?" a woman shouted, as I coughed a few times and took her in.

She was standing in a fighter's stance, as if she were preparing to attack me again.

"Did you just fucking throat punch me?" I clutched my neck as I straightened, standing a good foot taller than her.

She was petite, gorgeous, and without a doubt, a violent lunatic.

And what the hell was she wearing? She had some sort of cheetah print robe on, with a hood over her head.

"Damn straight, I did. I'll ask you one more time. Who are you?"

"I'm Easton's brother. Who the hell are you?"

"Oh." She dropped her arms and relaxed her body as she raised a brow. "I'm Lulu, Henley's bestie. You must be *Rafael*. You're one of the Chad-dicks. I thought you were staying in the guesthouse?"

"It's Rafe, and that would be Chadwick. Not Chad-dick." I rolled my eyes at the fact that she said my name with a shit ton of confidence, even though she was incorrect. "And yes, I am staying in the guesthouse. I thought you weren't supposed to move in until the end of the week."

"There's a storm coming, so I arrived a little early. I wasn't aware that I needed to run it by you. Do you always just let yourself into a home that isn't yours?" she hissed.

"Uncle Rafe. Are you okay?" Cutler called out from the kitchen, and I could hear the concern in his voice.

"Everything's okay, Beefcake," I said, my voice loud enough to carry down the hall.

"My God. You brought a child with you," she huffed, as she stormed past me in her ridiculous cat costume. "You do know that breaking and entering is a crime, right?"

I groaned as I followed her to the kitchen. "It's not breaking and entering when it's your brother's home and no one is supposed to be here."

"Henley knew that I was coming early." She stopped when she saw Cutler standing there, cowboy hat on his head, and chocolate smeared on his cheek.

"Beefcake. What are you eating, buddy?" I asked.

"I found some chocolate chips in the pantry. And I found the vinegar. And who did you find?" he asked, taking his hat off as he walked toward her.

"It looks like Henley's friend decided to move in early."

She shot me a glare over her shoulder. "Beefcake. I've heard so much about you. You're Easton's nephew, right?"

"Which also makes him *my nephew.*" I pushed past her and took the chocolate chips from Cutler, pouring a bunch in my hand before handing back the bag. "Damn, I forgot how much I like these."

"Okay, we need some ground rules. You can't just barge in here unannounced. I could have been compromised." She placed her hands on her hips, and damn, she was pretty. Not a stitch of makeup. I could tell she had blonde hair, even though it was hidden behind the ridiculous fuzzy hood.

"Compromised?" I asked.

"Yes. What if I wasn't decent?"

"I can't even imagine the physical violence that would have taken place if I'd walked in on you naked. The throat punch was a bit much, considering you were fully covered in a cheetah print costume, and there was no threat." And now I couldn't get the idea of her naked out of my head, although, she was basically wearing a bedspread over her body, so she wasn't giving anything away.

Cutler's head fell back in laughter. "Uncle Rafe, you can't say naked to a girl you just met."

Says who?

"Well, it's nice to see that one of you has manners." She closed the distance between us and put her hand out to Cutler, and he poured a bunch of chocolate chips into her hand. "Thank you. I'm Lulu, by the way."

She offered him her other hand, completely ignoring me.

"I'm Cutler, but my friends call me Beefcake." He waggled his brows. Damn, the dude had game. "Henley's my girl, and if you're her bestie, then I guess that makes you my girl, too."

Her lips turned up in the corners, and she was that breathtaking kind of beautiful, even if she was an angry little wildcat.

"That's the best offer I've had in a very long time. Consider me your girl, Beefcake. And how about you teach your uncle some manners about entering a home without knocking?"

More laughter from Cutler. Clearly, the kid had no loyalty when it came to a beautiful woman.

"Listen, *Wildcat*," I said, accentuating the nickname because if she was going to dish it to me, she should be prepared to get it dished right back. "You weren't supposed to be here. You arrived early. I'm living in the guesthouse of a property owned by my brother. And I took a pretty good hit to the throat, so I'd say I'm not the only one lacking manners."

She popped the last few chocolate morsels into her mouth and raised a brow. "If you enter a home I'm staying in unannounced, prepare to take a hit, buddy."

I moved closer, and she straightened her shoulders. "You knew I was staying in the guesthouse. You could have checked before striking."

"That's not really my style." She smirked.

"This is a small town, not the city. You need to take it down a couple dozen notches," I said, trying to contain my irritation because my throat was still sore. I glanced at Cutler, who was looking between us with concern.

We'd come for vinegar and baking soda, not to commit an armed robbery.

Her lips twitched the slightest bit. "You can never be too prepared for an attack. You've been warned."

"Not to worry. I won't be returning anytime soon. We got what we came for," I said, taking a step back and grabbing the baking soda and the vinegar off the counter. "Nice robe, by the way. It screams feral cat, so it's very fitting."

She narrowed her gaze. "Thank you. I wasn't looking for fashion advice from a man who looks like he shops at Baby Gap."

I glanced down at my clothes, taking in the navy long johns and gray hoodie that I've had on since we went sledding earlier.

The nerve of this woman.

Cutler found the comment hilarious.

"Uncle Rafe, she called you a baby."

"Let me ask you, Beefcake. You know your animals. Does Lulu here look like she's wearing a cat costume?"

He reached for my cowboy hat and popped it back on his head, before smiling up at her. "Prettiest cat I ever saw."

"Thank you, Beefcake." She sighed before turning to me. "Are you done robbing the kitchen? I'd like to get out of my *costume* and get dressed."

Damn. I wouldn't mind seeing her out of the robe, even if I found her incredibly annoying.

"We've got all we need. Thanks for the throat punch and the hospitality," I said, oozing sarcasm.

She ignored me and bent down to hug Cutler. I wasn't sure why he was getting special treatment. Hell, he was the one who wanted to make the damn volcano. He broke in here right alongside me.

"It was nice to meet you. Henley told me so much about you, and she was spot on. You are one cute kiddo."

He clutched his chest dramatically. "I'm all man, Lulu."

I chuckled and shook my head. "Let's go, little man. I'd say it was nice to meet you, Wildcat, but I can't lie in front of my nephew."

"Yes. Breaking and entering you're okay with, but lying is where you draw the line. I'm so impressed."

I winked as I pulled the door open, and Cutler jogged toward the guesthouse. Lulu stood there with her arms crossed over her chest, glaring at me.

"Look at that. You're already warming up to me." I smirked.

She flipped me the bird, and I chuckled as I let the door close behind me.

I'd definitely be staying clear of the little deviant.

2

Lulu

"I'm totally down with the small-town vibes here," I said, sipping my pumpkin chai latte with a shot of espresso and caramel drizzle. "And they even do custom orders at this adorable coffee shop."

Henley shook her head. "Well, aside from the fact that on your first day in town, you throat punched Easton's brother."

"Listen, that guy had it coming. He came slinking down the hallway unannounced, like some sort of predator. I can't help it if my bat senses were screaming *stranger danger*. Coach Jones was very impressed with my quick reaction when I told him about it." I leaned back in my chair, glancing at the cute chandelier hanging above. Rosewood Brew Coffee had this sort of French farmhouse vibe. I liked that everything was slower here. Calmer, in a sense.

Well, aside from the intruder a few days ago who turned out to be the brother of my best friend's boyfriend.

"Lu," she said over her laughter. "It's his brother's house. He's living in the guesthouse. He's far from a predator."

"And how would I possibly know that?"

She shook her head. "He said you were stronger than you looked. I don't think he'll be coming around anytime soon."

"He was downing chocolate chips minutes after. I think he'll be just fine." I quirked a brow. "*Rafael* seems like trouble anyway."

Her head tipped back in laughter. "Rafe is not trouble. He's a really good guy."

"He oozes big dick energy, and that's always a big red flag for me." I shrugged. "It's best to scare those types off right from the start."

"You're ridiculous. He's Easton's brother, so you better lighten up. He's got a big family, and you're coming to Sunday dinner with me tomorrow."

"Fine. But you know family dinners freak me out. Why do you think I arrived early? My family vacation was an absolute nightmare."

"Okay, so finish telling me what happened. I know you said that Charlotte was being judgy, per usual. She's always given off haughty vibes, but it sounds like she's getting worse."

Charlotte Sonnet was my cousin. She was my Uncle Charles's daughter on my father's side, and she's always had this edge about her. Normally, I enjoyed a woman with an edge, but not the bitchy kind of edge that my cousin had. She was four years older than me and acted like I was the dirt beneath her manicured fingernails. I've dragged Henley to plenty of family gatherings, and she's seen my cousin in rare form many times.

"Worse is an understatement."

"I mean, she did marry a congressman and have a wedding fit for a royal." Henley chuckled. "Her ego is clearly even bigger now. Let me guess, she brought up the fact that Beckett made a scene at the last family get-together?"

Beckett Bane was my ex-boyfriend, and also the lead singer of the biggest boy band of our generation, Tier One. He was a thorn in my side, a pain in my ass, and the bane to my existence.

All the puns intended.

We broke up over a year ago, yet whenever he returned from tour, he made every attempt to rekindle things with me, much to my family's disdain.

My father was still fuming about the holiday dinner that Beckett had crashed with my grandparents in the city, as he'd created quite the embarrassing scene. He flipped a table at Javier's Steakhouse with the paparazzi there to catch it all on film.

This was the thing about my ex. Most of his meltdowns had very little to do with his feelings for me. It was more about the attention that my last name garnered.

He thrived on media attention like a fraternity bro on spring break.

"Obviously, she brought it up ad nauseam. She made comments at every painful meal we were forced to eat together, asking if we should worry that someone might come in and flip our table." I rolled my eyes. "We were at the family compound in the Hamptons. That's not really the douchebag's hangout of choice."

Henley used her hand to keep her laughter quiet. "I've always thought she was jealous of you. She likes to act like she oozes confidence, but I think she's very insecure. And that husband of hers just goes along with whatever she says."

"Ya think? That jackass annoys the hell out of me. He does this thing where he repeats everything she says. As if we didn't hear her say it the first time."

"Nooooo. Example, please."

"Happy to oblige. She would say, 'I hope no one barrels through the door and flips the table.' Then he says, 'Yes, darling, I hope no one flips the table.' And then she says, 'This table is an antique and has been in the family for generations.' He looks me dead in the eyes and says, 'Did you hear that, Lulu? It's an antique and has been in the family for generations.'" I used my finger to pretend to make myself vomit.

"Yet you didn't throat punch him?" Henley asked with a chuckle.

"No. Because every time this would happen, I'd glance at my father, and he didn't appear irritated with them. All of his frustration was aimed at me." I took another sip of my tea and set my cup down. "As if I'm responsible for Beckett's irrational behavior."

"Listen, you can't control what he does when he comes into town. You've ended things. You've blocked him. Your father needs to stop blaming you for everything that asshole does."

"I know. And most of the time, I'm just trying to survive in this family. It's not easy being the black sheep, you know?"

"You're the only normal one in that family."

"Amen to that, girl."

"How was your mom? She brought Francois, right?"

Francois Tremblay was my mother's psychic and spiritual advisor. She relied on him for everything, and he had a weird obsession with my aura. She brought him to any family function with my father's side of the family because she said he helped keep her centered with the in-laws.

"She sure did. You best buckle up, Hen. This was the reading of all readings. My mother decided to have us all sit around the table, and he literally went from person to person, telling them who they were in their past life. And everyone got to hear what he said because it wasn't a private reading. It was mortifying."

"Ohhhh. I'd be lying if I didn't admit that I always love hearing what Francois has to say."

"That's because it's always been about the future. And apparently, my future is very bright. However, my past is shady as fuck, and he didn't hold back."

More laughter from my best friend as I sipped my tea.

"Tell me."

"Well, let's just say that Charlotte was some sort of healer back in the day. She cured some rare disease called Lakacocky, or something crazy like that."

"I've never heard of it," Henley said.

"Because she literally found the cure, and it's the reason that we're all alive today." I blew out a frustrated breath because my cousin's ego was already too big to fit through the doorway, and now she believed she was the reason we all existed. "And her jackass of a husband was some sort of general back in the day, and he conquered too many places to remember."

"Oh, boy. What did he say to you?"

"Apparently, I was a very busy lady back in the day. He painted me out to be some sort of colonial whore who had the hots for Ben Franklin," I hissed, trying hard not to laugh because I couldn't make this shit up. "Francois said that Ben reciprocated the feelings, but he chose to marry for status, and me being a commoner made it impossible for him to commit to me."

Henley had tears streaming down her face as she shook her

head and tried to speak over her laughter. "He did not say that."

"Oh, yes. And Charlotte could not have been more invested in my history, nor could her weird-ass husband, who kept staring at me while licking his lips."

"Well, all the cousins couldn't have been the reason we're all still alive today. Someone else must have had a shady past?"

"Wishful thinking. Barron was a king, and he had seven wives, yet for whatever reason, I'm being shamed because I had the hots for one man. And it appears that Cousin Barron hasn't changed at all. That dude has been engaged four times and never married, yet everyone focuses on my one bad decision of dating the world's biggest douchebag." Barron, my eldest cousin, is Charlotte's older brother, and the first grandson in the family to carry on the Sonnet name. The Sonnets were a well-known political family, as my great-grandfather had been the vice president of the United States back in the day. Two of my uncles were in politics, as well, and Hunter fit in perfectly as a congressman with aspirations of being president someday. Though I think he just liked saying it, and personally, I thought he'd probably hit the height of his career with this recent election.

But I just made jewelry for a living, so what did I know about political aspiration?

"Listen, you know that you're Gramps' favorite. And he's the best, so that's a win."

My grandfather is one of my favorite people on the planet, and he'd always been the one who saw me and appreciated me exactly as I was. Everyone else liked to focus on what I'd done wrong.

"That is definitely a win." I reached for my cup and took another sip. "And now I just have to figure out a believable reason as to why my very serious boyfriend isn't coming with me to Gramps' eightieth birthday. Charlotte was questioning me like she worked for the CIA."

"So they all think you have a serious boyfriend in Rosewood River, right?" Henley asked.

"Yes. My dad was losing his mind over Beckett's stunt. I already told them that I was seeing someone who was stable and reliable and respectable. I guess I got caught up in the whole thing, because he was ridiculously happy when I'd mention my mystery man. I was actually nervous that Francois would blow my cover."

Henley shook her head as she took a moment to process my current situation. "Thank goodness Francois was focused on the past."

"No. It gets even better. He actually helped me out. He told them all that they were going to love this guy, but then he shit on my parade by telling them that I'd be bringing my boyfriend to the big birthday celebration next week," I groaned. "Trust me, if it were anyone else's birthday, I would bail and make up an excuse about why I couldn't make it. But I can't miss Gramps' eightieth birthday. So I just need an excuse for my amazing, responsible boyfriend's absence, and Charlotte is going to be all over me like flies on shit."

"You could say that he's sick and you didn't want to risk getting your grandparents sick." Henley shrugged. "Did you give a name for this so-called dream boyfriend?"

"I had to think on my feet. I just called him Lover Boy, but of course, my mother, with her French accent, calls him, *Love Her Boy*." Now it was my turn to laugh. My mother was fabulously French and creative and quirky. I loved her fiercely, but she was like an attention-challenged whimsical fairy, which made it difficult to have an actual conversation with her about anything serious. My father was a much tougher nut to crack, and as his only child, his expectations were high, as was my ability to let him down. But at the end of the day, I knew they loved me. Being a Sonnet came with a load of pressure, and it could be very exhausting sometimes.

"Okay, so you tell them that Love Her Boy has come down with a bad case of Lakacocky."

We both fell back in our chairs in a fit of laughter.

"Then I'd have to hear how Charlotte cured the brutal disease," I said with a groan. "I'll drop the bomb soon that he's got a nasty virus. That way I'll prepare them for him not being able to attend the party."

Henley suggested, "You could just find a boyfriend and make things a lot easier."

"I need a break from toxic men at the moment." I shrugged.

"You need to get back out there, Lu."

"Well, that's going to be very tricky, seeing as I supposedly have a fake boyfriend now. I can't risk being photographed by the media on a random date. So I'm going to just read lots of dirty romance while I'm in Rosewood River and focus on the new designs for Luxe."

"I'm so proud of you, Lu. Luxe is the most exclusive department store in France, and they chose to partner with you. Your designs are going to be a known brand worldwide. You created MSL and look how many people love it."

"I just wish my father would finally recognize the business that I've built. He still sees me as the screw-up who dated the toxic rock star. Like what does it take to realize I'm not that girl anymore? Anyway, the fact that I have this amazing man in Rosewood River finally has him asking about my business, my designs, and my plans."

"Beckett sucks ass," Henley said, as she arched a brow. "You could barely stand him the last year you were dating him, not to mention how happy you've been in the year since you broke up with him. So, I'm thrilled that you've found a wonderful man to settle down with in Rosewood River, even if he is fictional."

I chuckled. My bestie was the one person who totally got me. She always had my back, and I always had hers. She was the sister that I always wanted. We met in boarding school in ninth grade, and we'd been inseparable since.

"Yeah. It's going to suck when I have to break up with Love Her Boy when I move to Paris for the launch in three months."

"Maybe you'll fall in love with small-town living and tell Paris to suck it." She winked playfully. "I'm proud of you. And I'll take the three months that you're here and enjoy every minute. I wonder how you'll break up with your soulmate."

I thought it over, because I'd eventually have to sell the breakup as hard as I sold the relationship. "It can't be messy. I think I'll make him a workaholic. I'll tell my parents he's too dedicated to his profession, and I just can't be with someone who's married to his job. Or I could blame the distance. Geographically undesirable. That's believable."

"The poor guy suffered from Lakacocky first, and then he's a miserable workaholic who lives on the other side of the world in the end. I do hope you and Love Her Boy are at least having lots of good fictional sex right now."

"Girl, of course, he's a fabulous lover. The man has the stamina of a high-end porn star. He's fictional, after all. We can make him anything we want."

"Sounds like you've really built this guy up. It's a good thing he's not going to meet your family." She chuckled.

"No man can fill the shoes of Love Her Boy at this point,"

I said, glancing out the window to see the snow coming down harder. "So what does one do with all that snow when you're living here? I haven't used a shovel in a very long time."

"Don't worry. Easton has someone who comes and shovels the driveway for you. He should be by later today. Or you could always have your hot lover boyfriend shovel for you."

"Yes. He's very manly that way. Big arms, big shovel... big dick."

Henley spewed coffee across the table as we both fell forward in laughter.

Three months in this charming, snow-covered small town, with my best friend and my fictional boyfriend, was exactly what I needed to get my life back on track.

3

Rafe

"I'm glad you made it back to Rosewood River. You probably shouldn't have ventured into the city this morning with the storm rolling in," my boss said through the Bluetooth speaker in my car. Joseph Chapman was a ball buster. He was claiming it wasn't safe for me to have come to the city today, yet he called me last night and demanded I be present for our meeting with our wealthiest client this morning.

"Four-wheel drive is coming in handy today." I turned down the final street toward my brother's house.

"Work from home tomorrow," he said.

Will do. Tomorrow is Saturday, so no one went to the office on Saturday. Including Joseph.

"I'll definitely work from home. And you've only got two

more weeks as a single man, huh?" I teased, because he was getting married soon.

"Yep. But I'm too old for bachelor parties, so I'll just be drinking whiskey with my brother at the club." He laughed, and a husky, deep sound rumbled through the speaker, probably due to years of smoking cigars.

"Sounds like a good plan."

"Denise mentioned that you RSVP'd for two. I guess we're finally going to meet this mystery woman you keep speaking about."

"Yep. She's looking forward to it. She's heard a lot about you over the last few months," I said, making a mental note that I needed to find a date to his wedding to play along with my story of being in a serious relationship. It had been the only reason I could come up with as to why I was unable to date his daughter Chloe.

Joseph had pushed it.

Chloe had pushed it.

I'd made it clear that I had a serious girlfriend, who would now be attending his wedding with me. I had a few women that I could ask to play along, but I hadn't reached out to any of them yet.

I'd be doing that this week for sure.

"All right, good work today. I'll see you on Monday," Joseph said.

"Yep. Have a good weekend."

I came to a stop when I approached the house and took in the scene playing out in front of me. The little hellion staying at my brother's place was wearing jeans, ridiculously high-heeled boots that came up to her knees, a white ski coat, and a white hat with a pompom on the top that was bigger than her head. She'd clearly never shoveled snow before, as she was slipping all over the place, and every time she scooped a little bit of the white powder, she tossed it over her shoulder and back onto the driveway.

Perhaps she should take fewer self-defense classes and learn how to use a shovel.

I parked in front of Easton's house and climbed out of my truck. I hadn't seen her since she karate-chopped me in the throat and accused me of breaking and entering.

I made my way up the driveway, shaking my head at the fact that she was making more of a mess shoveling than there was before she started. The snow was coming down hard, making it difficult to see. But she was sliding all over the place, so she was easy to track.

"Where's Janson? Easton hired him to shovel a couple of times this week, and today was supposed to be a shovel day," I called out.

She whipped around to face me, and I put my hands up to block her, just in case she decided to throw a punch.

"I'm not going to hit you, you big baby," she hissed, as she grunted and dropped the shovel. "Janson drove all the way over here and knocked on the door just to let me know that he couldn't shovel today."

"And did you hit him over the head with a bottle, kick him in the balls, cut off a finger maybe? What is the consequence for coming to the door?" I asked, trying to hide my smile because she was glaring at me.

"I don't attack people who knock on the door. Only those who break and enter when I'm coming out of the shower!" she shouted. "And apparently, Janson has a haircut appointment today, so he won't be shoveling. But he said he'd come by tomorrow, but only if his girlfriend doesn't want to *hang out*. I mean what kind of employee is he?"

"He's a seventeen-year-old teenager with really good hair." I barked out a laugh.

"Is this funny to you? My car is going to be trapped in the garage. I don't have snow tires."

"Well, here's a little tip, Wildcat," I said, quirking a brow as her honey-brown gaze locked with mine. "You don't wear heeled boots to shovel snow."

"These are the only boots I brought. I wasn't planning on shoveling. I thought plows did that."

"Plows clean the streets. The driveway is up to the homeowner. Why didn't you just call Easton?"

She swiped at her face as the snow landed on her dark lashes. "Because I'm not some damsel in distress. I can figure it out."

"That doesn't seem likely." I smirked, leaning down to grab the shovel.

She shoved me out of the way and reached for the shovel. "You don't know anything about me. Maybe I grew up in the snow. Maybe I'm a professional shoveler."

"For fuck's sake. Give me the damn shovel." I tried to take the handle from her. "You are just moving the snow from one side to the other. You clearly don't have a clue how to shovel."

Before I could process what she was doing, she stepped on the scoop side of the shovel as it sprung forward, aiming for her face. I quickly shielded her with my body as the damn thing hit me hard in the side of the head. I fell forward, taking the stubborn woman along with me, and we both landed in a bed of snow.

"Get off me, you big buffoon."

I rolled off her as I rubbed the side of my head. "Damn. You nailed me in the head, woman."

She pushed to sit up, and I groaned.

"Shit," she whispered. "Did it hit you in the head?"

"Yes."

"Well, why would you jump in front of it?" She studied me before turning my head to the side so she could look for a bump.

"Because it was going to nail you in the face, and I was trying to get you out of the way."

She used her teeth to tug her white furry mitten off her hand, and she dropped it in the snow. Her fingers moved through my hair, and it pissed me the fuck off that my dick responded immediately.

Great. Now I have a throbbing headache and *a throbbing erection.*

"You have a big goose egg on the side of your head." She winced.

"You don't say?" I oozed sarcasm. "You stepped on a metal shovel, and the handle slammed me in the side of the head."

"I thought I could catch it." She continued soothing the lump that was growing just above my ear.

"Clearly, you thought wrong," I said, sitting forward. "I'm fine. How about we agree that shoveling is not your forte."

"Fine. I'm retiring as a snow shoveler. I'd rather be with Janson getting a haircut."

"That's a safer bet." I moved to my feet and offered her a hand up. "Listen, I just got off work. Do you need to get your car out tonight?"

"No. I just thought I should keep up with it."

"Let me get inside and ice my head and make some dinner. I'll shovel it first thing in the morning, all right?"

"Thank you," she said, and her eyes kept looking toward the side of my head. Obviously, the ice queen had some sort of feelings because she appeared concerned about the shot I'd taken. "I'm sorry about the shovel to the head."

"Really?" I raised a brow. "It seems to be your thing."

She walked toward the main house, brushing her snow-covered jeans off as she moved. Her ass was impossible not to stare at. It was small, perfectly peach-shaped, and it almost made me forget that she caused me pain every damn time I saw her.

"What's my thing?" she asked, as she paused at the back door to the main house.

"Well, the first time I saw you, you punched me in the throat. The second time I saw you, you hit me in the head with a metal shovel. What are you going to do at our next meeting? Stab me in the dick?"

She surprised the shit out of me when her head fell back in hysterical laughter. *Lulu Sonnet actually laughed.*

And I was surprisingly mesmerized by it.

"Careful, Rafael. Don't give me any ideas." She smirked as she turned for the door. I watched as she stepped inside, and the door closed behind her.

I made my way to the guesthouse and pushed inside, rubbing my hands together to warm them up. I turned on the fireplace, grabbed a beer and an ice pack, and dropped onto the couch.

My phone vibrated with a text in the ongoing family group chat I had with my brothers and cousins.

Easton: *Archer, I thought you told me Janson did a good job shoveling for you last winter. The dude no-showed today.*

Archer: *Yeah, he bailed on me, too. He didn't have a girlfriend last winter.*

Clark: *Women are always a distraction.*

Axel: *He bailed on me too. Said he had a haircut, and he has senior photos next week, so he couldn't miss it.*

Bridger: *Stop being pussies and shovel your own damn driveways.*

Archer: *Don't have time to shovel. I have a child to take care of.*

Axel: *And this is why you need a nanny who isn't a hundred and seven years old.*

Clark: *The kid doesn't graduate for months. I highly doubt he's getting senior pictures in the middle of a snowstorm. Trust me, he's got a girlfriend, and he can't see straight.*

Bridger: *Women are nothing but trouble.*

Me: *Hey, I happen to love women. Well, aside from the heathen living across the yard from me.*

Easton: *Are we talking about Lulu Sonnet? Stay the fuck away from her. She's Henley's best friend, and she's off-limits.*

Me: *That should be easy enough since she beats the shit out of me every time I see her.*

Me: *<selfie of me with an ice pack on my head>*

Bridger: *Isn't this the same woman who throat punched you a few days ago?*

Clark: *She sure did. He was being dramatic when I stopped by that day. He kept coughing and saying she damaged his trachea.*

Me: *Dude. She karate-chopped the shit out of my throat. We're talking "Karate Kid," Mr. Miyagi type of shit.*

Easton: *I love that movie. But, how much damage could she do? She's half your size, you dicksicle. Man up.*

Me: *I'm going to throat punch you when you least expect it. <middle finger emoji>*

Easton: *Will you be hitting me with your tampon or your lipstick?*

Me: *Scratch that. I'm going to kick you in the dick. <eggplant emoji>*

Archer: *Back to the important question. Why do you have an ice pack on your head?*

Axel: *Inquiring minds want to know.*

Me: *She was shoveling the driveway in the most ridiculous heeled boots, and I tried to help her after she dropped the shovel. She decided to pick up the shovel by stepping on the scooper, and the handle would have knocked her ass out.*

Clark: *So you headbutted her?*

Easton: *That's a very gentlemanly thing to do.*

Me: *Fuck off, Lugnuts. I moved her out of the way, and the shovel hit me in the side of the head.*

Clark: *So this is really Janson's girlfriend's fault. <laughing face emoji>*

Bridger: *Why would anyone step on a shovel versus picking it up?*

Me: *I didn't ask when the metal handle was aiming for her face.*

Easton: *You are one chivalrous bastard.*

Archer: *Death by shovel is no way to go.*

Me: *Tell me about it. I took a good shot to the head.*

Clark: *I've taken many shots to the head on the ice. Try a cold beer with that ice pack.*

Me: *<selfie of beer and ice pack>*

Axel: *Sounds like Henley's bestie has it out for you.*

Clark: *He's not used to women hating him.*

Bridger: *Maybe you should ice your ego.*

Me: *I may have a concussion, but by all means, take this moment to shit on me.*

Easton: *Someone is feeling very sensitive.*

Bridger: *He hasn't been laid in a while.*

Me: *How the fuck would you know?*

Bridger: *Because you're always a moody prick when you go more than a few weeks.*

He was right, but I wouldn't tell him that. I hadn't been out much because I'd been buried at work.

Easton: *Your fake girlfriend doesn't put out?*

Me: *Don't you worry about me or my fake girlfriend. We're doing just fine over here.*

Clark: *Answer your door, assmunch. I came to check on you. We can order dinner.*

Axel: *Beware of any random shovels coming for your head, Clark.*

Easton: *Remember, someone is living in the main house. So if you two fuckers have a bunch of beers, do not wander over there. If you do, prepare to be punched in the throat.*

Archer: *My money is on Henley's friend. Sounds like she takes no shit.*

Axel: *Wait. Is she hot?*

I pulled the door open, and Clark walked in, holding up his phone.

"They want to know if Henley's friend is hot?"

I groaned. "Yes. The heathen is hot."

Clark: *He said the heathen is hot.*

Me: *I'm sitting next to you. You didn't need to type that. I could have answered.*

Easton: *The heathen is named Lulu. Consider her off-limits to all of you fuckers. But yes...she takes no shit. Don't mess with her.*

Me: *No problem. I barely know her, and she's caused me physical pain the two times that I've seen her.*

Axel: *Color me intrigued.*

Me: *<middle finger emoji>*

Clark laughed as I dropped my phone and finished my beer. My head had finally stopped pounding.

There was a knock on the door, and I pushed to my feet as Clark scrolled through the TV channels.

Lulu Sonnet was on the other side of the door when I pulled it open.

I narrowed my gaze. "Did you come to murder me, Wildcat? Because if you did, my brother is here, so there's a witness."

"Such a sensitive little flower," she said with a chuckle as Clark hurried over to the door to check her out.

"Hey, I'm Clark Chadwick. Would you like to come inside?" he said.

"You don't even fucking live here," I hissed.

"Neither do you. It's Easton's house."

"Hey." She snapped her fingers in front of us. "I'm not coming in. I was just unpacking my supplies to work on some designs, but I found some malachite and thought you might want to keep it nearby."

She handed me a green stone, and I studied it. "Is it poison? Do you want me to eat it?"

"You don't eat it, Rafael." She shook her head with disbelief. "These stones are a good form of protection. You know, because you're so accident-prone."

"Accident-prone? You throat punching me was not an accident. Nor was the fact that you stepped on a shovel and nearly killed me."

"You broke into the home I was staying in and then you dove in front of the shovel. You fell on top of me. You could have crushed me. So trust me, this is as much for my protection as yours. I can't have a walking disaster living in my backyard and not be concerned for my safety."

Clark was hysterically laughing now, and Lulu's lips turned up in the corners.

"I like this girl," my brother said, and I glared at him before turning my attention back to her.

"Does it ward off evil spirits?" I asked, quirking a brow as her gaze locked with mine.

"Are all the *Chad-dicks* this dramatic?" She smirked before turning on her heels and walking toward her house.

"Nice to meet you!" Clark shouted, and she held a hand over her head and waved.

I punched him in the stomach before slamming the door. "She just called you a Chad-dick, you dumbfuck. Do not flirt with the devil."

"My dick is not offended by the nickname. And she's fucking hot."

"Yeah. Spend a few minutes with her and see if you're still standing after."

He barked out a laugh, and I glanced out the window toward the main house across the yard. She was standing in the kitchen, and I hated that I couldn't stop staring.

She was fucking hot.

And that pissed me off.

4

Lulu

"So, you have dinner every Sunday with your family?" I asked as Easton drove us to his parents' house. Henley insisted I come with them because she wanted me to meet Easton's family. I'd already met Rafe, a.k.a. Rafael, and the man was infuriating. He brought on both incidents that had taken place, and he was blaming me?

I even offered him a malachite stone as a peace offering, and he managed to make that dramatic.

I'd also met the hockey player, Clark.

Obviously, I knew Easton, and aside from the ones I met at the hospital when Henley had had a rafting accident, there were only a few more Chadwicks to meet tonight.

"Yep. We've done it for as long as I can remember. But my

mom said she has something to talk to us about tonight, so buckle up, because you never know what will happen at these dinners," Easton said.

"Ahhh… I'm sort of an expert at crazy family dinners."

"I can vouch for her on that. You never know what will happen at a Sonnet family gathering." Henley laughed. "You're going to love the Chadwicks. Sunday dinners are my favorite. There's a game room, and they have your favorite game that includes balls and sticks."

"Stop it right now!" I squealed. "There's a pool table?"

Easton pulled into the driveway and turned around and looked at me over his shoulder. "I take it you play?"

"Do I play? Are you seriously asking me that?"

"Yes. I believe I just did." He chuckled as he put the car in park.

"Tell him, Henley," I said over my laughter as we stepped out of the car, and I was grateful that it had finally stopped snowing.

"Lu is kind of a shark. She loves to go to bars and pretend she doesn't know how to play, and then she smokes all these guys who think they're playing an amateur."

He quirked a brow. "So you're a pool hustler."

"Amongst other things," I said, as we walked up to the front door.

Easton barked out a laugh. "Let's not say a word to Rafe. He's the best pool player I've ever seen, and no one challenges him, so I say we just let things play out."

"I can't wait to see Rafael lose his shit when he gets smoked by a woman." I chuckled as we stepped inside.

It was chaotic and loud, but I thrived in these kinds of environments. Once I met and greeted everyone, I made some fairly quick assessments.

Easton's mom and dad, Ellie and Keaton, were the quintessential parents. Sweet, quirky, and charming. Like something you'd see on a family sitcom.

His brothers had notably different personalities, yet they finished one another's sentences. It was impossible to miss how close they were, even though they gave one another shit the entire time.

Keaton sat behind the bar, giving me the quick lowdown on all of his children.

Bridger was the oldest of the brothers. He owned an IT company and invented some sort of groundbreaking software two years ago, which made him a billionaire by the age of thirty. He was a man of few words—which I personally enjoyed.

Rafe was the second oldest, and apparently, he was some sort of numbers genius, working in finance for the top investment firm in the city. He drew the most attention in the group and was annoyingly charming.

I knew the type—and I made a point to avoid it at all costs.

Easton was a brilliant attorney, as was my best friend. He had a twin sister, Emerson, who was a pediatrician and now lived in Magnolia Falls. She was getting married in Rosewood River in a few months.

Next, there was Clark, the professional hockey player. He oozed confidence and absolutely adored his family.

Keaton handed me a glass of Chardonnay and continued telling me about his four sons and daughter.

"And those guys who just walked in are my nephews, Archer and Axel. Axel is the same age as Rafe, and those two always got into a fair amount of mischief growing up. But Axel builds custom horse trailers and is quite the artisan. People come from all over the country to work with him. Archer is the oldest of all these hooligans, and he's a commercial realtor. He's basically the only land guy in Rosewood River, so he knows everything that's coming to the area. That little angel, Melody, is Archer's baby girl, and we're all madly in love with her. And you already met my brother and his wife, Carlisle and Isabelle, and they live in the house right next door."

"I love how close you all are," I said, taking a sip from my glass as I watched Rafe scoop up his niece, Melody, as her head tipped back in laughter.

"Yeah, my family is my greatest joy." He took a sip from his beer bottle. "Are you close with your family? I understand you've got a pretty famous family, right?"

I chuckled. "We're close, but in a different way. We didn't grow up like this—you know, hanging out the way your family does. But we do get together often for holidays and celebrations."

I liked the comfort between them. My family didn't have that kind of comfort or closeness. I was on edge when I was at a family event. Endlessly seeking my father's approval. Preparing to be mentally challenged by my cousin Charlotte at all times. There was pressure to be on your game when you were at a Sonnet family gathering. My mother's side of the family was much more relaxed, but they lived in Paris, so we didn't see them as often.

"Okay, stop talking her ear off, and let's have dinner," Ellie said, and Henley came over and looped her arm through mine.

The dining room table sat the entire group, and I settled in the chair next to my best friend.

Rafe walked over and took the seat on the other side of me, quirking a brow as his gaze met mine. "Keep those utensils on the table please."

I rolled my eyes. "That's a bit dramatic. I've been told that you're in finance, but I think you missed your calling in the theatre."

The table erupted in laughter, but I hadn't even realized they were listening with all the side conversations going on.

"Hey, I'd react if someone came into my house unannounced when I was getting out of the shower, too," Ellie said, passing the basket of garlic bread around the table.

"People come to your house unannounced all the time," Rafe said, taking two pieces of bread and passing me the basket. His fingers grazed mine, and I pulled away quickly before he returned his attention to his mother. "I've yet to see you punch anyone in the throat."

"I think it's impressive," Isabelle said, winking at me. "A woman who knows how to protect herself."

"Thank you. I've trained in martial arts for the last year, and I like knowing I can protect myself if needed." I scooped the pasta onto my plate, and the smell of tomatoes and basil had my stomach growling.

"I think it's sexy," Clark said, waggling his brows, and Rafe glared at him.

"It's fine. My vocal cords have recovered. Now I'm just waiting for the concussion to go away."

More laughter.

"So, what's the big news you wanted to tell us?" Easton asked, glancing over at his parents.

"Well, you know your father is selling his HVAC company to Ronny," Ellie said, as she scooped two meatballs onto her plate.

"Keaton is retiring this year. Ronny is a guy who's worked for him the last ten years," Henley whispered to me, bringing me up to speed.

"I'm glad you're slowing down, Dad," Rafe said, and he put some noodles on little Melody's plate and winked at her.

"Me, too. And Mom and I were trying to decide what we

wanted to do. If we wanted to travel the world and where we'd want to go," Keaton said. "So, we've decided to follow our passion when the time comes, and we wanted you to be aware of our plans."

"What does that mean?" Bridger grumped.

"It means we're going on tour with Jelly Roll!" Ellie squealed with a wide grin spread across her face. "We love his music, and we're going to be groupies."

I coughed over the sip of wine I'd just taken, but I covered it quickly. I glanced around the table to see everyone gaping at them.

"What? You're going to follow a musician on his tour?" Easton asked, not hiding his shock.

"Have you heard Jelly Roll's music? It speaks to us," Keaton added.

"It's so deep and emotional. We just love it." Ellie reached for her wine glass. "So, yes. We're throwing caution to the wind and after Emerson's wedding in March, we'll be traveling to exciting new places and hitting all of Jelly Roll's concerts for a couple of months."

"I'm speechless." Bridger looked between his parents as if they'd lost their minds.

"Well, that's not saying much. You don't have a whole lot to say normally." Rafe barked out a laugh.

"We're going to meet them at a few of the shows. I just love his music, too," Isabelle said.

"I think it's great that you're going to do something that you love." Henley forked some pasta and popped it into her mouth.

"I'm also a big Jelly Roll fan," I said. "I saw him live once, and he was amazing."

"Yes, his music is just so beautiful." Ellie shrugged, and her husband winked at her.

"You dated a musician, didn't you?" Rafe asked, and the whole table turned to look at me.

"Are you stalking me now?" I flashed him my famous death glare.

"In your dreams. Clark brought the *Taylor Tea* rag over yesterday, and she said the new girl in town is some big deal in the jewelry world and used to date that boy bander, Barrett something, so I assumed that was you," he said, as he popped part of a meatball into his mouth.

"Beckett Bane," Henley said, bumping her shoulder into me. "We don't like him anymore, and they've been broken up for a long time."

"Good. I never cared for his music." Ellie winked at me.

"Why are you guys reading that trash?" Bridger grumped.

"I find it kind of entertaining," Clark said.

"And they haven't written about any of us in a while." Axel held up his wine glass. "Congrats on being welcomed to Rosewood River, Lulu. Henley made it in there when she first arrived here, too."

"I normally despise press and paparazzi, but I like the small-town gossip angle. It's kind of fabulous." I smirked as I raised my glass. "Thanks for having me."

The conversation flowed, and we drank more wine and finished off the delicious homecooked meal with apple pie and whipped cream.

Archer said he was taking Melody home to put her to sleep, and Isabelle and Carlisle walked them out and said they were heading home as well. Ellie and Keaton said goodnight as they went to their bedroom to watch a movie, and Clark refilled mine and Henley's wine glasses.

"Let's play some pool tonight," Easton said, and we all followed him to the large game room down the hallway. They had a pool table, a fully stocked bar, and two oversized couches that sat on each opposing wall.

We spent the next hour playing game after game, and I was in my element. I loved pool. Loved knowing how to put the balls where I wanted them to go. I've been playing for years, and it was a skill that had come in handy more than once. And tonight, it was a skill I was very grateful for. Rafe was by far the best player in the group, and I'd say we were evenly matched. We both knocked everyone off one at a time, as we'd played multiple games, and it finally came down to just he and I.

I welcomed the challenge.

He was a cocky bastard, the way he circled the table, studying the location of the balls and deciding his next move. He was very smooth.

Go figure.

The man oozed big dick energy, and he clearly knew how to handle his stick and balls.

Pun intended.

He almost won on his first break, as he'd been down to just one ball, and it had been a tough shot. A shot that I admittedly would have had a hard time making, as well.

But the guy wouldn't stop talking shit every time it was my turn.

Trying to get inside my head with his annoying comments.

Lucky shot.

Easy shot.

The ball practically put itself in that hole.

That one required very little skill.

I was down to one ball on the table now. The room had

grown quiet, as our heated banter had either entertained them or terrified them. I wasn't sure.

But everyone was sitting on the couches, watching this heated battle play out.

This shot would be tricky to make. Not impossible, but I wasn't overly confident. And I didn't want him to get another turn, because the thought of him gloating was all the motivation I needed to walk away with the win.

I bent down, eyeing the path from the ball to the right corner pocket. I rolled my stick through my pointer and middle finger, warming it up.

The large pompous ass standing at the end of the table was distracting me, and I didn't appreciate it.

"Can you please move out of the way? I'm trying to focus," I hissed.

"I'm behind the shot. I'm hardly in your way," he said, knowing he was getting under my skin. "Maybe it's too much pressure, and someone should stick to making jewelry."

Oh, no, he didn't.

Game on, Rafael.

I pulled back, determined to sink the shot.

But the stick slipped against my fingers, and I made contact too low with the ball. I put force behind it because I knew it was going to have to move quickly to make it across the table.

My eyes widened as the ball caught air and moved like a bullet, stopping only when it made direct contact with Rafe's groin.

My *ball hit* his *balls.*

He howled and then disappeared as his body hit the floor.

Damn it. This wasn't good.

Everyone was on their feet, moving toward him, and I hurried around the table and winced at the sight of the poor bastard covering his family jewels with his large hands.

"For fuck's sake, you heathen. What is your deal?" he shouted.

I bent down and studied him. "That was an accident. Did you not bring the malachite stone?"

He slowly moved forward to sit up and glare at me. "I did not bring that ridiculous rock with me because I assumed you would find a way to use it against me."

I tossed my hands in the air. "There you go. You have no one to blame but yourself."

"She may have a point. I took the stone off your counter, and I haven't been injured once," Clark said, winking at me.

"Everyone has lost their fucking mind." Rafe pushed to his feet and closed his eyes before taking a few deep breaths, which I guessed was an attempt to brush off the pain.

He marched to the other side of the table, setting the ball that had damaged his goods down in the center, and he didn't even hesitate. He pulled back his stick, sank the ball in the center left pocket, and dropped the stick onto the table.

"I win, Wildcat. Better luck next time."

I quirked a brow, my gaze locking with his dark eyes. "Well, I'm still leaving with a set of balls, which is more than you can say."

"That makes no sense. You don't have balls," he said, moving closer and invading my space.

"I don't know about that," Bridger said. "From what I can tell, this girl's got a big set of cajónes."

Laughter surrounded us, but Rafe's gaze never left mine.

Game on, asshole.

5

Rafe

I've never iced so many body parts in my life. My throat had recovered, but my head still hurt, and my dick had just taken one for the team.

I'd do it all over again to see her little hands fist when I sank that ball in the left center pocket and she was forced to concede.

I'd been up and working from home this morning for all of twenty minutes when someone knocked on the door.

Not once. Not twice.

At least a dozen times.

I made my way through the small space and pulled the door open to see my nemesis on the other side.

"Wildcat," I said, calm and ready for whatever she was going to throw at me today.

I reached into my pocket and found the green stone that I'd snatched back from Clark last night, and rubbed it between my fingers because I didn't trust that this woman wouldn't cause me pain once again.

"Rafael," she purred, her voice lighter and sweeter than usual, but her eyes looked slightly frantic. She was wearing a pair of jeans, a white turtleneck sweater, and some sort of colorful scarf tied around the top of her head. Long blonde waves fell around her shoulders, and I tried hard not to stare.

"What can I do for you?"

"Funny you should ask." She cleared her throat and pushed past me into the house, even though I hadn't invited her in. "I need a favor."

"That's rich. Why would I do you a favor?"

"Because my options are limited. So, basically, you're here, and I don't have a lot of time. So, if you do this for me, I'll owe you one."

"You'll owe me one? What does that mean? Are you saying that I can have anything I want?"

"It depends how well you play the part." She smirked. "But yes, within reason."

"Wow. You must be really desperate." I walked to the counter in the kitchen, picked up an apple, and took a bite.

"It's pretty simple, actually." She walked past me and grabbed an apple out of the same basket, acting like she owned the place before taking a bite.

The woman oozed confidence and sex appeal, and as much as I despised her, I would be lying if I said I wasn't intrigued.

And by intrigued, I mean that my dick was highly entranced with her.

And considering he'd been through a trauma—caused by

her—that was saying a lot.

"Take your shot." I leaned my ass against the kitchen counter and crossed my feet at the ankles.

"Okay. Time is of the essence, so try to keep up." She paced in front of me.

She was nervous.

I liked it because it meant I had all the power in the situation.

"I'll do my best."

"My family, well, they aren't like yours. Everyone is kind of… competitive."

"We're competitive. That's not unusual," I said.

"This is different." She came to a stop in front of me. "My cousin, Charlotte, is a real piece of work. But she's the shining star, so to speak, and she loves to point out that I'm sort of a black sheep."

"You don't say?" I said, not hiding my sarcasm.

Color me intrigued.

"Here's the short version. I dated a guy who became a famous rock star after we were together, and let's just say he's an unpredictable time bomb. He's pulled me into his endless drama, dragging my name into the press all the time." She shrugged. "But I've been done with that for a long time. However, no one seems to believe me. So, I stretched the truth a bit and said I had a very serious boyfriend in Rosewood River, and that's why I was coming here for three months."

"And you don't have a boyfriend here?" I asked, already knowing the answer.

"Correct."

"You didn't stretch the truth, Wildcat. You lied. I can't condone that kind of behavior." I smirked. "Is this because you're still in love with the boy-band shit show you used to date?"

"No. I can't stand the guy. But I haven't met anyone, probably because I kind of hate men at the moment. No offense."

"None taken. Being hated by you feels like a compliment."

She snapped her fingers in my face. "Focus, Rafael. I have no time for games. It's my grandfather's eightieth birthday next weekend, and they want me to bring my boyfriend to the family party. I've told them that he has a bad virus—you know, the kind that's super contagious. It's a reasonable explanation for why he can't make it. But they texted this morning and said that my cousin Charlotte, the ice queen from hell, is telling everyone I made the whole thing up and that my boyfriend is fake."

She gaped at me like this was the most incredulous thing she'd ever heard.

"So, Charlotte would be correct, then?" I arched a brow.

"That is not the point. I denied the allegations, of course. I told them that my boyfriend was in the shower and that we'd FaceTime them in twenty minutes. I don't have time to go find myself a fake boyfriend right now, so I need you to just come over to the house and act like the doting boyfriend. Tell them you wish you could come to the birthday party, but you don't want to risk getting my grandparents sick. Act like you are crazy about me, and that's it. Five minutes of your life. And I'll owe you a favor." She smiled like this was no big deal.

"What do they know about me?"

"What? Why does that matter? It's a five-minute call with people you don't know. Just roll with it. We know how theatrical you are already, so this plays into your wheelhouse."

"Don't try to flatter me. What do they think I do for a living?"

"I haven't told them. They just know that I'm ridiculously in love with a man who isn't a rock star and is an upstanding citizen. That's all they needed." She started to walk toward the door.

"So, if I agree to this, what do I get in return?" I already knew I would agree to it, I just wanted to see her squirm.

"What do you want?"

"Oh. If you put it that way, I could think of several things."

"Let's hear it."

"Hmmm... anything I want?"

She rolled her eyes, glancing at the watch on her wrist as if time was of the essence. "Try me."

"I'd like you to crawl to me and then settle between my thighs and give me the best blow job of my life." I knew that would piss her off, and I'd enjoy it. Not that I'd actually have her go through with it. She'd probably bite it off.

"You wish. I don't crawl for any man. And all sexual favors are off the table." She crossed her arms over her chest, pushing up her perky tits the slightest bit, and I internally scolded my dick for reacting.

Again.

"I figured as much." I chuckled. "So, I'll need you to agree to go to my boss's wedding with me in two weeks. Put on a show like we're ridiculously in love because he thinks I have a girlfriend."

"So you lied about the same thing, yet you shamed me for doing it?" she huffed.

"Correct."

"Is the wedding a one-day thing?"

"Not exactly. It's a weekend full of events. We already have a suite at the Four Seasons booked. Your man is already spoiling you."

"I'm asking you for five minutes, and you expect me to give you a weekend?" she hissed.

"It's a hard line for me. That's the deal."

"Fine. You get me my own room, and I get to order as much room service as I want, and you throw in a massage and a facial."

"Yes, to everything but your own room. My boss, Joseph, has a daughter."

"And this is my problem… why?"

"His daughter, Chloe, has been trying to close the deal with me for months. She'll be watching like a hawk. We have to stay in the same room."

"You'll order a cot?"

"Nope. She could find out. She's a persistent little thing."

"You'll sleep on the floor," she said, raising a brow as she studied me.

"I've sustained several injuries this week, and I'm not adding back pain to the list." I laughed. "I'll sleep above the covers, and you can sleep below."

"I agree to everything but the sleeping arrangements. I'll spend the weekend acting like you're an amazing boyfriend, but you sleep on the floor or the deal's off."

"Ah… someone's afraid to sleep in the same bed as me." I winked. "Fine. Done deal."

"Great. We'll work out the logistics after the call. Just follow my lead. And pour on the charm. They'll love that." She took one more bite of her apple and tossed it in the garbage before storming toward the door.

I followed, of course. My eyes were unable to focus on anything but her tight little ass.

I couldn't help myself.

She may be a heathen who'd caused me too much pain to overlook, but my fake girlfriend was hot as hell.

We stepped into the main house, and it smelled like vanilla and jasmine. There was a sketchbook on the table with drawings that I wanted to look at further, but she hurried me over to the couch.

"Okay, just agree with whatever I say. They can be very inquisitive, so keep it simple. But let them know how amazing I am and how crazy you are about me."

"Should I kiss you? Cop a feel? A little under-the-sweater action?"

"Are you high?" She gaped at me, pointing to the couch for me to sit before she settled beside me. I pitched my apple core in the kitchen and quickly washed my hands before joining her.

"No. I'm working from home today. I'm just trying to figure out what you want."

"If you attempt to kiss me or make a move, I will twist your balls so hard they'll fall off your body."

"As your fake boyfriend, I feel inclined to tell you that you're very difficult to be in a relationship with." She turned to look at me, adjusting the colorful scarf on her head.

"I am not."

"I've dated plenty of women before you, and no one has ever caused me so much discomfort without giving any sort of affection back to me." I shrugged, trying hard not to laugh.

"Put your arm around me and get into character."

"Oh, I'm there, Wildcat. Don't you worry. Parents love me. I've got this. Cousin Charlotte is going to be a jealous little beeyotch after she hears about us."

This earned me a laugh. A genuine, from the belly, real laugh.

I puffed up my chest. I was already winning the boyfriend game.

She dialed her phone and waited for the screen to display her parents.

Wow. The apple didn't fall far from the tree. She looked just like her mother, but a younger version. Her father was a good-looking man, in that stately, wealthy sort of way.

"Hey there. I wanted you guys to meet Rafe. He's definitely very real, so you can let Charlotte know that there are no fake boyfriends over here," Lulu said, and I pulled her a little closer, as my arm was wrapped around her shoulder.

"Rafe. Hello. It's so wonderful to meet you. I'm Noemie, and this is my husband, William," her mother said, with a French accent.

"It's wonderful to meet you both. I can't believe anyone would accuse my girl of having a fake boyfriend. I promise you, I'm very much real," I said, winking at the phone. "And I'm crazy about my little wildcat."

Both of her parents chuckled before her father spoke. "We're just happy that she's no longer in that toxic relationship. That man, if you can even call him that, has caused her and our family more trouble than I can say."

Lulu sighed. "It's been over for more than a year, Dad. I wish you'd stop bringing it up. I can't help it if every time he does something, it embarrasses you. I'm with Rafe now, so that's all that matters."

"Yes, sweetheart. I know it's not your fault. But then Charlotte was telling everyone in the family that she didn't believe your boyfriend was real because he missed the holidays and now he can't attend Grandpa's eightieth birthday party." Her father lifted his Starbucks white-and-green to-go cup and took a sip.

"It is such a shame, Rafe. We'd really love to meet you in person. And we'll all be staying at the beach house in Los Angeles, so the weather will be so lovely. You're sure you can't make it?" her mother asked.

Did she say beach house?

"He's had that virus, Mom. We don't want to get Gramps sick at his own party, not to mention Grandma as well."

"Rafe, you look well to me," William said. "And both of my parents have stronger immune systems than the rest of us."

"Thank you, William. I am feeling much better." I moved my hand to play with the ends of Lulu's hair. I wasn't even acting at the moment. I wanted to see if it was as silky as it looked.

Her blonde tresses did not lie, unlike the little deviant who was having me pretend to date her.

Glass houses and all that, because I'd be doing the same thing at my boss's wedding in the not-too-distant future.

Her fingers found mine, and she made it appear that she was being touchy-feely with me, but she dug her nails into my knuckles, an obvious attempt to make me stop touching her hair.

"But he was sick for quite a while, so I'm sure he's just exhausted. This poor guy has had the shits for days. We almost had to put him in a diaper," Lulu said.

I was pissed that I was meeting her parents for the first time, and she was giving me a bad case of the shits?

I wasn't going down that way.

I didn't give a shit if this was fake; a man had his pride. I placed my hand behind her head, tucking my fingers into the back of her hair before pulling her closer to rest her cheek on my chest. "It was rough, but actually, it's been two days with no incidents. My doctor cleared me to go back to work today. So, my little wildcat can put those diapers away, at least until we're in our eighties and need them again." I kissed the top of her head as her fingers dug into my thigh in the most painful way.

I released her, and she sat forward.

"Oh, this is fabulous news. Is this why you wanted to FaceTime us, Lulubelle?" her mother said.

Lulubelle? That little tidbit was going in the vault for a later date.

"No, actually. I was FaceTiming just so you could let Charlotte know that you met my boyfriend in person."

"You know she never gave us your name before now, Rafe." Noemie chuckled. "She called you Love Her Boy."

William and I both chuckled like we were old friends.

"She does like to call me that. She's got so many pet names for me, it's adorable." I winked at my fake girlfriend. "But I believe my little wildcat kept my name from you because she's desperate to protect this special thing we've got going."

Lulu's foot pressed down so hard on mine that it was challenging not to wince. "The nickname is actually *Loverboy*, Mother. It's just one of many things I like to call my man." She slapped her hand down a few times on my thigh, and it still stung from where her blade-sharp nails had tried to draw blood. "But I can't ask him to put his health and the health of our family at risk."

"Nonsense. We've got a private plane to fly you both to the beach house in a few days, so he wouldn't even need to go to the airport or subject himself to any illness there. We'd be pleased to have the family meet you, Rafe. It's about time our daughter brings home a man who has an ounce of class to the family gatherings." Her father kept his lips in a straight line, giving very little emotion, which made him hard to read.

"William, I assure you, I am overflowing with class," I said, with a playful chuckle.

"So you'll come, then?" Noemie clapped her hands together. "It'll mean so much to all of us."

"I wouldn't miss this special occasion for the world. Gramps is turning eighty, after all. Lulu talks about him all the time," I said.

"We're looking forward to it. The whole family will be there. And you can show Charlotte for yourself that you're very much real," William said.

"Personally, I think Charlotte has always been a little jealous of our Lulu. Hopefully, she will let it go now." Noemie smiled and then swiped at an invisible tear below her eye.

"I can't wait to meet you all in person and start making some good ole Sonnet family memories."

"We look forward to it. See you both in a few days."

Lulu had gone completely silent over the last part of the conversation, and I wasn't sure that she was still breathing.

"You okay, Wildcat? Just overcome with emotion about your parents and I finally meeting?" I asked, winking at the phone screen.

She nodded. "Yes. That's exactly it. We'll see you soon."

"Love you, Lulubelle," her mother said, and her father gave a curt nod.

"Love you, too," she said.

I said my goodbye, just as she ended the call and turned her imminent rage in my direction.

"What the hell was that?" she shouted.

I leaned back on the couch and reached into my pocket, pulling the green stone of protection out and holding it in front of me to ward off her attack.

She slapped it out of my hand and pushed to her feet as it rolled beneath the coffee table. "You were supposed to spend five minutes impressing them. Not agree to fly to Malibu with the family, you jackass. Charlotte will sniff you out like a vampire at a blood bath. She's not oblivious like my parents, and she isn't easily fooled."

Lulu paced in front of me.

"You're overreacting," I said over my laughter. Her parents were great. People loved me. This would be a piece of cake.

"What if we find a reason to have you admitted to the hospital? We could use the pool stick to break one of your kneecaps," she said, her hands on her hips like she was completely serious.

"My God. You would harm me just to keep me from going to Malibu for a few piña coladas and some family fun?" I reached for the malachite stone on the floor and tucked it back into my pocket. "Good luck with that. My kneecaps will remain unharmed. I'm going to meet Gramps for his big day, and I'll charm the shit out of the ice queen, Charlotte. And then you'll return the favor and pour it on thick the following weekend. We kill two birds with one stone."

"What if I choose to save the birds and kill you instead?" she hissed.

"You're shit out of luck. I've got the green stone, Wildcat. And I'm looking forward to meeting your family and enjoying some warmer weather. You had me at beach house."

6

Lulu

"I cannot believe you're taking him to Gramps' birthday weekend," Henley said over her laughter, as I listened from the other end of the phone.

"Tell me about it. All he had to do was remain quiet and play along, but he couldn't follow simple directions."

"That's not really Rafe's speed. He beats to his own drum. But the good news is he's the life of the party. People love him," she said. "If anyone can pull this off, it's him."

"Well, he better. I'm not going to just stand by while Charlotte accuses me of having a fake boyfriend," I hissed. "Even if it's true, she will not be the one to figure it out."

Henley chuckled. "I couldn't agree more. And you leave tomorrow? What's the plan?"

"I ignored him for the last two days because I was seething that he messed up the plan, but I stormed over there this morning and told him that we were having dinner tonight so we could come up with a *new* plan. You know, learn about the other so we don't look like we're faking it."

"You know, this might actually be great. You always get stressed at these family gatherings and having Rafe there, on team Lulu, might make this weekend easier."

"He's hardly on team Lulu. The man can't stand me. And the feeling is mutual. And now he keeps holding up that damn stone to me like a shield, as if I'm the source of all his pain. He's ridiculous!"

She was laughing hysterically when the back door pulled open. "Hello, lover. I'm home."

"Ah... he's here, and once again, he entered without knocking." He wore dark jeans and a white button-up, and his dimples were on full display.

The sexy bastard was working my last nerve.

"I'll let you two go fight it out. I love you. Call me after and let me know how much you know about your new man." She chuckled.

"You're very lucky I love you. I'll call you later." I ended the call, and my gaze locked with his. "So you think you can just walk in here now? Even though I've shown you my moves and that I'm capable of dropping you to your knees?"

"Oh, I'll drop to my knees anytime you want me to, Wildcat." He pulled out the stone and held it up. "But, if you attempt to drop me for any other reason than to pleasure you, just know that I've got protection. So don't even try it."

I rolled my eyes and motioned for him to sit at the table. I'd set out two place settings, and I always kept fresh flowers on my table no matter where I was, and with the candle that was burning on the kitchen island, it started to feel like a date. So, I blew out the candle and moved the flowers to the counter. The table looked very bland now, which made me feel better. I'd also intentionally prepared a very unromantic dinner to keep things platonic. I set a baked potato in a large bowl in front of each of us, and all the toppings were set between us. Chili, cheese, sour cream, and chives, along with a basket of cornbread muffins. Delicious and also warm on a cold evening. And it screamed *platonic relationship*, because who in their right mind would eat chili on a date?

No one.

"What's all this?" He rubbed his hands together.

"It's a potato bar."

"Ah... this is information I should know. You wouldn't have struck me as a potato bar kind of girl."

"Which proves you know nothing about me. What would you have guessed I would be serving?" I asked, half irritated, half curious.

"I don't know. What do fancy people eat? Maybe caviar or sushi, or you'd sacrifice some extinct animal right before you served it to me."

I gaped at him. "I like fancy clothing and handbags, but I keep my food simple. In fact, I love themed meals."

"What qualifies as a themed meal?" he asked, as he loaded his potato with all the fixings.

"You know, hot dog bar, potato bar, taco night, a little pasta extravaganza."

"Ah... so a ball gown and a hot dog. Not what I was expecting, but good to know."

"So, we're going to have our work cut out for us. We leave

first thing in the morning, and between my cousin Charlotte, my father, and Francois, my mother's spiritual advisor, we're going to be under a microscope. Francois is a psychic, but if we know enough about one another, I think we can make him believe we're dating."

He finished chewing. "This Francois dude comes to all the family gatherings?"

"Yes. My mother can't travel without him. He's basically part of the family at this point, aside from the fact that his readings are often offensive."

"Interesting. So, what do you want to know?" he asked.

"Well, according to what I've shared with them, we've been dating for a few months. We should know a lot about one another."

"A few months? I just met you; how is that possible?" He waggled his brows.

"Remember, my mother thought your name was Love Her Boy." I chuckled before adding some more cheese to my potato of deliciousness. "So we've been together for a while, as far as everyone knows, and that's why I came to Rosewood River for the next three months."

"Ahhh… It's clearly been challenging for you to stay away from me. You packed up your shit to cozy up with Love Her Boy."

I rolled my eyes and laughed at the same time. "I made a list of questions, like basic things we should know. Here's a copy for you and a pen in case you need to take notes."

"I'm a numbers guy. All the notes stay right here, in the vault." He tapped his fingers to his forehead as he looked down at the piece of paper I handed him. "Okay, number one." He paused and reached for his water because I was not serving alcohol when I was determined to keep things very platonic. It had everything to do with the fact that he was sexy as hell, even if he annoyed the living crap out of me. "*How many siblings do you have?* Obviously, you already know that I have three brothers and one sister, and my two cousins are more like brothers. How about you?"

"I'm an only child. But Henley has always felt like a sister to me."

"You two met at boarding school? You both went away for high school, right?" he asked.

"Yes. We were roommates, and we've been besties ever since."

I thought he'd move to question number two, but God forbid he followed any kind of direction. Of course, the man would go rogue. "Was it lonely being an only child?"

"I've always been independent and good at taking care of myself." I scooped some more potato onto my fork and popped it into my mouth. "Next question."

"You didn't answer the one that I asked. I didn't ask if you were independent, I asked if it was lonely. Did you ever sit in your room alone and wish there were other people there?"

I groaned, but I thought it over. "Yes. I used to wish for siblings. My parents are very social people, so they weren't around a ton. But I always knew that I was loved, so it was fine."

He studied me for an uncomfortable amount of time, which was probably just a few seconds, but it felt like forever. "All right. This is helpful."

"Number two…" I cleared my throat. "Favorite place to travel."

"If I'm being honest, my favorite place is Rosewood River. I love the mountains and the water, and most of the people I care about are all here. I'm not a big traveler, but I commute to the city most days for work, so I get to experience a very different world when I'm there. How about you?"

I couldn't wrap my head around that answer. I didn't even know where I'd call home. I grew up traveling all the time. We had homes on the West Coast and the East Coast. I was homeschooled most of my life before going to boarding school.

"If I were to narrow it down to two places, I would choose Paris and Cabo." I chuckled. "I like to mix it up."

"Good answer. Number three. Favorite candy and road trip snack. Now this can tell you a lot about a person." He took a sip of water as he thought it over like I'd asked him to tell me what the meaning of life was. "My favorite road trip snacks and candy are beef jerky, Funyuns, Bugles, pickles, Snickers, and french fries dipped in a chocolate shake."

My eyes widened. "That was both disgusting and unusually specific."

"Hey, this should be a judgment-free zone. You can't judge a dude you aren't even dating. And those are some top-rated snacks right there."

"I don't even know what Funyuns and Bugles are."

His eyes darkened as he quirked a brow. "Oh, Wildcat, you haven't lived if you haven't tried them. They are not only deliciously crunchy, but Funyuns are addicting, and you won't be able to stop with just one, and the Bugles make perfect finger hats. Now tell me yours."

My head tipped back in laughter at his ridiculous answer before I shared mine. "Gummy bears. Popcorn. M&M's. I like the M&M's in the popcorn. It's a nice mix of sweet and salty."

He winced. "Lame. But I won't judge."

"Calling me lame *is* judging. And you have to know that gummy bears are a big part of my life. I always keep some in my purse, in my car, and in my home. Anyone dating me would know this. I also never eat popcorn without the M&M's. I wouldn't have either alone."

"Gummy bears. Got it. Popcorn and chocolate together is a must. It's all in the vault."

We discussed our favorite colors. His was red, and of course, he made fun of mine being periwinkle, which he said should just be called blue.

But I didn't like most blues.

I was a girl who had very specific tastes.

"So, why is your company named MSL?" he asked, before reaching for another cornbread muffin.

"That's not on the list," I said.

"I'm aware. These are very basic. I wouldn't ask any of these questions to someone I was dating. I've dated plenty of women, and I've never known their favorite road trip snack or their favorite color. But this would be the first thing I would have asked you if we were on a real date, after asking about your family and what you do for a living."

I wasn't a big fan of detouring from the plan, but he had a point.

"MSL stands for My Silver Lining. It's a tribute to my grandfather, who happens to be my favorite person on the planet. He's just always sort of gotten me, you know?" I reached for my water and wished it was a glass of wine because I was relaxed and actually having an easy conversation with my fake boyfriend.

"I get that."

"I wasn't a particularly easy kid," I said.

He chuckled. "You don't say?"

"I was headstrong and always trying to keep up with my older cousins at family events. And when I got frustrated that I couldn't beat them at tennis or board games or ride on the larger horses that my grandparents kept in the stables because I was much younger and smaller, I would go sulk and sit by Gramps. He'd tell me that if I looked hard enough, I'd see the silver lining. It became a game for us." I shrugged.

"Like seeing the positive in a frustrating situation."

"Correct. So, when I didn't get to ride Bruno, my grandfather's stallion, he would remind me that I was the only one who would get to ride and train the pony he'd gotten for me, and she'd grow up knowing me the best. Which is true. Penelope is the most beautiful horse I've ever seen, and she and I have a connection."

"She's your silver lining. I got it."

"And every piece of jewelry is unique at MSL, and I like to think that there's something special in each piece for the customer. I work hard on the designs and add custom stones and metals and details to everything I come up with. So the name works."

"It does."

"So, tell me what you do. I know you work with numbers. What does that mean?"

His lips turned up in the corners, and I'd never noticed how plump his lips were before now. This man definitely had no problem getting women to fall at his feet. A great reminder that he was the type of man I made a point to avoid.

Even if I was horny as hell lately, this was not the avenue we'd be taking to pleasure town.

Hell, I'd become a pro at pleasuring myself. I did not need to depend on any man for that.

"I'm a financial advisor. So, I assess the financial needs of my clients, provide recommendations like investments and life insurance, and help them build financial wealth."

"Ahhh… you help the client so the math is mathing."

He barked out a laugh. "I've never said that before, but sure, I guess I do that in a way."

"When was your last relationship?" I asked, wanting to finish the last question on the list.

"Would you ask someone that on a first date?"

"We aren't on a first date. They think we've been dating for a few months. We'd definitely know this." I reminded him.

"College was my last serious relationship," he said, wiping his mouth with his napkin. "But I date often. I enjoy women."

I rolled my eyes. "You just don't enjoy them for long periods of time."

"I'm not opposed to a serious relationship. I'm not a guy determined to be single." He shrugged. "I haven't been knocked on my ass by anyone, I guess. I watched it happen to Easton, and I think it's fucking amazing what he and Henley have. If I find that, great. If I don't, I'm pretty content doing what I'm doing for now."

He was a straight shooter, that much was clear.

But most playboys liked to say that they'd straighten their act for the right woman. The problem was, it was usually about the challenge, and then they'd lose interest.

I'd learned to think like a man… and I had my own big dick energy.

"Good answer. So, you'll make sure my family thinks I've knocked you on your ass."

"I can do that." He winked. "I'm guessing your last relationship was the rock star douchebag?"

"Correct. But I've gone on a few dates since, even if Beckett likes to come to town and act like we're still together. We haven't been together in over a year, and we never will be."

"How can you be so sure?" He leaned forward, invading my space.

"Because the night that I broke up with him—" I let out a breath because I didn't even like talking about Beckett anymore. "Let's just say, he made it so I'd never look at him the same. That ship has sailed. And I'm not looking to reboard any ships, so to speak. I like being single."

"Really. You're not looking for the fairytale?" He chuckled.

"Hells to the no. I know how to ride my own white horse. I don't need a man to rescue me. I like my life. I love my company, and at the moment, that's the only relationship I want to be in."

"Well, you kind of need me to rescue you, now, don't you?" he asked.

"I wouldn't call it rescuing. I would have been fine going by myself and just saying you were sick. You're the one who got yourself invited."

"Last question, Wildcat."

"I thought we were finished, but go ahead."

"When was the last time you had sex? Really good sex." He smirked, his dark eyes locked with mine.

He was good. But I was well trained at not being affected.

"You don't need to know that. It's a fake relationship."

"Hey, if you want me in character, I need to know these things about my lady," he said.

I leaned forward, my lips a breath away from his. "It's been a while since I've been with a man. But I know how to take care of my own needs."

"Last time you got yourself off?" His voice was gruff now.

We were going to be spending the next few days together. We agreed to get to know one another. This wasn't really necessary, but I never minded torturing a man.

"About an hour before you arrived, *Rafael*," I purred. "How about you?"

"As my fake girlfriend, you should know that I have a very healthy libido." He shifted the slightest bit in his chair. "Don't worry yourself with the last time I got myself off; just know that the next time will be about thirty seconds after I leave here."

And then he pulled back and smiled.

Did it just get hot in here?

7

Rafe

We had just boarded a private plane heading to Malibu, and the flight would be short, but it would give us more time to go over a few more questions that she'd apparently come up with during the night.

"Good morning, Miss Sonnet. Your grandfather sent me a list of snacks for you and your special friend, and I will bring them out as soon as we're up in the air," an older woman wearing a navy skirt, white blouse, and red cardigan said.

"Thank you, Beverly. This is my boyfriend, *Rafael*," Lulu said, rolling the last syllable ridiculously long before trying to cover her laugh.

I smiled. "You can call me Rafe."

Lulu moved to the two seats in the center aisle, and I sat

beside her as the older woman disappeared in the back.

"You gave them a list of snacks?"

"Yes," she whisper-hissed. "He always requests a list, and if I didn't list anything for you, it would look suspicious. Suck it up, Buttercup. And start gushing because Beverly has worked for the family for two decades, and she's always watching."

"Hey, Lu." A man opened the curtain and peeked his head out. "I heard you brought your boyfriend along for the birthday celebration. I'm happy to see you doing so well."

"Hi, Jerry. I was hoping you'd be flying us today. This is Rafe, and I promise he's much tamer than the last one I brought home," she said with a chuckle.

My jaw ticked, and I didn't know why I was suddenly irritated at the mention of her ex.

I was here now.

Or at least they thought I was.

So show me some goddamn respect.

"Nice to meet you, Rafe. Everyone, buckle up, we're cleared for takeoff."

"Nice to meet you." I checked my seat belt before reaching over and pulling Lulu's tighter around her waist as I whispered in her ear. "That's the last time we mention the ex. If this were real, I wouldn't tolerate it. You want me to play a role, then you best do the same."

Her eyes widened, and she glanced over her shoulder before slapping my hand away and loosening the seat belt. "You're suffocating my bladder."

I winked. "I'll do it tighter if you mention him again."

"Now you're playing the jealous boyfriend?" She kept her voice low so only I would hear, and I winked at her because I knew I was getting under her skin.

Good. She was getting under mine, so if she wanted to play dirty, I'd do the same.

I made sure to allow some time to get myself off in the shower this morning before spending the weekend with this sexy as hell, aggravating, pain in my ass.

Yet I was still wound tight. I closed my eyes, and we were both silent through takeoff.

Beverly brought out two bottles of sparkling water and two glasses of champagne, along with a basket full of snacks, including a bowl with popcorn, and a bag of M&M's for Lulu, along with a giant bag of gummy bears.

My brother, Bridger, had a shit ton of money, and I'd been on private planes and helicopters many times, but that had never included personalized snacks. The Sonnets were definitely next level.

"Bugles are an all-time favorite of mine, too, Rafe," Beverly said with a big grin on her face.

We both thanked her before she walked away. "See, even Beverly favors my snacks."

"Fine. I'll try one Bugle and one Funyun, and you have to try mine, and we'll see who has better taste."

"Give me your hand," I said, holding mine out to her after I took a sip of champagne. "Damn, that's the good stuff."

She rolled her eyes and held out her hand after I tore open the bags. I placed a Bugle on each of her fingers, and she did not hide her irritation. She pulled her hand to her mouth and ate one. And then another. "You gave them too much credit. I tried two, and I'm unimpressed. Take these ridiculous Bugle hats off my fingers."

I leaned down and covered her middle finger with my lips, making sure to go much farther than I needed to. I sucked on the bottom part of her finger before pulling my lips over the crispy goodness and chewing. She stared, acting completely unaffected before glancing over her shoulder to see if Beverly was around.

"That was smooth, lover. But no one is watching right now," she whispered.

I leaned down and took her ring finger into my mouth and did the same, holding her hand firmly in mine, before doing it one final time. "You never know, Wildcat. We need to be ready."

She licked her lips and tugged her hand away, taking a sip of her champagne. "For the record, when I referenced my ex, it was because the last time he flew on this plane, he got wasted and vomited everywhere before passing out. He was obnoxious and awful, and when I got off the plane in the Hamptons—because we were celebrating back East—I had Jerry fly Beckett back home. He woke up in California and wasn't too happy about it."

That had the corners of my lips turning up. "What an asshole."

"You have no idea."

We made small talk for the next twenty minutes, and I tried her food options, and unlike her, I told her she had good taste in snacks because the popcorn mixed with the chocolate was fucking perfection. "The gummy bears are not my favorite. They get stuck in my teeth."

"Well, that makes it a snack for later," she teased.

"Do you need anything else?" Beverly asked as she moved beside where I sat in the aisle seat. "Jerry said we will be landing soon."

"I think we're good. We'll tuck the rest of the snacks into our backpacks," Lulu said, as Beverly cleared away the champagne glasses.

We continued talking until we were on the ground.

"Remember, if you think of any random fact that might come in handy, just text it to me as you think of it, and I'll do the same. There's still a lot that Charlotte could ask that we haven't covered," she said, keeping her voice low.

"It's a birthday celebration for your grandfather, right? Do you really think anyone is going to give a shit about what's happening here?"

She chuckled. "I've been the topic of conversation most of my life. I don't quite fit the mold of the Sonnet family, and thanks to my trainwreck ex, my cousin has taken a deep dive into my failures. She's also not super close with Gramps. I think he sniffs a fraud. She acts sugary sweet but is anything but, and I think she resents my relationship with him. So, buckle up, Rafael. You've got your work cut out for you."

My God. She acted like we were heading into battle.

We said goodbye to Beverly, and Jerry gave Lulu a big hug as we made our way toward the exit.

"I'm happy for you. You look well," he said before offering a hand to me. "You're a very lucky man. She's the best."

"You don't have to tell me. I pinch myself daily." I leaned forward and wrapped a hand around the side of her neck and kissed her cheek.

"Oh, my. Aren't they darling? Your parents are going to love him," Beverly said.

Damn. I was clearly cut out for being a fabulous fake boyfriend.

There was a car waiting for us on the tarmac because the Sonnets appeared to be modern-day royalty. A man in a black suit put his arms out, and Lulu took off running toward him as I pushed both of our suitcases toward the car.

He spun her around. The dude looked to be in his mid-seventies, he was tall and thin, with a smile that showed how genuine he was.

"There's my favorite girl. I heard you brought someone special home. I hope this doesn't mean you won't be flirting with me anymore when you steal all my money at backgammon."

Once he set Lulu back down on her feet, she turned toward me. "I'll never stop flirting with you, Milty. This is my boyfriend, Rafe. Rafe, this is Milty. He's been driving for my grandfather since before I was born. I spent several summers with my grandparents, and he'd always take me for as much ice cream as I could eat."

"Hello, young man. You can call me Milton. This one just gets away with the ridiculous nickname because she knows she's my favorite." He extended his hand, and I shook it.

"She's told me lots about you," I lied.

She quirked her brow, which I read as, *I told you so*. There's still a lot we didn't cover.

I insisted on loading the suitcases into the car, and we climbed in the back as Milton drove us to their beach house. We were making small talk with the older gentleman when my phone vibrated.

Wildcat: *How the hell did we not cover Milty and ice cream? My favorite flavor is key lime, and cherry is my second favorite. Tell me yours. And then delete these messages. Charlotte has been known to go through her husband's phone, and I wouldn't put it past her to check ours.*

Jesus. What the hell was I about to walk into?

Me: *Is key lime even an actual flavor of ice cream? I don't know anyone who likes cherry ice cream either.*

Wildcat: *My mind is blown. These are the best flavors. What is yours? Time is ticking.*

Me: *Mint chocolate chip. The most popular, of course.*

Wildcat: *Very basic. I expected more from you, Rafael.*

Me: *I believe my ice cream flavor is enjoyed by most humans, while yours is unknown for a reason.*

"So, how long have you two love birds been together?" Milton asked.

"A couple of months," we said at the same time and then smiled at one another.

We've got this. It's in the bag.

"If you hurt our girl, I'll hunt you down, Rafe," Milton said, his tone light, which was followed by a laugh. But when his gaze met mine in the rearview mirror, I got the feeling that he meant it.

"I wouldn't dream of it," I said as I typed a quick message to her.

Me: *When we break up, you're going to have to be the bad guy. I will not have Milty angry at me.*

Wildcat: *I've already got this figured out. We'll blame the distance. We can stop pretending after your boss's wedding, but my family doesn't have to know it ended until I leave Rosewood River. It's not like they subscribe to the Taylor Tea. They'll never know. When I move to Paris in three months, I'll say that we grew apart. Just focus on today, and stop worrying about tomorrow.*

Me: *I prefer my woman to be slightly more empathetic. You're a bit harsh for me, Wildcat.*

Wildcat: *<middle finger emoji>*

We pulled through a gate that led down a long driveway with the ocean in the distance. I wouldn't even call this a house. This was definitely what people referred to as an estate or a mansion. The large home wrapped around the property, and I'd never seen anything like it.

Milton was out of the car, and I turned to Lulu before opening my door. "You didn't prepare me for the palatial mansion. I feel like you're my sugar mama now."

She rolled her eyes. "Just pull your shit together, and act natural."

"You're quite possibly the meanest sugar mama around." I pushed my door open and hurried to the back of the car. "Don't you dream of grabbing those bags, Milton. I've got them."

He opened Lulu's door and was laughing about my comment as I lifted our suitcases out of the trunk.

"It's my job," the older man said, reaching for the handles.

"I'm trying to impress my girl." My voice was all tease.

"All right. I'll never stand in the way of love. Are you sure you want to bring those in?" he asked.

"Yes. We've got it," Lulu said, moving beside me.

"All right. I'll be back to see if you need to go anywhere later. I've got to go run an errand for your grandfather."

Lulu gave him a quick hug, and I extended my hand. "Great to meet you, Milton."

"You, too." He turned to the woman standing beside me. "I think this one's a keeper. I've never said that before."

Lulu forced a smile and leaned her head on my shoulder. "I couldn't agree more."

We waved goodbye as he pulled back down the driveway and made our way up the steps to the oversized double doors.

"That is one smart dude."

"Yeah, well, don't get cocky. He's going to be the easiest one to win over, outside of Gramps and my mother." She quirked a brow.

"But he knows good people. That's all I care about."

"Focus, Rafael. It's game time."

She pushed through the front door, and a gentleman greeted us.

Another man wearing a suit, although this one was in his mid-fifties, so a bit younger than Milton.

Either way, these people were clearly very formal.

"If it isn't my favorite lady." He kept his voice low as Lulu jumped into his arms. Obviously, the staff loved her. It was her family she seemed concerned about.

"Cam! I've missed you." She hugged him and then pulled back. "This is my boyfriend, Rafe Chadwick."

"A pleasure to meet you, Mr. Chadwick." He extended a hand and chuckled. "You've got your hands full with this one."

"And that's why I'm your favorite." Lulu smirked.

"You're not wrong about that." He took our coats and told us he'd have someone bring our luggage to our room.

Were there more staff working here? It was a home, not a hotel.

"Give me the quick lowdown. What's happening?" Lulu whispered to Cam.

"Well, Charlotte is in a mood because your grandfather has been anticipating your arrival all day. Your mom is in a session with Francois, and the rest of the family seems to be downing the Bloody Marys this morning."

"That means they're on their way to three shades of liquored up," she whispered to me. "Okay, we're going in."

She slipped her hand into mine and glanced up at me. "Let's do this, lover boy."

8

Lulu

We made our way to the great room first, where Hunter and Charlotte were playing chess. I scanned the room to find my grandfather and my dad pushing to their feet when they noticed us come in. My hand was in Rafe's, as I knew that Charlotte would be watching every detail.

And if she thought she was going to accuse me of faking a relationship, she had another thing coming.

"Lulubelle is home!" Gramps shouted, and I dropped Rafe's hand and threw myself into my grandfather's arms. He was the most affectionate family member I had. Everyone else was a bit stiff, but Gramps and I were clearly cut from the same cloth.

"Happy Birthday, Gramps."

He set me back down on my feet as I turned to give my

father a quick hug. He wasn't big on affection, and he patted my back stiffly.

"Yeah, yeah, yeah. Now, introduce us to this new fella of yours," Gramps said.

"This is Rafe Chadwick." I quickly moved beside him and took his hand again when I felt Charlotte's eyes on me. "You're going to love him as much as I do."

"Oh, my, this is news... She loves him now?" A sarcastic laugh filled the space around us as Charlotte and her husband, Hunter the douche-kabob, made their way over to us. My grandfather and father shook Rafe's hand, and they were already making small talk.

"Guilty as charged." I smirked before forcing the next words out of my mouth. "It's good to see you both."

"I'm sure it is. Grandfather has been talking about this boyfriend of yours *ad nauseam*. I was waiting for you to call and say he couldn't make it due to his—what was it, Hunty? A rare virus?"

"Yes." Hunter let out this deep chuckle that screamed politician. His dark hair was covered in a thick layer of gel, and his blue eyes scanned my outfit from head to toe in that particularly creepy way he always did. "I didn't think he'd show either."

"You must be Charlotte and Hunter." Rafe turned and extended a hand when my grandfather and father left to let Mrs. Weston know that we were in need of a round of champagne. "I've heard so much about you both. And I wouldn't have missed this for the world. I was just worried about giving you that nasty virus. I'd hate to see you locked up in a bathroom for days. But I was lucky because I had my girl to take care of me."

I used my hand to cover my mouth because Rafe Chadwick knew how to handle himself, and that gave me less to worry about.

"I see. So, this is serious enough to include caretaking? What is it that you do, Rafe? I think I heard something about you being a cashier? Or a bank teller?" Hunter asked, in that one-of-a-kind condescending tone that annoyed the hell out of me.

"I'm actually a wealth management advisor. But I've done all of those things before doing this, so you aren't wrong. And you're a congressman, right?" Rafe asked. He could have stuck it to him and said something snarky, but he was respectful that way.

"Yes. I am."

"That's impressive." He turned to Charlotte next. "Lulu mentioned that you are very active in philanthropy. I'd love to hear more about that."

Her expression softened. My cousin was so difficult and combative in her relationships that she didn't know how to handle it when someone wasn't coming for her.

"Yes. I mean, I plan to have children soon, and I'd like to be home to raise them."

"Ahhh... honorable work right there. My mother stayed home with all five of us kids, and I give her a lot of credit. It's not an easy job; the hours are long, and the pay is terrible." Rafe barked out a laugh.

Charlotte's lips turned up in the corners as if she couldn't help but smile at the charming man beside me. I didn't even know Charlotte's lips could move upward. I assumed her filler had just given her a bad case of resting bitch face. But apparently, she saved that particular look for me and the rest of the family.

"I couldn't agree more. Some women are cut out for motherhood, and others are just—not. Like Lulu here, she's all about her career, just like her mother was."

What the actual hell?

"A woman can have both a career and a family. There is no right or wrong way to do it," I said, trying to tamp down my irritation. "I think if you want to stay home and raise your family, it's very honorable. But I also think it's just as wonderful if you want to work outside the home."

"I wouldn't allow my woman to work outside of our home," Hunter said, and I cringed at his backward way of thinking. "I like my wife to have time to make herself beautiful and have dinner on the table when I come home. Not to mention that she'll be the one to educate our future children. Can you think of a better teacher for your future nieces and nephews?" he asked, as he looked at me.

Ursula and Maleficent would give her a run for her money.

"Really?" Rafe gaped at him. "You don't think your wife should choose for herself?"

"Men have been the breadwinners since the beginning of time. I say, if it ain't broken, then don't fix it." Hunter barked out that horrific laugh of his.

"Well, I think that's the argument," Rafe pressed. "Limiting a woman's options is a very broken way of thinking. Would you like it if Charlotte said you had to stay home and raise the children, if that wasn't what you wanted to do?"

Hunter smirked like Rafe was kidding. Most of my family was appalled by the way Hunter spoke to his wife, aside from Charlotte's parents and her brother.

"Come on now, we all know a woman's place is in the home." And then he leaned down between me and Rafe and whispered loud enough for Charlotte to hear. "Particularly in the kitchen and in the bedroom."

More obnoxious laughter from the jackass standing in front of us. Charlotte's lips were in a perfectly straight line, and I gave her a sympathetic smile, because as awful as she was, she didn't deserve him.

"Come on, Congressman," Charlotte said, her voice even as she cleared her throat, most likely in an attempt to hide her irritation. "I think you've had one too many scotches. Let's go get you some water and check on lunch."

"He may be the worst person I've ever met," Rafe said, his lips grazing my ear. "But I like your grandfather and your father. They're very nice."

"Yeah, they're great."

"Lulubelle," my grandmother called out as she strode over with my father's sister, Aunt Jaclyn. Her children, Meredith and Jasper, were much more tolerable than Charlotte and her brother, Barron.

I made introductions, and Rafe pulled them into a hug one at a time, which they seemed to be just fine with. They, in turn, hugged me, which wasn't really the norm. *I guess Rafe and I aren't the only ones faking it at the moment.*

Rafe was charming the hell out of my entire family, so I'd clearly picked the right guy for the job. Beckett had stood out like a sore thumb at these family events. He'd get drunk and just give everyone a lot to work with when it came to critiquing him.

But Rafe Chadwick was the gold medal of boyfriends.

I glanced over at him wearing that fitted gray V-neck sweater with a white tee beneath, and his dark jeans that accentuated his long legs. His hair was wavy but cut shorter on the sides and a bit longer in the front. His peppered jaw had a bit of scruff, but in that polished sort of way, and those dimples had a way of charming the hell out of everyone in the room. His large hand was wrapped around mine, and I glanced down at the size of it.

And then I glanced down at his feet.

Also large.

I wondered if the old saying was true.

"Hello, my darling," my mother said, wearing a bright, colorful caftan dress, pulling me from my dirty thoughts.

"Hey, Mom." I hugged her and then pulled back. "This is Rafe."

"I just greeted him, my dear. Wow, you must have had your head in the clouds." She chuckled before gushing all over him, and of course, he hugged and flattered her, winning her over with ease.

My mother turned back to me. "After you say hello to everyone and have lunch, I'd like to sit in on a session with you and Rafe and have you meet with Francois."

I groaned. "Mom. We just got here. Can we skip the psychic readings until tomorrow?"

"What? No. He's dying to meet with you both. He wants to get inside those heads of yours. Rafe already agreed to it."

"Of course, he did. He has no idea what we're getting ourselves into."

Rafe did the most unexpected thing when he turned me to face him. He bent down so he could rub the tip of his nose against mine. "Baby, we'll be fine. There isn't anything about you that I don't love."

What the swoony hell?

This man was so good that I almost forgot we were pretending.

His hand moved to the side of my neck.

"This must be the new man everyone is talking about." My cousin Meredith's voice brought me back to reality.

"Yes. Hey." I pulled back and faced her, and her brother, Jasper, and his girlfriend, Serena, were walking in behind her. "Meredith, Jasper, Serena, this is Rafe Chadwick."

They smiled, and Meredith waggled her brows at me over his broad shoulder when he pulled her in for a hug. Serena was my favorite, and I was thrilled she was here, as she rarely came to family gatherings anymore.

"He's so pretty," she whispered in my ear as she hugged me.

"I've always had an eye for pretty things, right?" I asked, my voice all tease.

Jasper and Rafe were talking away, and I was happy to see that he'd have someone to talk to who wasn't a pretentious prick like Hunter and Barron.

Speaking of the pretentious pricks.

"Rafe, I want to introduce you to my brother-in-law, Barron Sonnet. I thought you two would have a lot in common," Hunter said as he walked back into the room.

Rafe shook Barron's hand, and I waited for it. Neither Barron nor Hunter could go long without saying something offensive.

"Nice to meet you. Are you in finance?" Rafe asked.

"Let's just say, you're good at managing the money, and I'm good at making it." Barron chuckled before turning to look at me. "Another blue-collar worker for you, Lu?"

My mother shook her head. "Rafe is in finance. And Bucket may have been awful, but he's a rock star, so he's hardly struggling financially."

I didn't have the energy to correct my mother about Beckett's name, as I'd need all my strength to get through this weekend.

My grandmother announced lunch and insisted everyone meet in the dining room, but of course, Barron lingered.

"You're an asshole, Barron," I hissed.

"You don't need to stick up for me, baby. My father is a blue-collar worker. So is my cousin. I'm sure your cousin doesn't mean it offensively. Only a man with a very small dick would

need to knock another man down to feel good about himself."
Rafe reached for my hand and interlocked his fingers with mine.
"Your dick can't be that miniscule, can it, Barron?"

My cousin's cheeks were a dark shade of red, and he pulled
his scotch to his lips. "I assure you, my cock is as big as my bank
account."

Rafe winced. "Oof. Most of the intelligent and wealthy men
that I work with are pretty smart about investing their money
and keeping their bank accounts lean. You might want to keep
that analogy to yourself for multiple reasons."

I barked out a laugh and glared at Barron, and Rafe and I
followed the rest of the group into the dining room.

The table was large, and we always sat in the same seats,
with me beside Gramps. Rafe sat in the chair beside me, and
everyone was taking their seats just as Uncle Dalton arrived. He
was married to my Aunt Jaclyn. He was a decade younger than
her, and their union had been a bit scandalous back in the day,
as she'd married her masseuse, though he now owned one of the
largest luxury spas in Malibu.

He'd clearly arrived earlier, as it was obvious he'd already
seen everyone else, and he beelined right for me.

"Hello, angel. Is this your new beau?" Uncle Dalton kissed
my cheek and turned to greet Rafe.

"Yes. This is Rafe Chadwick. Rafe, this is my Uncle Dalton."

"Great to meet you," Rafe said. "I heard your spa is amazing.
My sister has been there, and she raved about it."

A chuckle escaped Barron's lips. "Not shocked that these
two would have a lot in common."

"Barron, do you remember when I told you that you talk
too much?" Gramps interrupted, and everyone quieted as Uncle
Dalton took his seat next to his wife.

"Yes. Is there a point?" my cousin snipped, and I wanted to lunge over the table at him for disrespecting our grandfather.

"There sure is." Gramps gave him a hard look. "Don't do it. No one likes an arrogant prick."

Rafe choked on the sip of water he'd just taken, just as my mother waltzed into the dining room with Francois as she sat beside my father, with her spiritual advisor on the other side of her. I think Francois had become a safety net for my mom at these functions. When she couldn't handle any more family time, she'd claim she needed to have a reading. My mother was a unique kind of amazing. Her attention was all over the place, yet she was charming and warm and a brilliant creator when it came to business.

"Your grandfather speaks the truth," Francois said in his very strong French accent.

"Thank you, Dr. Ful-of-shit. I don't take advice from a man who reads crystals for a living." Barron clapped his hands, which was his way of telling Mrs. Weston that he was ready to eat. She's run the kitchen for my grandparents since I was young. She traveled with them to each house, which most of the staff did not do. But our family had become her family in a way.

"I agree, darling," Aunt Louisa said, as she took her seat beside Uncle Charles. They were the proud parents of the two biggest assholes in the family.

"Let's all try to be on our best behavior as we have a new guest, and it's Grandfather's birthday," my father said.

Always the diplomat.

Mrs. Weston had plates with silver domes over each one brought out by her staff, and they placed them at every seat and waited behind us for each of them to be set down.

"I'm starving," Rafe said as he lifted the dome off the plate. "What do we have here?"

"Like I said, blue-collar worker," Barron said under his breath.

Rafe looked up at my cousin and held up his thumb and his pointer finger about an inch apart. "Like I said. You keep showing your hand, little Barron."

Jasper, Meredith, Serena, and I all chuckled.

Everyone else looked a little confused as champagne flutes were passed around, and my grandfather raised his glass.

"Thank you all for being here to celebrate my eightieth birthday. We've got a big crowd coming to the party tonight, but I'm happy to have this time with all of you now. Welcome to the family, Rafe." He waited for everyone to raise their glasses, and we clinked them together.

The staff stood behind the table and raised the silver domes, and everyone started eating their kale-cranberry salads.

"It's a little soon to be welcoming him to the family, isn't it?" Charlotte asked, as she took a sip from her flute and held her pinky out.

"I don't think so. They seem very happy," Meredith said, and she couldn't wipe the smile from her face.

"How long do you plan to stick around, Chadwick?" Barron asked as he quirked a brow.

"As long as my girl will have me, Barry." He winked at me.

My grandfather beamed. My mother and Francois clapped their hands together. All the ladies, including my grandmother, who tended to be a bit chilly when meeting new people, were swooning at the man beside me. Even my father looked slightly amused.

Rafe Chadwick was everything a boyfriend should be.

I hit the jackpot, and I was going to enjoy every minute of it.

Well, at least for the next three days.

Then I'd go back to being annoyed by him.

9

Rafe

I could handle crazy. I grew up in a large, loud, wild family with colorful personalities.

But the Sonnets were next level.

You had the sweet grandfather, who clearly favored his youngest grandchild, Lulu.

He appeared disgusted by his eldest grandson, Barron, who was possibly the biggest dickfucker I'd ever met. His brother-in-law, Hunter, was a close second.

I knew the type. I worked with a lot of men like these two. Barron was clearly a trust fund kid because he'd still yet to answer what he actually did for a living, aside from saying he made money.

I asked Lulu, and she said he managed his and his sister's trust funds.

Yet he was busy pointing his finger at everyone around him like they were beneath him.

I'd never been that guy. I didn't give a shit what people did for a living or how much money they made. It's more about doing what you love. I wasn't surrounded by people who compared or looked down on others, so the dude instantly rubbed me wrong. Lulu had already prepared me for him, and she hadn't exaggerated.

She was in the bathroom getting ready for the party, as we were sharing a room, which could potentially be awkward as fuck, seeing as there was only one bed. There was a couch at the end of the bed, and I assumed that was where I'd be sleeping.

The bathroom door swung open, and Lulu walked out, and I quickly tried to straighten my features.

Because holy fucking shit, this woman was stunning.

Long blonde waves fell over her shoulders, and she wore a black sparkly dress that dipped low in the front.

And by dipped low, I mean that it dipped down *real* low.

The rise of her breasts peeked out of the opening, and I wasn't sure how the fabric was staying in place.

I couldn't stop staring, and she clearly noticed because she snapped her fingers in front of my face. "You can't be looking at my boobs as if you've never seen them before."

"Well, they're kind of hard not to stare at."

"Fine, get it over with. Once we walk out the door, you need to look at me like you've seen me naked hundreds of times." She shrugged, placing her hands on her hips and motioning for me to check her out.

"I'm not going to just stand here and stare at you. That's ridiculous," I said, scrubbing a hand down my face.

"You already were staring, so I don't know why you're acting all weird now. You're clearly attracted to me." She smirked.

"Listen. Don't make it a thing. You've got great tits. That's all it is."

Her eyes moved down to my black dress pants, which were clearly tented.

For fuck's sake.

My dick could give Benedict Arnold a run for traitor of the century.

"You sure you can handle this tonight?" Her voice was all tease.

"Yes. I'm absolutely fine."

She moved closer, brushing nonexistent dust from my suit coat. "You look handsome, Rafael. You wear this suit well. And you handled my jackass cousin well, too."

"Barron is an asshole. And Hunter is, too," I said, as I stood in front of her and took her up on her offer to take her in. "You look really beautiful tonight, Wildcat."

I didn't miss the way her chest rose and fell quicker at my nearness. Pear and vanilla wafted around me, and I swore her scent was some kind of aphrodisiac.

"Thank you. And I'm sorry about Barron and Hunter. Keep your eye out for Charlotte; she's a quiet kind of evil."

"They seem to be hyperfocused on you. Has it always been that way?"

"With Barron and Charlotte, it has. They don't like my mother, and they don't care for me either. At times, it feels like they are gunning for me. Always trying to dig around for things and bring it up at family gatherings." She shrugged, as if that were perfectly acceptable.

"Fuck them," I said. "I've got your back if you need me tonight."

"It's fine. I don't need saving, Rafe. I can handle myself. We need to go. The party starts soon." She started to turn, and I put a hand on her shoulder.

She was the most intriguing woman I'd ever met.

She was beautiful and vulnerable and fierce all at the same time.

"You do know that someone can have your back without it meaning you need to be saved, right? I don't give a fuck if this is fake. Just know that if you need me, all you have to do is say the word."

Her gaze narrowed as if she were surprised by my words. "Just say the word? And you'll be there for me even if we're not together? Even if I'm not sleeping with you?"

"Yes." There was no hesitation. Because I would.

She was Henley's best friend. Hell, we lived on the same property. When she wasn't causing me physical pain, I found her very entertaining.

She's also starred in every dirty dream I've had lately, and I spent quite a lot of time in the shower with thoughts of her.

"Careful, Rafe Chadwick. Don't go falling in love with me while we're faking it." She smiled, her red-covered lips plump and taunting.

"I'm the last guy you need to worry about. That's not really my thing."

"Oh, trust me, I know."

There was a knock on our bedroom door, and Lulu moved across the grand room and pulled the door open.

"What are you two doing here?" Lulu said. "We were just coming downstairs."

"Francois has ten minutes to sit down with you two, and nothing is happening downstairs. Everyone is just arriving and having cocktails. He wanted to meet with you and just, you know, talk for a few minutes," Noemie said, as she pushed into the room and took me in. "You look very handsome, Rafe."

"Thank you. You look lovely, as well." Lulu's mother wore a black velvet dress that was long and stopped at the floor. Her blonde hair was tied back at the nape of her neck, and she was wearing a lot of sparkly jewelry that I imagined cost a ton of money.

"Hello, Rafe," Francois said, taking both of my hands in his and closing his eyes briefly before opening them and quirking a brow. "I know we met briefly at lunch. But we didn't get a formal introduction. I'm Francois Tremblay, and you've got some magnificent energy."

"Mom, we need to get to the party," Lulu said, as another knock came from the other side of the door.

"I brought the party to you," Noemie said as she waggled her brows. A woman I recognized from our lunch walked inside with a tray holding four champagne flutes.

She walked over to the table in the corner that had four chairs surrounding it, and Noemie and Francois took their seats as Lulu groaned and led me there, as well. There were fresh flowers in the center of the table, which Francois slid to the side before taking a sip of champagne.

I thanked the older woman for the drink, and she left the room.

"We have a few minutes before we get swamped downstairs," Noemie said.

"I planned to meet with you tomorrow, Francois."

"Tomorrow is going to be busy with the family photos and the interview," her mother said as she took a sip of her bubbly.

"The interview?" Lulu gasped. "What are you talking about?"

"The press is coming. Hunter and Charlotte set this up, claiming it was an interview for Hunter and Uncle Charles, with him just being reelected. But obviously, it now involves the whole family with us all being here. And your father thinks it would be great to have Rafe present. You know, it would be a good thing to make your relationship public, so everyone can stop talking about Bucket and see that you've moved on."

I noticed Lulu's shoulders stiffen, and I reached for her hand beneath the table. She glanced at me, and my gaze locked with hers, and I tried to reassure her without speaking.

It's fine. We're fine. We've got this.

"We will sit in on the photos, but we're not being interviewed. We aren't politicians. We're here to celebrate a birthday, not give political statements," Lulu snipped.

"I couldn't agree more," Francois said as he continued studying me. I didn't mind it. He appeared to be trying to see into my soul, and I was fine with it. I was an open book. No way he could tell this relationship was fake just by looking at me, but Lulu seemed uncomfortable. She left her hand in mine, which made it obvious she was definitely nervous. Francois finished his thoughts. "It doesn't surprise me that Charlotte wanted to turn a family celebration into a photo shoot and press event."

"Yet you made sure she got the better reading at the holiday dinner." Lulu pulled her hand away from beneath the table, clearly more comfortable now. "Come on, Francois. You basically said that Charlotte saved all humankind, and you made me some kind of colonial whore. What the hell was that about?"

My head tipped back in laughter, and I had no idea what we were talking about, but she was funny as hell.

Her mother gasped. "I knew you were upset about that."

"I never said you were a whore. Charlotte was the one who said that. I said you were a lot of fun, and you had the hots for Ben Franklin. That's not a bad thing, Lulu. And just because your cousin was a healer in her last life doesn't mean she's a saint in this one," Francois said, tossing a wink at her.

He was probably in his mid-sixties, had long, dark wavy hair, and was wearing a black velvet suit with a pink floral button-up beneath.

Lulu sighed. "Whatever. Ben Franklin was hot, so I can live with that."

"Are you getting a feel for these two, present day?" Noemie asked, looking between us, like this man could tell her everything she needed to know.

"Yes. It's very strong. The connection between them. They don't even know how strong it is." He chuckled. He then continued to stare at us and smile and then closed his eyes and smiled some more. "Wow. This is better than I imagined."

"It is?" Noemie asked, a wide grin on her face.

Lulu was chewing on the corner of her lip, and she peeked up at me.

"I'm happy for you, Lu. You went through your fair amount of drama with the last one, but this is going to be fairly easy," he said, clasping his hands together and turning to Noemie. "Yes. Yes. Yes."

"Yes?" she asked.

Lulu shrugged and reached for her champagne flute, so I did the same. We clinked them together, and I watched as she tipped her head back and drank the whole thing. I did the same. When we set our glasses down, they were both staring at us.

"Lulubelle, do you know that when Francois met your father for the first time, he told me that he was my forever? Did I ever tell you that?" Her mother dabbed at her eyes with a handkerchief that Francois had just handed her.

"Yes. You've told me, and it's very sweet." It was clear that Lulu wasn't fully on board with Francois and his predictions, but she was appeasing her mother.

"He never saw you and Bucket together. He saw flames and disaster and darkness," Noemie said.

"Yes, Mother. I recall him telling Beckett and me that over a Christmas dinner once." Lulu chuckled. "That went over like a whore in colonial times."

Damn, she was cute. Funny and sexy and confident.

"He sees it. He sees it!" Noemie squealed, and Francois shook his head and clapped his hands together as he turned toward us.

"I do see it. Congratulations. I know you two don't see it," he said, quirking a brow as if he were in on something. "But you must trust me."

"Of course, they don't see years down the road. They're young and in love, and it's all new. But this is wonderful news."

"My work is done." Francois pushed to his feet. "You can stop worrying, Noemie. She's in good hands. Rather large hands, if I do say so myself." The older man winked at me, and I barked out a laugh.

Her mother pushed to her feet, as well.

"I'll stop bothering you now. Let's go enjoy the party," Noemie said, as she hurried around and hugged me. "Welcome to the family, Rafe."

"Mom, please stop," Lulu groaned.

Noemie paused in front of her daughter. "I love you, my beautiful girl. We've been worried about you for a long time. About your choices. But you've figured it out professionally and personally. All I want is for you to be happy."

Francois reached for my hand and held it between both of his. He pushed up and whispered in my ear. "You're a lucky man. Don't mess it up. She's not as tough as she pretends she is."

They both left the room, and Lulu pushed the door closed and leaned against it before bursting out in laughter.

"Damn. He hates most men. He told Charlotte she would be married twice," she said.

"Well, after meeting her first husband, I don't think that's the worst news."

"He announced it at the table at her rehearsal dinner." Lulu was laughing now. "It was a whole thing. But she's determined to prove him wrong. He then basically said that Beckett was the devil, and I should stay away from him. And now he embraces the guy who I'm not really dating. This is like a psychic's worst nightmare. He's completely wrong, which means, maybe I'm the one who healed the sick in colonial times."

I barked out a laugh. "Listen, I wouldn't have been hanging out with you in colonial times. I would have avoided your cousin like the plague."

"Well, she was busy curing the sick back then." She reapplied her lipstick. "Shall we go dazzle them?"

"I mean, we already have the dude who can see into our minds and souls on board; I think we're going to crush it."

She paused with her hand on the door handle. "Thanks for doing this. I'll return the favor at the wedding next week."

"I would have done it either way." I shrugged, because it was the truth.

Her brows pinched together. "Why?"

"Because I get to stare at your boobs in that dress. Totally worth it."

Her head tipped back in laughter as she placed her hands over each breast. "I never thought they were that powerful because they aren't super large. I mean, don't get me wrong, I'm a fan. They're perky, they don't get in the way if I'm playing sports, and they look good in low-cut blouses, but you're acting like they're the best boobs you've ever seen."

Her words went straight to my dick, and I closed my eyes and cleared my throat. "All right. No more talking about your perfect tits, or I'm going to be walking around with a boner all night." I motioned her toward the door.

"Okay, Rafael. It's game time," she said.

Let's do this.

10

Lulu

I've attended more family events in my life than I could begin to count. But tonight had been the best one yet.

My fake boyfriend was a hit.

I spent years dating a guy I always thought was the life of the party. The yin to my yang. But it always ended in drama. Beckett was sloppy and selfish, and he always found a way to bring a good night to a catastrophic end.

But Rafe Chadwick… he was the whole package.

He rocked a black suit like he just stepped off the runway for a luxury brand. He charmed all the women, including my grandmother, who was a hard nut to crack. He spun her around on the dance floor before getting her a cocktail and helping her to her seat.

My grandfather had taken him and my father to his den to

smoke a cigar, which had Charlotte seething because Gramps had never done that with Hunter.

My mother couldn't get enough of my fake boyfriend.

Even Francois Tremblay was enamored.

But my father talking to him was the biggest surprise. He was skeptical of anyone I brought around him, and always had been. But he seemed to be very comfortable with Rafe. He stopped asking him endless questions, and they were just having normal conversation last I checked.

I stepped out of the bathroom and leaned against the wall, typing out a quick text to Henley.

Me: *Hey, Hen! Rafe is killing it. They love him. Thank you for dating Easton and finding me the best fake boyfriend ever. Even freaking Charlotte can't come up with anything negative to say.*

Henley: *I'm not surprised. He's very loveable. What about Francois?*

Me: *He sees a long future for us. The whole fairytale bullshit. We freaking did it. We pulled it off. One more day to go, and we'll take a few photos and head home.*

Henley: *Wow. This is the first time I've ever talked to you when you were at a family event that you weren't miserable. You should take Rafe with you to all of them.*

Me: *No can do. We have big plans to break up the day after his boss's wedding. <laughing face emoji>*

Henley: *Damn. This is the best relationship you've ever had. LOL.*

Me: *Seriously, how sad is that?*

I looked up to see Rafe striding toward me. Long legs. Broad shoulders. Those dark eyes bored into mine. His lips turned up the slightest bit in the corners and those dimples on full display.

"I've been looking for you, Wildcat." His voice was gruff yet playful.

I could tell he'd had a few drinks. His cheeks were slightly flushed, his tie had been loosened, and he'd undone one more button on his dress shirt.

His lips parted when he stopped in front of me, and he smiled. *Damn.*

Maybe it was that I'd had too many glasses of champagne to count, but it was taking everything I had not to tug his head down and kiss him.

"Did you have fun with my grandfather and my dad?" I asked, fidgeting with my hands to keep from touching him.

"Sure. They're great. But the party is winding down, and your mom wants us to get in one last dance. I requested a song, and they said they'd wait to play it until I found you."

We already danced our asses off tonight, but who was I to say no to one more?

"All right. One more, and then we call it a night," I said.

"I'm not in a hurry to get back to the room, so I may hang out in the cigar room for a while until you're asleep," he said, extending a hand, as mine slipped inside his.

"What? No. We need to go up together. It will look suspicious if I leave without you. You want to stay out?" I asked.

He came to an abrupt stop, and he ran a hand through his hair before leaning down close to my ear. "There's only one bed. My dick is very responsive to you, especially after seeing you in this dress all night. I'd rather not embarrass myself again."

I squeezed my thighs together in response to his words.

"Don't worry about it. I know how to take care of that."

He chuckled. "If it involves your tits or your hands, count me in."

"There you are," Serena said as she and Jasper called out to us from the other end of the hallway, pulling us from a very questionable conversation. "The DJ is anxious to play the last song. Your boyfriend picked it especially for you. Everyone is waiting to leave."

"Let's go, lover boy."

I tugged him down the hallway, but his words were still ringing in my head.

If it involves your tits or your hands, count me in.

That was hot and sexy and honest.

Damn him.

If I had a penis, I would definitely have a boner right now.

Of course, my fake boyfriend would have to be the first man in a very long time to turn me on. I used to love sex. But then for the longest time, I didn't enjoy it, and I've been in a rut ever since.

Would it be so bad to just give in to it?

We were clearly attracted to one another.

We'd be fake dating for another week.

So what if he was my best friend's boyfriend's brother?

So what if we lived on the same property and would have to see one another all the time?

"Stop overthinking. We're fine. I can tame the big guy down. Don't worry about it," he whispered in my ear as if he could read my thoughts. He led me straight to the dance floor.

He thought I was bothered by the fact that he had a boner around me.

Hell, I was far from offended.

I kind of loved it.

The music started playing, and it was one of my favorite songs.

"Rumor" by Lee Brice.

I chuckled when he tugged me against his body and he swayed us both to the beat.

The lyrics were all about a couple who were friends but were suddenly finding it hard to stay away from one another.

He started singing in my ear, his words slurring the slightest bit. No one else would notice, but I recognized the slight drawl in his words.

He was singing about the way people were talking about us.

About the rumors swirling around.

And then he sang the line about making the rumor true.

Giving them something to talk about.

I pulled back and looked at him, and he was smiling down at me. He glanced around and my eyes followed to see everyone watching.

And then he sang the last verse loudly as he looked down at me, and everyone joined in and sang along.

He was putting on a show.

And I was getting lost in it.

I knew better. I'd made it my mission not to allow things like this to happen. Getting lost in a charming man.

I swayed my hips and smiled, reminding myself it was just a game.

One that I asked him to play.

The song came to an end, and there were a few whistles and lots of clapping, and we both laughed.

"Kiss her already!" someone shouted, and his eyes searched mine.

Play along.

His mouth came down over mine, and it was soft and sweet. His hand found my lower back as he dipped me down and then pulled back.

No tongue.

No nipping or biting or franticness.

It was lukewarm at best.

He smiled and led me off the dance floor.

My grandparents were waiting, and Gramps smiled. "That was some dance. Nice to see you two having so much fun. Tomorrow, we've got the photographer and some press coming to do a story on Uncle Charles and Hunter. We'd like Rafe to be there with us, as he just feels like part of the family now."

My chest squeezed, suddenly feeling guilty about lying to Gramps.

"Yes, of course. We'll be there, but we'll just be on the sidelines, if that's okay."

"Whatever you want, my love. Thanks for making today so special. Love you." He kissed my cheek, and my grandmother smiled and patted me on the shoulder before walking away to say goodbye to their remaining guests. Most of the older people had left about an hour ago, so it was just the younger generation still here drinking and having fun.

My parents came over and said goodnight. I watched as they hugged Rafe, and a tinge of guilt flooded. They liked him.

It felt good to be with someone that everyone liked.

I had just wanted to get them off my back about all the negative press that had tied me to a guy I hadn't been with in a very long time. But I didn't know they'd be quite this enamored with the man.

Hell, I didn't know *I'd* be this enamored with him either.

"Goodnight. We'll see you in the morning."

They walked away, and Rafe quirked a brow. "That last dance made you the talk of the party."

"I think my boyfriend made me the talk of the party," I said.

"I'm going to bed," Charlotte said as she approached, a scowl on her face. "We need to all be dressed appropriately for the interview tomorrow. It's important."

Her eyes scanned the front of my dress, and I chuckled. This was a party. She wore a dress that rivaled my grandmother's and was more age-appropriate for a woman in her eighties.

"We'll be there," I said.

"This is a big deal for Hunter," she said. "You can be in the background, as I know Grandfather will want you there."

"Well, she is part of the family, so I would guess everyone wants her there." Rafe found my hand and interlaced our fingers.

"Of course. But you should know, seeing as you two seem to be inseparable—" She paused, glancing at me before looking at Rafe. "Lulu tends to steal the thunder from others, and tomorrow is not about her."

I was ready to rip into her when Rafe squeezed my hand and looked over at me. It was a look that I understood.

Allow me.

"Well, scheduling a media circus when it's your grandfather's eightieth birthday celebration for your husband's personal gain sounds like you're pretty good at stealing other people's thunder yourself, Charlotte. My girl doesn't need to steal anyone's thunder. She manages to shine all on her own by simply existing."

Oh, this was good.

He was pouring it on.

And I am here for it.

My fake boyfriend could hold his own against anyone.

"Yeah. Exactly what he said." I squared my shoulders. "We'll see you in the morning, if we can even get out of bed because this guy tends to keep me up all night."

I laughed when we walked away.

"You told her, Wildcat," he said, as he led me up the steps and into the room. "And just so you know, what I said to her wasn't me putting on a show. It's the truth. Your cousin is jealous of you. And that's because you're fucking amazing."

My teeth sank into my bottom lip, and I shook my head. "You're not so bad yourself."

"Thank you. Do you want to use the restroom first? I need to take a shower."

"A cold shower?" I asked, as I waggled my brows. "One where you think about these perfect tits of mine?"

"Lu, stop fucking around. I'll be out in a little bit." He pulled the green stone from his pocket and set it on the dresser, which made me laugh.

"Wait," I said, grabbing his hand. I was still slightly buzzed and on a high because it was the first time I wasn't the center of attention for the wrong reason. I hadn't brought a date who made a scene or embarrassed us both. I wasn't alone and feeling self-conscious about it. I just had a great night. And I was with this sexy man and feeling turned on for the first time in a very long time, and I wanted to be reckless. "What if you take your shower, and I'll come in and wash my face and do my beauty routine while you're taking care of business?"

His lips turned up in the corners, his eyes dark, looking almost black, as his hand moved to the side of my neck. "You want to watch me get off to thoughts of you?"

"I can't read your mind, so your thoughts are your own. And

I won't be staring, I'll just be—" I paused to think over my word choice. My voice was breathier than usual.

"Turned on?" he asked.

"Maybe."

"Do you think that's a good idea? You're the one with all the rules," he said, his thumb stroking the line of my jaw.

"Listen, we aren't going to do anything about it." I sighed. "So here's the thing… I used to really like sex. And then I didn't like it. I haven't liked it for a while. I've dated, but I've had no desire to do anything more than kiss anyone. I don't know, maybe after you come off a relationship that ends terribly, you're cursed in a way."

"You're not cursed, Wildcat. You're healing. You don't trust easily because you've been hurt. I get that." He paused and studied me for a few beats. "So you haven't wanted to have sex because you don't like it anymore. But you want to watch me shower?"

Well, hearing him say it like that was a little mortifying.

"No. What I'm saying is that I was feeling something tonight. Even with that lame kiss you gave me on the dance floor… I don't know." I chuckled. "You're sexy and attractive, and we don't have to cross the line to have some fun, right?"

He smiled, and my stomach flipped.

I was not a girl who got the tummy flutters from a guy.

But here I was, fluttering away.

"All right. But just like our original deal, there has to be something in it for me, too, right? This can't all be one-sided."

I raised a brow. "You get to think about my perfect tits, remember?"

"I remember. And I'll do that on my own. But if I'm going to have an audience, I think you should sweeten the pot."

Interesting.

"How would you suggest I do that?"

"Take a shower with me. Make yourself feel good, and I'll do the same. We'll do it together."

"You're joking."

"You asked me if you could watch me get off in the shower, and you find it offensive that I want to do the same?" His voice was gruff, his chest pressed against mine.

"No touching," I said.

"No problem. Seeing you will be more than enough." His tongue swiped along his bottom lip.

Dear God. Have I ever been this turned on?

"We never discuss this. We wake up tomorrow and put on a show for my family, and it never happens again."

"There's nothing to talk about. It's not like it's something we both haven't done before. We're just doing it at the same time. Chances are we've done it at the same time at some point in our life before; we just weren't in the same room."

"The same shower, you mean," I said.

Why was I panting?

"Listen, we're two good-looking people pretending to date, and we're not with anyone else. We're not crossing any lines. We're just going to enjoy a friendly shower. Tomorrow you can go back to being annoyed with me, and I'll do the same."

"I can easily do that tomorrow."

"All right, then, let's do this," he said.

I turned and walked to the shower. I could do this. I was a twenty-eight-year-old woman. I hadn't had sex in close to a year and a half.

I was just going to take a shower, and he was going to shower at the same time.

I was a conscientious environmentalist anyway.

Why waste the water on two showers?

I was doing my part to protect the ecosystem and wildlife habitat.

That's what I was doing.

Taking one for the team.

11

Rafe

They say that Christmas only comes once a year, but seeing as I just celebrated that holiday a month ago, I'd beg to differ.

Because right now, I was standing under a spray of hot water, watching Lulu undress through the glass. She insisted I get in the shower first.

She watched me remove every piece of clothing and drop it on the floor.

She watched as my dick pointed right at her like he was picking her out of a lineup. Her eyes had widened, lips parted, and I didn't miss the way her legs shifted together as if she were trying to dull an ache that wouldn't go away.

Glass houses, Wildcat.

I've been hard as steel all night. I planned to take a cold shower alone, but instead, I'll be taking a hot shower with the hottest woman I'd ever laid eyes on.

I'd call that a win.

She pulled her long blonde hair into some sort of blue scrunchie on top of her head before she reached behind her back and unzipped her dress. I stared through the water droplets covering the glass shower door.

Holy shit.

I'd imagined those tits dozens of times tonight. A perfect handful. With perfect pink nipples that looked like they were dying to be sucked.

My cock throbbed beneath the spray of water, but I wouldn't touch it until she was in here with me. I sure as shit didn't want things to go too fast.

Her stomach was flat and toned, and she wore a pair of black lacy panties.

I watched as her fingers slipped beneath the thin band circling her hips, and she slowly peeled them down her legs.

Her eyes locked with mine as she stepped out of the panties and walked toward me. I opened the door, and I swear my dick doubled in size with her nearness.

She glanced down and sucked in a breath. "Obviously, you're not the only one who's happy to see me."

"And your pretty pink nipples look like they could cut glass, so I'd say we're in the same boat."

She tipped her head up and let the water run down her beautiful face.

"I'd like to say something. For the record, that kiss sucked ass because I thought you'd knee me in the balls if I gave you a real kiss. If I'd kissed you the way I wanted to in that moment…

let's just say we'd be doing more in this shower than what we agreed on."

Her breath hitched, and I fucking loved it.

She was always so in control, and I liked seeing her react to me.

"You were probably smart to keep it tame," she said, reaching for the soap and rubbing her hands over her gorgeous tits. My mouth watered at the sight. She knew what she was doing to me. She had a wicked grin on her face, and her teeth sank into her bottom lip playfully. "How would you have kissed me if you'd done what you wanted?"

I soaped up my hands and moved closer. "I would have covered your mouth slowly at first, waiting for your lips to part on a breath." I stroked my dick, and I could see the way her chest was rising and falling. "I'd slip my tongue in and find your greedy tongue waiting for me. And I'd fuck your mouth, in and out, driving you crazy with desire. I'd pull you closer so you'd feel how hard I was for you. How bad my cock was throbbing just having my mouth on yours."

She was breathing heavily now, but she squared her shoulders. "I think I'd probably have liked that. But then I'd have gotten all turned on while we were on the dance floor, and I'd be desperate for your fingers to slip beneath my dress and see how wet I was for you."

Fuck. Me.

She was playing along.

"Put your fingers between your legs. I want you to come with me," I said, deep and commanding. She shocked the shit out of me when she actually did what I asked her to do and didn't argue. Her hand moved between the apex of her thighs, and she leaned back against the wall, her eyes still on mine. "You have no fucking idea how badly I wanted to slide my hand beneath your dress. To fuck that sweet pussy with my fingers while I continued to fuck that greedy little mouth with my tongue."

"Holy shit," she whispered, as her hand continued to move between her legs, and I tightened my grip on my cock and slid up and down faster now.

"Would you like that, Lulu? Would you have liked me to get you off on the dance floor without anyone knowing what I was doing to you?"

"Yes."

"And what would you do about it?"

"I'd ride your hand and beg you to pull me into the bathroom so I could unzip your suit pants and grip that beautiful dick of yours. And then I'd wait until you were just about to go over the edge, and I'd drop to my knees," she said, her words breathy and sexy, and I was struggling not to lose it.

"I'd insist that you slide your hand between your legs while I fucked that sassy mouth of yours." My words were barely audible. "Because I'd refuse to come until you were right there with me."

"I'm right there with you now," she whispered as she stared down at my hand that was sliding up and down my shaft as I chased my release.

"I know you are, Lu. Come with me, right fucking now," I said, as her body started to shake, and her head fell back against the wall, eyes closed, as she came apart on a moan right in front of me.

It was the hottest fucking thing I'd ever seen.

"Fuck," I growled, as I came so hard I could barely see straight.

We both continued moving, riding out every last bit of pleasure.

It was the most erotic thing I'd ever done.

And probably the most tortuous thing I'd ever done, as well.

Because I couldn't touch her.

Couldn't kiss her.

Her honey-brown eyes opened, and she smiled. She reached for the soap and started showering as if we hadn't both just gotten off, and then she passed me the soap to clean myself up.

I turned off the water and handed her a towel before drying myself off.

"Well, at least we got that out of our systems. I feel fan-fucking-tastic. I think I'm going to sleep like a baby," she said, as she wrapped the towel around herself and moved to the bedroom to slip into her pajamas.

"Speak for yourself. That was hot as hell. And now your scent is going to be surrounding me in the room." I walked behind her and found some clean briefs in my suitcase and slipped them on.

"What are you, a basset hound? My scent is going to bother you? Please. We didn't even touch each other. It was just an orgasm shower." She tossed some of the throw pillows on the floor, and when she bent over, her little sleep shorts rode up the slightest bit, exposing her perfectly round ass cheeks.

"I'm a man. And I just watched you get off in the shower, and I'll never forget it. So, yeah, I'm going to be uncomfortable now."

She turned around and hit me in the face with a pillow. "Shake it off, Rafael. We agreed to never speak of it, and you just keep bringing it up."

"It just happened. My dick is still in awe of you."

She made her way to the couch, covering it in a blanket and tossing a pillow there. "I can sleep on the couch, and you can have the bed." She shrugged. "Apparently, I've tortured you enough tonight."

"I'm not an asshole. I'm sleeping on the couch." I moved to the dresser, grabbed the green stone, and carried it with me to where I'd be sleeping.

"You're sleeping with the stone?" She chuckled.

"Maybe it will keep the boner away."

She climbed into bed and clapped her hands together twice, and the room went dark.

Like I said, these people are fancy. They have a hand signal to turn off their lights.

"Tomorrow is a new day. My family loves you. They've got me up on a pedestal at the moment, and I'd like to keep it that way. Let's get some sleep."

I was lying on my back, staring at the ceiling.

"Have you ever done that before?" I asked, my voice low as I glanced over at her silhouette lit up the slightest bit from the sliver of light peeping through the opening of the curtains.

"Have I ever showered with a man while simultaneously giving myself an earth-shattering orgasm?" She didn't hide her sarcasm. "No, I haven't. Let me guess, you do it weekly?"

"No. I've never done that. And not touching one another was challenging."

"I didn't notice. I was fine just touching myself," she said over a fit of laughter.

I sat forward and glared at her, even though she couldn't see me. "You noticed. Your eyes never stopped staring."

"What can I say? You're pretty to look at." She cleared her throat. "Go to sleep. We have to be on tomorrow."

"I'm not tired now."

She sighed. "If you go to sleep, I'll flash you my boobs in the morning."

"Deal."

But now all I was doing was thinking about her boobs.

Her breathing slowed, and I knew she was asleep.

I counted down from one hundred to zero.

I counted sheep.

I counted pigs.

I counted forward and backward before sleep finally took me.

And I dreamed of perfect tits and hot water and a beautiful woman with honey-brown eyes.

A pillow hit me in the chest, and my eyes flew open.

"You need to get up. We've got to be downstairs for breakfast and the photo shoot in thirty minutes," Lulu said, standing over me looking stunning. She wore a black lacy top that once again dipped low in the front, showing off her slight cleavage. She had baggy faded jeans and boots on. Her hair was pulled back in some sort of messy knot at the nape of her neck, with a few waves that were loose around her pretty face.

I pushed the covers back, and she gaped at me, which had me glancing down to see my eager erection had woken up before me.

"It's morning. It's perfectly normal," I groaned as I sat forward.

"My God. I had no idea my boyfriend was such a horndog." She chuckled. "Are you always like this?"

"No. Maybe it's the fact that I showered with a naked woman who happens to have perfect tits, who, by the way, I wasn't allowed to touch. And then I had to sleep a few feet away from her and not touch her."

"We fly home tonight. This is almost over. Then you won't have to see me until the wedding next week. You're almost rid of me." She placed her hands on her hips, and damn, this woman was so cute, I wanted to scoop her up and toss her onto the bed.

"Now get dressed and make yourself charming and handsome and meet me downstairs."

"You're leaving?"

"Yes, Rafe. Last I checked, you know how to dress yourself. My mother sent a text that Francois wanted to speak to me." She quirked a brow. "The gig might be up. He's probably going to call me out. I'll be better at playing the game and telling him he's wrong if I'm alone."

"Fine. I'll be down in half an hour."

Her gaze moved to my briefs once again, where my dick was pointing right at her. "Take a shower if you need to. Do not bring that thing with you to the photo shoot," she said, waving her hand back and forth in front of my erection.

"My dick. You'd like me to leave him here in the room?" I walked toward the bathroom.

"I'd like you to stop being a baby about this and—"

I closed the door before she could finish her statement. I wasn't in the mood, and she was being cocky and unaffected, and I didn't like it.

"Very mature!" she shouted from the other side of the door.

I heard the outside door close, and I bent over the sink and closed my eyes. I needed to rein it in. We'd be back home tonight.

We'd forget all about this.

I brushed my teeth and quickly dressed, wearing my dark jeans and a black sweater, before making my way downstairs. Lulu was already walking toward me with wide eyes.

"Are we busted?" I whispered in her ear, and the smell of pear and vanilla had my body reacting all over again.

"Nope. He wanted to tell me that you have a lot of Benjamin Franklin characteristics, and that's why I'm so drawn to you." She was shaking her head and smiling. "We're still good. However, my cousin failed to mention that this interview is a bit more serious than she let on."

"What does that mean?"

"It's a reporter from the *Weekday Morning Show*. So it's sort of a big deal."

"The *Weekday Morning Show*, as in the most popular morning show in the US?"

"That's the one. So, we need to keep a low profile. We'll take the photos with the family, and we'll say we want to go take the boat out on the water so we can spend some time together. Just follow my lead. They're here for my Uncle Charles and Hunter. They just want a photo of everyone, and then we can slip out."

"Wow. I'm shocked when I'm in the *Taylor Tea*. I can't imagine being talked about on the *Weekday Morning Show*."

"I actually love the *Taylor Tea*," she said. "It's small town meets *Gossip Girl*. The anonymous factor makes it much more charming. It's like having your neighbor talk about you, but the whole world isn't listening. I like it."

The *Taylor Tea* was a sore subject for my family, since we were constantly a topic of conversation in the gossip column that had become a Rosewood River guilty pleasure.

"Of course, you do," I grumped. I was trying to tame down the boner that wouldn't go away, and this woman was getting under my skin. And now I had to think about everything I said because there was a reporter here.

"What's with the attitude? We need to join everyone in the library, so you best start doting on me now, you big baby. Your penis will recover, I promise." She chuckled as she slipped her hand in mine. "Now, turn on the charm and look at me like you can't live without me."

I barked out a laugh. "You're absolutely insane."

"You got that right." She waggled her brows. "Let's do this."

She led me into the room where a camera crew was set up, and her entire family was sitting on the two couches and chairs, looking like the Kennedys. The men were all in sports coats, and the women were all dressed fairly formal.

And then there was us.

Me and Lulu.

She wore her cute jeans that were cut off at the bottoms with heeled boots, and I was dressed for a casual Friday at the office.

We stood out like sore thumbs.

And everyone had their eyes on us.

12

Lulu

"There's my Lulubelle," Gramps said, as he pushed to his feet and pulled me into a hug.

"Good morning. We're just going to take some photos with you, and then I'm going to take Rafe out on the boat." I was putting it out there early so we could slip out shortly after the photos.

"Well, you certainly didn't dress for family photos," Charlotte snipped as her eyes scanned me from head to toe.

Of course, she was wearing red-and-blue-plaid dress slacks and a white collared shirt with a navy cashmere sweater. Her blonde hair was perfectly styled in a sleek bob, ending at her chin.

"It's called fashion. This top and these boots are Laredo, and both were actually designed by my mother," I said, before flashing my wrist that was covered in gold bangles. "And these are mine. So we've got all sorts of family representation here."

"And you certainly wear them well, darling," my mother said as she took me in. She strode over in a cream cashmere maxi dress and heels.

"If that's the case, I think it would be best if we spoke with Lulu first—you know, just ask a few quick questions before we shift to politics," Ray Coffee said. He was one of the hosts of the *Weekday Morning Show* and a man who graced most people's televisions every single day while they had their first cup of coffee.

"Of course," my mother said. "She'd be happy to answer a few questions. You know her line just got picked up by Luxe, the largest retailer in Paris."

Charlotte's hands fisted at her sides, and I saw the veins on her neck pulse. "This interview is not for my cousin."

Ray turned slowly, his mouth in a straight line. "I was very clear with you, Mrs. Wellington, that the only way we were going to do this story about Hunter was if we included your father and the rest of the family."

"That would be Mrs. *Sonnet*-Wellington," Charlotte hissed. "This isn't a story about jewelry and lace bodysuits. My husband is making a difference in the world."

"I happen to be a big fan of lace bodysuits," Rafe said, and my head fell back in laughter. Talk about a gift for breaking up the tension.

"And you are?" Ray asked, extending a hand.

"I'm Rafe Chadwick. The lucky guy who gets to date this woman." Rafe wrapped his arms around me, and my heart raced. We needed to be careful because we didn't need that mentioned in the story.

"I heard you were dating someone new." Ray leaned closer to

us. "I'm happy to hear that, Lulu."

I'd met Ray a few times at parties and events that my mother had been hosting.

"You're not the only one, Ray," Rafe said with a chuckle.

Ray looked completely enamored, and Charlotte was busy ordering everyone around for the photo shoot.

"Why don't you go grab some breakfast, and I'll take the family photo real fast, and then you and I can sneak out on the boat." I shot Rafe a warning because Ray would start asking him questions if he seemed open to it.

"Nonsense," my mother said. "We all want Rafe in the family photo."

"What?" Charlotte gasped. "They aren't married. We don't allow non-family members in the family portraits."

"They aren't married *yet*," Francois said, walking into the room holding a champagne flute. "I feel comfortable having him in the photo."

"You aren't even in the photo. In fact, I don't know why you're here," Charlotte snipped, and Hunter placed a hand on her shoulder to try to calm her down.

"He's here because my wife wants him here. And that's all we need to know," my father said.

"Listen, I can take photos with and without Lulu's boyfriend, and you can decide which you would like to hang in the library," Delilah said. She was a world-renowned photographer and the daughter of some famous French actor, and my Aunt Louisa had insisted she take our family photos for the last decade.

"I'd like Rafe in the photos," Gramps said, eyes hard. "It's my birthday photo, and I have the last word. Let's get this and the interview done so we can enjoy the day before everyone heads home."

"This is ridiculous." Charlotte stormed over to me and whispered in my ear, "You always ruin everything."

Why did I care what she thought?

She was a miserable human being. She treated people terribly. I've known her my whole life, and she's always gone out of her way to be cruel to me.

We all took our positions around the hunter-green velvet sofa in the library. It was Gramps' favorite room in the house.

Charlotte and Hunter were sitting in the center of the couch, where the grandchildren always sat, and the aunts, uncles, and grandparents stood in the back. Jasper, Serena, and Meredith were on one side, and I moved to sit on the other side, tugging Rafe along with me, but Delilah didn't like the layout.

"I'd like Lulu and Rafe right here in the center. It doesn't look balanced this way. Charlotte and Hunter, you move down to the end, please," the photographer said.

No. She. Didn't.

Serena and Meredith chuckled, and I tried not to look at Charlotte, who was not making any attempt to tone down her anger.

I squeezed in beside Jasper and made as much room as I could for Rafe, but he was a big guy, and Charlotte wasn't allowing space for him to sit.

"I'm going to be on your lap if you don't move over, Char-Char," Rafe said, which caused everyone outside of Charlotte's direct family to laugh hysterically.

Charlotte Sonnet-Wellington did not like nicknames.

"We could actually have Charlotte and Hunter stand on the end if that's more comfortable," Delilah said, completely unaware of how badly she was offending my cousin.

Charlotte moved over enough to make room for Rafe, but

her hands were fisted so tight that her knuckles turned white.

"Okay, this works." Delilah stepped back as Ray watched with Francois, both admiring the bookshelves in the background. "Yes. Yes. This is it. Natural smiles to start, please."

We spent the next thirty minutes taking endless photos. Delilah had moved Rafe's hand to rest on my knee, and every few minutes, he'd take his thumb and stroke the inside of my leg gently. As if he knew I was uptight and anxious and wanted to soothe me.

I appreciated it.

I was coming off the world's best orgasm from last night, which was saying a lot, seeing as I was the only one touching myself. But it was the view in front of me that had gotten me there.

This tall, strong man stroking his erection as he watched me.

It was so hot, I'd never be able to get it out of my mind. I slept like a baby after that because it had been a long time since I wanted to be touched by anyone—a long time since anyone had made me want to even touch myself.

"Okay, that's enough for me. Time to move on," Gramps said.

Everyone agreed, and Charlotte asked to take a few photos without Rafe in them, but my parents stepped in before my grandfather did.

"We're done, Charlotte." My father's eyes were hard, and Uncle Charles nodded in agreement, which surprised me.

"Okay, I'll just hang out and take some candids while you all do the interview," Delilah said.

Rafe gave me a look as he started to head for the kitchen to grab some food.

"Not so fast," Ray said. "How about I start with Lulu and Rafe so they can take the boat out while I finish up with everyone else?"

"You have got to be kidding me," Charlotte hissed. "Is this some kind of joke?"

"This is me doing my job. Laredo and MSL are huge brands, and not everyone is as interested in politics as you are, Mrs. Sonnet-Wellington." Ray quirked a brow before turning back to me. "It won't take but a few minutes. But I'd love to speak to both of you."

Forty-five minutes later, he asked us far more than we were prepared to answer. Sweat dripped down my back the entire time, but Rafe handled it like a pro.

He never wavered or seemed nervous.

He told a great story about how we met, and I had no idea where he pulled that from.

He talked about my jewelry line with pride, as if he'd studied my website.

He talked about my gummy bear obsession, and then he pulled a mini bag of gummy bears from his pocket and handed them to me, making a joke about how he was always prepared.

Blasphemous.

This man was brilliant.

We made our way out to the kitchen, with my cousin Charlotte glaring at me when I told everyone we'd be back in a while. Mrs. Weston quickly packed up a few sandwiches that she was making, a large bottle of sparkling water, and some fruit in a basket, and we took it out to the boat.

"This is not good," I whispered as we walked side by side toward the pontoon boat.

"What do you mean? I thought we did great."

"Let's get out on the water first," I said.

We walked across the dock, and I stepped aboard, reaching my hands out to him for the picnic basket. Once we were both on,

I moved to the front, and he offered to drive, telling me he grew up on boats on the river.

I nodded and pointed in the direction of my favorite peaceful spot on the water. The sun was out, but it was January, so I reached for two blankets beneath the seat and pulled them out. There was a cover on the boat, so it provided protection from the wind.

I pointed to the cove for him to pull into. He turned off the engine so we could just float out here. No one was out today, so it was quiet.

He moved to sit beside me, and I pulled the picnic basket between us, and we both started eating.

"So, what's the problem? We killed it," he said, and I tore open the bag of gummy bears he'd given me and popped a few into my mouth. They always helped me relax, like a shot of straight dopamine.

"That was the *Weekday Morning Show*, Rafe. The whole world is going to think we're dating. This is a lot more than just my family and your boss." I blew out a breath.

"So what? It's not like we're dating anyone else. No one is going to get hurt. Who cares?"

"I don't think you realize how much attention this could get. I mean, maybe they won't focus on us. Maybe the story will be about my uncle and Hunter, and we'll barely be mentioned. He just asked you so many questions, and I'm afraid they are going to make it a big deal."

"We're fine. You worry too much." He took a bite of his sandwich and groaned as he leaned back on the seat.

"What if your family hears about it? What if the press comes to Rosewood River?"

"We already have the *Taylor Tea*." He chuckled.

"Shit. I dragged you into this," I said, rubbing my hands over my face. This was going to be a big deal. I knew it in my gut.

"Lulu, relax. People thinking that I'm dating you is not a bad thing. I'm single right now. My boss thinks I'm in a relationship. It's fine."

I studied him for a few seconds.

Man, this guy was too good-looking for his own good.

"Rafe."

"Lulu," he said, his voice all tease.

"If Beckett hears about this, he's going to lose his shit and make this a big deal. He loves a good show. The press will play into that. You're going to be dragged into my shit, and I feel bad about it."

"So, flash me your tits, and we'll call it even." He smiled, and damn if a rush of butterflies didn't flutter in my stomach.

"This isn't a joke. Maybe we can keep it under the radar. Charlotte is on a mission to make this about her father and Hunter. Hopefully, she gets her way this time."

He reached for my bag of gummy bears and set it down before handing me some bread and cheese. "Eat something solid. You can't live on gummy bears alone."

His words startled me, and I didn't even know why.

He was right, but no one had ever really commented on the amount of gummies I ate as an actual meal replacement.

I ate a bite of my sandwich and then reached for the fruit. "You're much nicer than I thought you were when I first met you."

"Really? Would that be when you karate-chopped me in the neck? This is such a surprise. I thought that meant you liked me," he said, making no attempt to hide his sarcasm.

I chuckled. He was funny and easy and smart and handsome.

"So, why aren't you in a relationship? I mean, you're unfairly good-looking by most women's standards. You're funny and charming—even Ray Coffee was captivated, and he hates everyone."

"I don't know." He shrugged. "I've dated plenty. I just haven't really found anyone that I wanted to get serious with since college. And even then, I was one foot out the door the minute she mentioned moving in together after we graduated."

"Commitment-phobe?" I asked, taking another bite.

"I don't think so. I've never been unfaithful. I'm a straight shooter when I date a woman." He shrugged as he took a sip of the sparkling water right from the bottle before passing it to me. "My dad told me that when he and my mom were dating, she was about to leave to study abroad, and a sick feeling came over him. He said in that moment, he just fucking knew that she was the one, you know? And I guess I'm waiting for that."

"So, did she study abroad?" I asked.

"Yep. But they admitted their feelings or something like that, and they talked daily that semester and have been together ever since." He handed me a strawberry, before popping one into his mouth, as well. "How about you? The rock star tainted all men for you?"

"I just realized at some point that my life was revolving around a very selfish man. I wasn't giving my business the attention it deserved at that time because I was being pulled in every direction. I have goals that I want to achieve, and I don't want to be resentful for giving them up because my partner doesn't support me, you know? So, I'm committed to My Silver Lining and growing my company. I date, or I did before I made up this whole relationship, but at this time in my life, I prefer to keep it casual."

He nodded. "I get that. You mentioned that you hadn't been

with a man for a while, is that because of your ex?"

"Beckett has a ton of addiction issues, so we didn't even have sex the last six months that we were together. And before that, it wasn't great. It hadn't been great for a long time. But we had this history because we dated all through college, and I think I felt this need to save him in a way, if that makes sense."

"Explain," he said, handing me back my bag of gummy bears as if he was pleased with the amount I'd eaten.

"When he started touring with the band and his fame grew, so did his problems. That was when I started trying to save him. He'd guilt me about not being there because I was building my company, so I'd neglect the things that were important to me to help him. And then the sex was awful because he was always wasted. He was sloppy, and I didn't enjoy it. But I didn't want to rock the boat when we only had a weekend together every couple of weeks. And weeks turned into months. And then one day, I woke up, and I was done. I just wanted out of it, and I didn't care how uncomfortable he'd make me. But it hasn't been easy, and I do feel bad because my family has been embarrassed by it."

"Stop apologizing for something that you have no control over. You can't control people from your past or your present. You dated a guy who was obviously a good guy in the beginning, and then he got famous, and he changed. It's not your job to fix him. The only one I feel bad for is you. You're the one who got the short end of the stick. And he's a fucking moron for letting you go."

I sucked in a breath. I was so used to being judged for dating Beckett and being dragged into the media. But Rafe was right.

I didn't owe anyone an apology.

Well, aside from myself.

13

Rafe

We got home late last night, and I actually missed Lulu after I'd gone to the guesthouse. I was used to her being snarky or frantic about putting on a show or vulnerable like she was on the boat.

This woman. Man, she was multifaceted in every way.

I enjoyed her family, aside from Barron, Charlotte, and Hunter.

My phone vibrated for the hundredth time, and I rubbed my eyes and rolled over in bed to grab my phone.

Easton: *Holy fuck. Has anyone been on the internet this morning?*

Axel: *I work on a ranch. I see horses long before I check the internet.*

Clark: *I had a game last night. I was actually trying to get some sleep, but my phone kept vibrating. Thanks for that, fuckers.*

Archer: *I'm making Melody breakfast, and I just survived getting her hair into two buns because Missy Lowell wears two buns. It's been a morning over here.*

Bridger: *I'm guessing you're referencing our now-famous brother?*

Easton: *Of course, he isn't answering. I'd drive over there, but it's snowing like a bitch this morning.*

Axel: *I work outside, dickhead. It's not that bad.*

Clark: *Rafe, where the fuck are you?*

Archer: *Is someone going to fill us in?*

Me: *What the fuck is going on? I've been out of town and was trying to get some sleep. It's barely 7 a.m. What's the emergency?*

Easton: *Did you take part in a family photo shoot with the Sonnets? Did you do an interview with the most popular morning show and forget to mention it to anyone?*

Me: *It was a family thing. They asked me to sit in. It was no big deal. The dude asked a few questions.*

Easton: *You're going viral, brother. Everyone is posting photos of you and Lulu. Something you want to tell us?*

Me: *You seem to know more than me. Why don't you fill me in?*

Easton: *Okay, it says here, and I quote, "I always keep gummy bears in my pocket because my girl loves them. And I love her, so I'm always packing the gummies."*

Bridger: *I just threw up in my mouth.*

Clark: *Wait a hot fucking minute. The girl beats the shit out of you, and you're terrified of her, and now you're dating her and in love?*

Axel: *Hey, she's hot. It happens. Has she cut off your balls yet?*

Archer: *Now I'm online, and I just read a quote posted on an entertainment account, and the comments are all saying: Swoon. Swoony. I'm swooning. Apparently, they are all swooning for you, buddy. Whatever the fuck that means.*

Easton: *What was the quote?*

Archer: *Rafe was asked how long they've been together, and his answer was: "It's not about time, Ray. It's about feelings. And to me, it feels like forever."*

Bridger: *What the fuck is happening?*

Clark: *I'd say that forever is happening.*

Me: *Fuck you. I can explain, but I need a minute.*

Axel: *Do you have to talk to your lover before you answer us now?*

Bridger: *I'm so fucking confused.*

Easton: *Hey, that's how relationships work.*

Archer: *Wait a hot fucking second. She hit you in the balls with a pool ball a couple of days ago and you were cursing her name. And now you found your forever? It makes no sense.*

Clark: *Love doesn't always make sense. <laughing face emoji>*

Easton: *Mom is blowing up my phone. She's mad at me for not telling her that you have secretly been dating Lulu.*

Bridger: *You better get your story straight, brother.*

There was a knock on the door, more like a pounding that wouldn't stop. I set my phone down and trudged through the small space to the front door to see Lulu standing there in her sleep shorts, slippers, and tank top as the snow was falling all around her.

"Jesus. Get in here, it's freezing out there." I reached for her hand and tugged her inside.

Her teeth were chattering. "The shit has hit the fan, Rafael. The whole world knows we're dating."

"Come here." I led her to the bedroom and lifted the blanket for her to climb in. Hell, we'd showered together; this hardly felt inappropriate at this point. And she was freezing. I covered her with a blanket before padding back out to the front room and reaching into my coat pocket for what I knew she needed. I tossed a mini bag of gummy bears onto the bed before climbing in.

She quirked a brow. "Our problems are much bigger than gummy bears."

"Relax. It's not that big of a deal."

"He barely posted anything from the interview with my

cousin or uncle. It was all about us. And people are zooming in on us sitting together in the family photo with your hand on my thigh." She shook her head like we'd been photographed naked.

"Well, at least they don't know about the orgasm shower. Isn't that what you called it?" I reached for the gummies and tore open the bag.

Damn. These weren't as bad as I remembered.

"Holy shit." She fell back on the bed. "I've made a mess of things. It's a disease, you know? I tend to do this all the freaking time. I'm trying to break free from a lunatic ex, and now I've dragged my best friend's boyfriend's brother into my drama. You had a normal life before you met me."

"That's a bit dramatic, Wildcat. I've never been normal." I fell back to lie beside her.

"What are we going to do? The press is going to be here the minute Beckett makes a statement and turns this into a thing."

"You don't know that."

"Rafe." She sat forward, her eyes wild and frantic. "I grew up in a very public family. I know how this works. They will come here and dig into this relationship. And Beckett is going to fuel it even more because he thrives on drama. This is so bad."

She was clearly in a state of panic now. So, I did the only thing I knew to do.

I leaned her back on the bed and tickled her senseless until she was laughing hysterically.

She wasn't yelling anymore, so I pulled back.

"I hate being tickled," she hissed.

"You were spiraling. Take a breath. It'll all be okay."

"Well, you should have just said that everything would be fine. You didn't need to grope me like a wild fucking animal." She pushed to her feet.

"I think you like that I knew how to calm you down."

She crossed her arms over her chest. "Are you drunk?"

"I just woke up; I'm far from intoxicated. But I might be on a sugar high from the gummy bears." I chuckled.

"This is not a joke, Rafe. We need a plan."

"The plan is that we're dating. We have to keep it up until next weekend anyway. More people just know about it now. It's not that big of a deal. People date all the time. They'll think we dated for a little while, and then we'll say we broke up and remained friends. You are making way too much out of this."

She marched toward me, pointing her finger in my face. "This is complicated, Chadwick. People are going to be watching now, so we need to be very careful. No more tickling and no more orgasm showers. We need boundaries. Clear-cut boundaries so this doesn't get any more complicated than it already is."

I picked up my phone to see seventeen messages from my mom. She went from asking what was going on to deciding that I was in love.

"Well, buckle up, girlfriend. You're having dinner with my parents tonight," I said, as I read through the messages. "Apparently, they're very hurt that we've kept our love affair a secret, and they want to talk to us."

"What the hell are we going to tell your parents?" she said, as she paced around the bedroom. "This is such a mess."

"I'll just tell them that we're having fun. I'll be honest. We did go on a trip. I do find you attractive, even if you have caused me more physical pain than any woman I've ever known and you're always yelling at me. I'll just pussy foot around the truth."

"Did you just say pussy foot?"

"It's one of my favorite kinds of foots." I barked out a laugh.

"You're disgusting."

"And I'm all yours, baby." I grabbed a T-shirt from the drawer and pulled it over my head before tugging on some gray sweatpants. "Come on. I'll make us coffee, and then we'll come up with a plan."

. . .

"It's not every day you read on the internet about your son being in a relationship," my father said.

"But I'd be lying if I didn't say we were thrilled about it." My mom winked at me.

"I'm sure you're used to this kind of stuff, Lulu, growing up in such a public family," Dad said.

"Yes. But that doesn't make it right. I'm so sorry that you found out the way that you did," Lulu said.

"You have nothing to be sorry about," my mother said, reaching for Lulu's hand.

"Listen, I'm a grown man. I don't go running to my parents every time I date someone. We weren't at the point where we were ready to tell anyone what was happening because we wanted to see where it was going first. And then the interview was sort of sprung on us," I said, reaching for another breadstick.

"I'm really sorry about all of this." Lulu blinked several times, before straightening her features and scooping some salad onto her plate. "I didn't mean for it to come out like this."

My mother was on her feet and coming around the table. She wrapped her arms around Lulu and squeezed. "Honey, no. This is not your fault. We aren't upset about any of it. I told Keaton the night we met you, when you shot that ball off the table into Rafe's family jewels, that there was something special about you. I saw the spark there. I just didn't know you two were already together. You put on a good show pretending you couldn't stand one another."

Apparently, our acting skills preceded us.

Mom walked back to her seat and sat down.

"Thank you for being so understanding. I think you should know that this is all my fault," Lulu said, and I could tell that she was about to confess because she looked over at me and gave me that look.

"Stop. It's not your fault." I grabbed her hand beneath the table and squeezed it. "Listen, it's still fairly new. Lulu just moved here for a few months. We didn't want the added pressure. So let's just not read into it too much and see what happens."

My father nodded as he reached for his wine glass and took a sip. "I couldn't agree more. The last thing you need is pressure. So, tell us about your jewelry business. Henley was filling us in on how talented you are."

"Thank you. I love it. I've designed every piece that we sell, and we were just picked up by a big department store in Paris called Luxe. I'll be moving there in a few months, as the jewelry market is booming there, and I've got a team here in the US that can oversee everything."

My mother's brows cinched together, and I could see the wheels turning. They thought we were dating. If they read everything on the internet, I'd boasted about being in love with her. And now she was moving to another country.

"You're moving there permanently?" my mother asked.

"I love to travel," Lulu said, glancing over at me in panic. "So, I'll be back and forth quite a bit. I just want to get the office there off the ground."

"It's amazing," I said. "Seeing what you've created. That you've taken a design from a drawing to an actual piece of jewelry, and you've got your pieces in stores all over the world. That's something, Wildcat."

"Thank you. I'm thrilled about all of it. I'm working on a few new designs while I'm here, and with all this snow, it gives me plenty of time to sit down and draw." She chuckled.

"I love that you can just see something and then put it on paper before making it come to life," my mother said. She held up her wrist, showing us the dainty gold and jade bracelet she was wearing. "I bought this in New York last year when Keaton and I were on vacation and didn't even realize that it was your company until this morning. Does this mean that you designed this piece?"

Lulu's smile spread clear across her face. "That is actually one of our best sellers. It's the first piece that I ever designed, so it's very special to me."

"I remember when you saw it," my father said. "She lit up and couldn't stop looking at it. I had the lady wrap it up and surprised her after she'd left to use the restroom."

"You've still got the moves, Dad." I laughed. "Very smooth."

"You're very talented, Lulu. And Henley has told us so much about you. We're just thrilled that you and Rafe have found your way to one another." She held up her hands and smiled. "No pressure. I'm glad you two are enjoying your time together."

"Very subtle, Mom." I shook my head and winked at her.

We spent the next two hours talking and laughing. My parents were the best people I knew, and Lulu seemed to be very comfortable with them as the dinner went on.

She fit right in.

It didn't matter if it was real or fake.

Because in this moment, there was nowhere else I wanted to be.

Than sitting right here next to my fake girlfriend.

14

Lulu

"I know things are a little messier than you planned, but I think it's actually okay," Henley said, as she lay next to me in the oversized king bed.

The snow had continued to fall, and I was over it.

I was also over the mess that I made. The mess that I dragged Rafe and his family into.

My best friend's boyfriend's family.

So, this morning when I woke up to news that Beckett had decided to use his social media platform to speak to millions of his fans about how heartbroken he was to hear the news that I was in a serious relationship, I called my best friend immediately in a full-blown panic.

Things would be even bigger now.

My family was well-known. People were interested in the Sonnet family.

But Beckett Bane's fame was next level.

The trolls would come out. The attention would be on a much larger scale now.

Henley had come right over and found me in a heap under all the covers, where I wished I could stay and hide for the next few weeks.

"How is any of this okay?" I croaked.

"Well, you've been telling Beckett that you're in a relationship for months, and he never believed you. Now you have an actual person in photos. A man who told a reporter that he was crazy about you. That changes things. The good news is, I don't see him coming and flipping any tables now that there is another man involved."

"A man that's been lying on my behalf." I sighed.

"Yes. And you're going to go put on a show on his behalf tomorrow." She stroked my hair away from my face after she pulled the blanket back. "He's a grown man, Lu. He seems completely okay with the arrangement."

"And now his family thinks we're together. And they're all so nice and normal," I said with a wobbly chuckle. "I'm an awful human being."

She reached for my wrists and pulled me forward to sit up. "Lulubelle Sonnet, you are the best person I know. You are honest and kind and fierce and strong all at the same time. You have a famous ex-boyfriend who won't leave you alone. Your father puts an abnormal amount of pressure on you, and your family is in the public eye. You're doing the best you can, all while building an empire."

"Wow. When you put it that way, I sound like a badass." I

swiped at my eyes and chuckled.

"Exactly. And as far as Rafe's family goes, I'm fairly certain that his siblings and cousins know that there's a story here. His parents are sweet, and if Rafe wants them to think you're dating, let it be. He's dated women before, and the relationship ends without any drama. You're my best friend. They will love you while they think you are together, and they will love you after. I promise it's all fine."

I nodded. "Okay. I just fear that the attention will get to be too much. We planned a quiet breakup, but now with the whole world watching, I won't be able to keep any of it quiet. We're going to be under a microscope."

"Stop overthinking. I don't think Rafe is in any hurry to do anything. He seems much calmer than you are about it. Easton said he's been in a great mood. I guess his boss reached out because he saw the news online, and he couldn't believe that Rafe had kept it a secret that he'd been dating *The Lulu Sonnet.*"

I couldn't help but smile. "Really? Okay, that makes me feel slightly better. I just don't know if Rafe realizes how big this could get. And this is Easton's family, too, and I know how much they mean to you. And you mean the world to me."

Her gaze searched mine. "What's going on, Lu? This isn't like you to be so stressed out. I'm fine. Easton is fine. Rafe is fine. Your parents are on cloud nine. Why are you so upset?"

She was right. This was out of character. I dealt with the madness of dating a rock star for years.

My family was used to this kind of attention.

But Rafe was not.

Rafe was different.

"Rafe's a really good guy," I said with a shrug.

Her eyes widened, and she laughed. "You hate most men.

I've never heard you call anyone a good guy, outside of your grandfather. Even when you dated Beckett for years, you never said that."

"That's because Beckett is a complete douchebag. I was young and dumb and thought I could do a douchebag exorcism and fix him. And Gramps is a good guy. I've also said that Easton is a good guy—I mean, after I threatened to cut off his balls if he hurt you."

"Right, but that's because Easton is my boyfriend and I love him, so you love him. But I thought Rafe annoyed you?" She quirked a brow. "Did something happen?"

I've never lied to Henley. I've withheld one little thing in all the years that I knew her, and that was mainly because I was afraid of what she'd do if I told her about the day I ended things with Beckett. But showering with Rafe was not something I could share. He and I had promised we'd keep it between us, and there'd been no touching, so it was innocent. It didn't mean anything.

"What? No. Nothing has happened outside of pretending to be dating and putting on a show. And of course, he totally annoys the shit out of me. But he can still be a good guy and annoy me." I smirked. "I don't want to do anything that hurts the people that you love."

"Hey. I love you. I'm not going anywhere. Obviously, I would prefer that you and Rafe don't make things complicated because he is Easton's brother. I mean, unless you actually like him?" She waggled her brows.

"Hen."

"Lu," she pressed.

"I'm moving to Paris. And he's got all that big dick energy. He hasn't been in a relationship in years. I've been down that road, and I'm not doing it again. Plus, I like being single."

"I get that. And if you wanted to have a fling, it's probably best not to do it with a guy who is going to be in your life for years to come, because he's going to be in mine."

Good point.

But an orgasm shower is not a fling.

Even if I couldn't stop thinking about it.

"I can't even have a fling because now I'm in a relationship with a man I can't sleep with."

Her head fell back in laughter. "Come on. Let's get you dressed and bundled up and go grab breakfast at the Honey Biscuit Café."

I pushed to my feet, and she followed me into the bathroom as I pulled my hair into my favorite periwinkle velvet scrunchie and then pulled on a turtleneck and a pair of jeans and boots.

We loaded into her SUV and drove the short distance to the restaurant.

"You know you're going to be the topic in the *Taylor Tea* tomorrow with all this media attention," she said when she put the car in park.

"I'll be at the wedding. We're leaving first thing in the morning, so you'll have to call me. That's the only newspaper I'm excited about being a subject of. I feel like I've really made it now." I laughed.

We jogged inside as the snow continued to fall. When we pulled the door open, Oscar was waiting for us with his arms folded. "You two are dating brothers? Was that planned before you moved here?"

I was about to answer him, but he continued.

"Of course, it was. You've been seeing that man behind our backs," he grumped.

He barely knew me, and now he was offended?

"Welcome to small-town living," Henley whispered in my ear.

"We didn't want to add pressure to our relationship, Oscar." I held my chin up defensively.

I was defending a relationship that wasn't even real.

"Leave them alone, you big jackass." Edith came out from the kitchen. "Those Chadwicks are easy on the eyes. I'm not surprised at all."

"No. You're just jealous because you make a fool of yourself falling all over them when they're here," he grumped.

"Hey, I have no shame when I see a beautiful man, yet I still picked you, you stubborn ass," Edith said, as she walked us to the booth in the back.

We took our seats, and she handed us each a menu before walking away. Henley's phone rang, and I knew she was working from home today, so she told me she needed to take the call as I scanned my phone.

There was a new text from Rafe.

Rafael: *Hey. I know you're freaking out about everything, and I know you need to work today, but I want you to come with me somewhere.*

Me: *I'm not freaking out. I do need to work, but I'm currently getting harassed at the Honey Biscuit Café because Oscar is furious that we didn't tell him about our relationship. <head exploding emoji>*

Rafael: *He just lives for giving people shit. Don't worry about it.*

Me: *Where do you want to take me?*

Rafael: *Oh, Wildcat. That was not the right question to ask. I could name several places that I'd like to TAKE YOU.*

I chuckled as my teeth sank into my bottom lip.

Me: *Where do you need me to come with you?*

Rafael: *Holy shit. Does everything you say sound sexy? I could also name quite a few places I'd like you TO COME.*

Me: *I'm having breakfast with Henley, you fool. Just tell me what you need.*

Rafael: *I'll come over to your place in an hour and get you. It's a surprise. You'll love it. Trust me.*

Me: *I trust very few people. We aren't there yet.*

Rafael: *Dress warm, Wildcat.*

I set my phone down just as Henley ended the call, and we placed our orders.

"Are you feeling okay? Your cheeks are flushed," she said, as she reached for her coffee that had just been set down.

"I'm not flushed. I'm fine. Maybe it's the blizzard outside that's wreaking havoc on my skin."

She rolled her eyes. "Whatever. Your cheeks were not that pink when we walked inside. Who were you texting?"

"What? Who was I texting? Who were you talking to?" I was the queen of deflection, and it usually worked.

"That was a client," she said, and thankfully, two plates of pancakes and bacon were set down in front of us, so we never circled back to who I was texting.

Because if my bestie knew that my fake boyfriend was dirty texting me, she'd be very concerned.

We enjoyed our breakfast, and she told me all about the wedding plans that were happening for Emerson, Rafe and Easton's sister.

"Well, if it isn't the two city girls taking over Rosewood River," the annoying dude who owned the grocery store called the Green Basket said. The guy gave me the creeps, and the way he was looking at both of us only convinced me more that my bat senses were correct.

"Hi, Josh," Henley said, her voice cold, which was out of character for her. She'd already shared what an asshole this guy was.

And now he turned his attention to me. "I'm curious. You went from dating a rock star to a Chadwick. That's a big slide in the wrong direction. You're far too beautiful to settle. I think you can do better."

Henley's hands fisted on the table, and I saw red. "And I would say that you sound like a jealous douchebag."

He startled at my words, as if his weren't equally offensive. "I was just complimenting you."

"No. You were cutting down my boyfriend, and I'm not down with that. You might want to tuck those insecurities away before everyone catches on," I said, holding his stare.

"All right. We'll see how long it lasts." He smirked.

"I would say you've outstayed your welcome, Josh," Henley said as she glared at him.

"Have a nice day, ladies." He chuckled as he walked away.

"What the hell is wrong with that guy?" I asked.

"He's a miserable asshole. But you really put him in his place."

"I try."

"Was that little pissant giving you girls trouble?" Oscar

asked, suddenly outraged on our behalf. Apparently, he was the only one who was allowed to harass the customers.

"We're fine. We sent him away with his tail tucked between his legs," I said.

"Good. We love to see it." Oscar smiled, and it made me laugh because he always appeared so grumpy.

"Ah... Oscar, you're my kind of guy."

"Well, I'm spoken for, Lulu. But if I wasn't old as dirt and married most of my life, I'd ask you out for a burger."

My head fell back on a laugh, and Henley did the same.

We finished our meal, and she dropped me off at home before I quickly changed into the warmest clothes I had. I didn't tell Henley that I had plans, but it was only because I didn't know where I was going.

"Wildcat, you here?" Rafe called out from my kitchen.

That bastard came in without knocking on the door once again.

I hurried out to where he was standing in a huff. "You can't come in without knocking on the door."

"I did knock. You didn't answer, and I was freezing my balls off. Plus, the whole world thinks we're in love. It would be weird if I stood outside and kept knocking."

"You're in the backyard. No one can see you. Everyone thinks we're staying in the same house."

"My point exactly. Plus, I've already seen you naked, so it's not like I'm going to walk in and see something new." He smirked.

"Where are you taking me?" I crossed my arms over my chest.

"The happiest place in Rosewood River, and we're picking up my favorite girl."

"You're bringing a date?" I quirked a brow.

"If that's what you want to call her."

He walked over and zipped my coat up to my neck before taking my hat from my hands and tugging it over my head and leading me to the door.

I feigned irritation like a pro.

But my stomach fluttered once again because I couldn't wait to see where he was taking me.

15

Rafe

"All right, Princess. This is a big day." I tightened the hood over Melody's hat and took her little hand in mine.

"Because I'm four years old now, right? Right, Uncle Rafe? You promised when I'ze gots to be four, you'd take me to your special place."

"I sure did. And we've got fresh snow, so the timing is perfect." I smiled down at her. My cousin Archer's daughter was the most adorable kid on the planet. Where Cutler Heart was a cool cat, Melody Chadwick was a sweet angel girl. I was there the day she was born, and I've never felt love like I did the first time she was placed in my arms.

I'd walk through fire and slay dragons for this girl without hesitation.

"I love your pink coat and hat and mittens," Lulu said, as she bent down to help Melody get all bundled up.

God forbid her nanny, Mrs. Dowden, who was in her early eighties and rivaled the energy of a geriatric sloth, did anything to help. She was sitting on the La-Z-Boy in the family room, watching her "programs" as she sipped the hot chocolate she asked me to make her when I arrived.

Our office was closed today because my boss, Joseph Chapman, was getting married tomorrow, and he'd declared it a company holiday today. When I had the day off, if my cousin was working, I'd always come to see my girl.

"And I love your pretty face," Melody said to Lulu, in that soft little voice that made my heart squeeze.

"Rafe," Mrs. Dowden called out.

"Yep."

"How about you top me off with a little more whipped cream in this mug before you take off? I'll probably get in a nap if you're going to be a while."

Lulu pushed to stand, clearly sensing my irritation. "I'll get that for her."

"You can probably take off, Mrs. Dowden. I'll keep Melody until Archer gets off work."

"Well, I need the hours, so I'll just stick around," she said as she thanked Lulu for the top-off. I was seething at the blatant way she took advantage of my cousin.

She was too old for the job.

Archer was paying Mrs. Dowden and having us come over to relieve her as often as possible because he knew she counted on the income.

Lulu came striding over, holding the can of whipped cream, just as I was about to snap back. She held up her finger and smiled. "Open."

I did as I was told because I'd probably do just about anything this woman told me to do. She sprayed the cream into my mouth, and Melody burst out in a fit of squeals.

Lulu bent down. "Don't tell me you've never had your mouth filled with this yummy goodness."

"I've had the creams on my chocolates," Melody said, dark brown eyes wide as saucers.

"Open up that sweet mouth, love," Lulu said.

Melody opened her mouth, and Lulu squirted just a little bit onto her tongue, and Melody waved her hands excitedly. Lulu pushed to stand again, tipped her head back, and filled her mouth with whipped cream.

For whatever reason, my dick woke up and joined the party.

She took her time swallowing and winked at me before waltzing back into the kitchen and putting it away.

"I likes your girlfriend, Uncle Rafe," Melody whispered.

"Yeah, me, too, kiddo. Just don't tell her I said that."

That earned me a fit of giggles as Lulu came walking back. "Looks like Mrs. Dowden is already asleep. Shall we head out?"

"You knows where we are going, Lulus?" Melody asked as I took her hand and led us outside to my truck.

"Nope. Uncle Rafe hasn't told me."

I kept a car seat in my truck at all times. It was pink, and I always had a mesh bag in the back seat filled with stuffed animals and little toys for my girl.

I opened the back door and set her in her car seat, buckling her up. I opened the passenger door for Lulu, and she climbed right in. Once I was inside the truck, I cranked up the heat and reached inside the center console. I pulled out a bag of fruit snacks, tore the top open, and handed it to Melody. I glanced over to see Lulu smiling at me before I handed her a bag of gummy bears.

But the way this woman was looking at me, it was like I'd just given her a diamond ring.

They were tiny, processed bears made of gelatin.

We pulled up to the bottom of the best snowy hill in Rosewood River. I glanced out the window to see the snow still falling from the sky, so there'd be nice powder for us to slide on. It was the end of January, and the snow would be ending soon, so I wanted to get Melody out here before it was too late. And Lulu Sonnet needed to have some fun. She'd been stressed out ever since news broke that we were together.

"Are you two ready for the most fun you've ever had?" I asked, my voice teasing, as the little angel in the back seat squealed and the little angel in the front seat looked equally excited.

We got out of the truck, and I scooped up Melody into my arms and pulled the large toboggan behind me, calling out for Lulu to follow as we made our way up the hill.

When we got to the top, I set Melody down on her feet and put the toboggan down on the snowy hilltop.

I bent down, getting eye level with my niece. "You've been talking about me bringing you here for months. You ready, baby girl?"

"Yeps." She tucked her lips between her teeth, and I could tell she was nervous.

"Hey, Uncle Rafe would never take you to do something you weren't ready for, okay?" I assured her.

She nodded, her lips turning up in the corners, and her little cherub cheeks were bright pink.

I turned to Lulu, who was watching the interaction intently. "You ready, Wildcat?"

"Absolutely." She waggled her brows, and I helped her onto

the front, placing Melody in the middle, and I slid onto the back. "Are we ready?"

"Yes!" Lulu and Melody shouted at the same time.

I laughed my ass off as I wrapped my arms around my niece, and my legs were long enough to hold Lulu in place, as well.

"One. Two. Three!" I shouted, as I used my hands to get us going, and we took off flying down the hill with snow falling all around us.

The wind hit us in the face, and the snow made it difficult to see, but I couldn't stop smiling as I listened to both my girls squealing and laughing the whole way down the hill.

We continued moving fast once we got to the bottom until we came to a stop. I leaned forward just as Lulu turned around, both of us making sure Melody was good. Melody jumped up and dove on top of me in a fit of laughter.

"I knew you'd love it, my little adventurer," I said, pushing to my feet and setting Melody down in the snow. She dropped onto her back and started making a snow angel through a fit of giggles.

"What did you think, Wildcat?" I asked against her ear.

"I think it is the best place in Rosewood River."

"Yeah? Is this better than city living, or what?" I winked, and those honey-brown eyes were brighter than usual, as her plump lips turned up in the corners, and she nodded.

"I mean, I do enjoy a good department store and a fancy restaurant, but yummy pancakes and a snowy hill are definitely a lot more fun than I expected."

"Stick with me, Lulu Sonnet. I'll show you a good time." I smirked.

"I have a feeling you're right about that." Her teeth sank into her bottom lip, and for whatever reason, I had to fight the urge to kiss this woman. It was getting more challenging. Maybe it was the game that we were playing. I didn't know anymore. I'd never experienced a discomfort like this.

Wanting someone who was off-limits.

Yet pretending that we were together.

"Let's go again, Uncle Rafe and Lulus!" Melody clapped her hands together.

I scooped her up and grabbed the toboggan, and we took off for the top of the hill again.

We went down three more times until we were cold and wet and ready to get inside.

I called Archer, and he was home from work, so we dropped off Melody and headed home.

When we pulled around the corner toward the house, there were two cars parked out front.

I parked in the driveway and glanced in my rearview mirror as two men came out of both cars at the same time, cameras in hand.

"Shit," Lulu groaned. "They're photographers. They have no shame."

"What do they want?" I asked, my voice harsher than I meant it to be. But I didn't like the fact that they were just waiting here for us. What if she'd come home alone?

"A photo of us because they can get a good paycheck for it at the moment."

"Stay in the car. I'll be right back."

"Rafe. You can't reason with these people," she said, and I hated that I could hear the underlying fear in her voice. It pissed me the hell off that her ex put her in this situation and that these two men thought it was appropriate to stalk her for a photo.

"Listen, we're going to the city tomorrow. We'll be out in public, and if someone is there and gets a photo, so be it. But they won't come to your home and park outside to photograph you. That's creepy as fuck. It might fly in the city, but Rosewood River is a small town, and the same rules don't apply."

She nodded. "I know you think that. But one time I left a concert with Beckett and I was hit in the face with a camera, which required a few stitches. So I just want you to know that they are persistent and unreasonable."

My hands fisted at my sides as I processed what she said. I would lose my shit if someone hit a woman in the face with a camera in front of me.

"That's bullshit. Stay put." I pushed the door closed and made my way to the two men standing on the sidewalk. They held their cameras up, and I used my hand to motion for them to put them down.

"Listen, guys. This is Rosewood River. You can't park in front of someone's house and take random photos." I held up my phone. "I grew up with the sheriff, and you've got two options here. You can hold that camera up again, and I'll knock it out of your hands and have you escorted out of this town immediately, only after I destroy the card in that camera."

"Dude. We just want one photo. We drove all the way out here. We have to feed our families, too," one of the guys said.

"Well, I'm all for taking care of family, but this isn't the way to do it. Not here."

"What was the second option?" the other guy asked.

"We're going to be in the city tomorrow night for a wedding. We'll be staying at the H Hotel downtown. If you pull up in the valet tomorrow evening at 5:00 p.m., we'll pose for a photo. You'll be the only ones to get the photo because no one else knows we're going to be there. It's a public place, so that's what we're willing to offer. But you won't come to this house again. Because this is me taking care of my family," I said. My voice was firm and unwavering.

They glanced at one another and nodded. "Yeah. We could do that."

"Good choice." I crossed my arms over my chest and waited for them to climb back into their cars and drive off.

I made my way back to the truck, turned off the engine, and came around to open her door.

"What happened?" she asked, looking over her shoulder to make sure they were still gone.

"They'll be at the hotel tomorrow when we head to the wedding at 5 p.m. We'll pose for one photo in a public place. They took the deal."

She caught me off guard when she lunged at me, wrapping her arms around my neck. "Thank you."

I held her there for a few beats. "I didn't do anything."

"You did. You made today really fun, and you didn't have to include me. You haven't been even slightly annoyed by the fact that I've turned your world upside down. And then you actually stepped in and made the paparazzi leave without following us to the door." She stepped back and shrugged. "You are quite possibly the best fake boyfriend a girl could ask for."

And there it was. The constant reminder that we were playing a part.

None of this was real.

I was staring at her, and she was staring at me.

And then she abruptly turned to walk inside, and I followed. Once there, she shoved her hands into the pockets of her jeans. "So, um, tomorrow morning we leave, right?"

"Yeah. I talked to Bridger, and we're going to take the helicopter into the city so we don't have to drive on the icy roads to get there. I got us a suite, so there's a couch, and I can sleep on that."

"Oh, yeah, that's great. Thank you."

"I'd get you your own room, but I'm afraid someone might notice."

"No, I think the suite is a good idea," she said.

Why was I just standing here like an idiot? She was waiting for me to leave.

This was a business deal. Nothing more.

"If you need anything, I'll be right next door." I took a step back. Okay, that was dumb—she obviously knew that.

"Sounds good. I'll be fine. I'll see you bright and early."

"One more weekend as a couple, and you're off the hook. You're almost free of me, Lulu Sonnet." I winked.

And even as the words left my mouth, I wanted to take them back.

Because a weekend wouldn't be long enough for me to get this woman out of my system.

But I was starting to wonder if I even wanted her out of my system.

16

Lulu

We arrived in the city by helicopter, and Rafe had a car waiting for us when we landed, which took us straight to the swanky hotel near the wedding venue.

We were in the room unpacking, and he was quieter than usual.

"Are you nervous about today?" I asked, suddenly curious about his relationship with his boss.

"I'm ready for this night to be done. I know we're going to have a lot of eyes on us, and Joseph is an intense and unpredictable guy, so you just never know what you're going to get."

I dropped to sit on the bed after I hung up my black satin evening dress in the closet. This was a black-tie affair, and luckily, these types of events were in my wheelhouse. I loved getting all dressed up, as most days I worked from home and lived in athleisure wear.

"Do you like working for him?"

"Not really. He's arrogant and pretentious, but he also hired me when I was first starting out, and his firm is one of the best in the country, so I'm grateful that he took a chance on me."

"And you've been there for years?"

"Yes. I started working for him right out of college. I've been able to achieve all the certifications I wanted during that time, and the goal is to break off on my own and have my own team eventually." He moved to the closet and hung his sleek black suit beside my dress. "Just trying to decide when to do it."

"What's your hesitation?" I asked as I reached for my sketch pad and opened it to the new design I'd been working on.

"I don't know if I'm ready to manage a team. If it's financially wise to do it now, which logically, I know it is. I've been saving for years. But I do really well where I am right now, so there's always a risk. In the big picture, this is the move I need to make. But it'll be slow in the beginning, probably a little scary if I'm being honest. I'll be the one responsible for employees, so it's just a lot to weigh, you know?"

Rafe Chadwick was a multifaceted man.

He was charming and flirty and funny in one breath, but listening to him talk about his professional life—there was a more serious tone.

Professional Rafe was all business. And it was attractive to see how driven he was and how seriously he took his work.

"I get that." I sighed as I found my favorite pencil and started drawing. It always relaxed me. "Change is scary. I went to Juilliard and always thought I'd be a professional dancer. But that didn't work out, so I had to find another plan."

"What happened?" He sat on the edge of the bed and glanced

at my sketch pad curiously.

"I tore all the ligaments in my ankle during training, and I was just never the same. Plus, it's hard to make a living as a dancer, and it's physically taxing. So I had to figure out what I wanted to do. The easy answer was just to go work for my parents. Laredo is hugely successful. I could have stepped into a posh position with a ridiculous salary, but I just didn't see myself doing that for the rest of my life."

He studied me. "What made you choose jewelry?"

"Well, I love jewelry." I chuckled. "I think it can make such a statement. I've always worn lots of rings and bracelets and layered necklaces. I love pieces that have meaning and stones that complement and add to the design. At the end of the day, I need to be creative. I would have just been an executive at Laredo. I want to build something, create something of my own."

He nodded. "I get that. And I think it's pretty cool that you didn't take the easy path."

"I almost did. I had just graduated, and I was dating Beckett, and he'd just signed with a record label. He wanted me to go with him on tour and work remotely for my parents. I actually considered it for a brief moment, but I didn't want to be in someone's shadow, you know? I wanted to create my own magic."

"And how did he handle that?"

"Like a spoiled rock star." I chuckled. "It was the beginning of the end. We were different people in college, and in his defense, which I don't often give him any defense, but his fame came on quickly. It's a lot to handle. I'd grown up with money, and Beckett hadn't. And suddenly, he had a lot in a short period of time. Not everyone can handle that."

"So you started building your company, and he went off on tour?"

"I'm not proud of the fact that I didn't go all in on MSL in the beginning. Beckett was spiraling, and I had a lot of guilt that I wasn't there to help him. I would fly out to see him, and he was growing dependent on alcohol and prescription drugs and who knows what else, and he'd beg me to stay. So, I neglected my own dreams and plans for the first two years, and I will never do that again."

"You were worried about someone you loved, and you put them first. That's not a bad thing, Lulu." His lips turned up in the corners, dimple on full display.

"That's the thing. I don't even know if it was love the last few years. Maybe it was loyalty or history, but as he deteriorated, so did our relationship. I woke up one day and saw a photo of him with another woman in the press, and it was just like one of those lightbulb moments. I was done. I had zero feelings for him, and he wasn't my responsibility anymore. So, I poured myself into work the last eighteen months, and I've seen what I can do when I put my mind to things."

"That's fucking amazing. I'm glad you put yourself first."

"It's funny because I've always been very independent. I grew up in an unconventional home, traveling the world as a kid and attending boarding school in high school. I have always been driven and have known who I was and what I wanted. But I let someone derail me, and it scared the shit out of me that I could allow that to happen."

"It doesn't help that he's a douchebag who keeps coming around and dragging you back into his drama, long after you've been over."

"I think that's why I wanted my father, in particular, to think I was dating someone else. He used to look at me like I set the sun, like I could take over the world. And it actually made me feel like I could. But after Beckett started dragging me into the press by making scenes at events and embarrassing himself, along with me, I felt like he looked at me differently. But last weekend, it felt different. Like his confidence in me was back. And it's sad that it took a fake relationship to do that, even though I've built this company that I'm so freaking proud of all on my own, but I don't even care. Shamefully, I want his approval. So even though I have no desire to invest in a man ever again, for whatever reason, when I brought you home, I think my father saw that as me moving on from being this rich socialite party girl in a relationship with a trainwreck rock star."

His dark gaze softened. "Nothing wrong with wanting your parents' approval. I love my parents. Love my family. And making them proud is important to me, as well."

"Not sure they're going to be proud of you being dragged into the media and tied to a socialite party girl."

"Did you see them the other night? They loved you." He chuckled. "And nothing about you fits that description. I see a woman who is passionate about her company. A woman who cares about each piece of jewelry she creates. A woman who is about to expand her business when she moves to Paris. You're the fucking rock star, Lulu Sonnet. You were just hanging out in someone's shadow for too long. We've all done that. We just don't do it publicly. Nor with family pressure about how we appear in the media. That's a lot to navigate when you're young."

A lump formed in my throat.

For whatever reason, getting Rafe Chadwick's approval also meant something to me. And that was a bit of a red flag because I shouldn't care what this man thought.

"Thank you."

"You found your silver lining, Wildcat. You left a toxic

relationship, things are changing with your family, and your business is taking off."

"This fake relationship ended up being my silver lining in a way. Thanks for putting up with me."

"Thanks for being here this weekend."

"Of course. So there was a moral to that torrid story I just shared," I said with a shrug.

"Let's hear it."

"I wouldn't have taken this leap to start MSL if I hadn't gotten injured. Dancing was my safe place. But it wasn't going to allow me to grow the way this does."

He nodded. "I get that. Getting injured forced your hand."

"It did. But you already know what you want to do. So don't let fear keep you in someone's shadow. You were born to lead, Rafe Chadwick."

He studied me for a few beats before his lips turned up in the corners. "That might be the nicest thing you've ever said to me. I must be growing on you."

"Like a fungus," I said, my voice all tease. "Anyway, tell me what to expect tonight and what you need from me."

"Well, just you being here will get Joseph and his daughter off my back, and even after we're officially over," he said with a wink, "I'll be able to tell them that I'm not ready for anything serious for a long time."

"Are you going to play the wounded bird after this is over?" I arched a brow.

Something crossed in his eyes, but I couldn't read it. "You aren't leaving for Paris for a while, so I'll still be around. I told you that I remain friends with all my exes."

"So we'll stay friends. I've never really had any male friends."

"Really?"

"No. I always think men have an ulterior motive. I'm not very trusting."

"You don't say." He barked out a laugh. "Let me see that drawing."

I spent the next twenty minutes telling him the meaning behind the new "Forever" bracelet. It was all about loving yourself and being okay in your own skin. Because when you start loving yourself, you allow others to do the same.

He listened intently, as if my words mattered.

My ideas mattered.

Rafe Chadwick was more than just a sexy, charming man. He was a good man. A kind man. And I would be lucky to call him my friend.

We realized the day had gotten away from us, and I set up a makeup area in the room at the desk so he could take a shower. I was not going to cross that line again, even though he'd made several jokes about me joining him.

Things had shifted between us, and I liked him. I felt close to him in a way I couldn't even begin to explain. This crazy situation that had brought us together, connected us in a way.

Which meant I needed to be careful.

I curled my hair before pulling it into a low chignon at the nape of my neck and applying my makeup. I did dramatic eyeliner and a smoky eye.

I wanted to make him proud to have me on his arm tonight.

It didn't matter that it wasn't real, he'd shown up for me when I needed him, and I intended to do the same.

He came out of the bathroom looking like he'd just stepped off a photo shoot for *People Magazine's* "Sexiest Man Alive" edition.

He sat on the edge of the bed tying his shoes, and I tried not to stare.

His jaw was chiseled, and his hair was gelled tonight into a sleek style that worked with the fitted slim-cut suit.

"Henley and Easton sent us a screenshot of the *Taylor Tea*. Would you like me to read it to you?" His voice was all tease.

I applied my lipstick and moved to my feet to slip into my dress. "Ohhhh, yes, please. I'll get dressed in the bathroom and leave the door open so I can hear you."

"I've seen you naked. Just get dressed out here, and I won't look if you don't want me to," he said, shaking his head as he stared down at his screen and then peeked up at me to see if I'd listened.

"Fine, you big baby. If seeing me in my bra and panties does it for you, have at it." I tugged my dress from the hanger and dropped my robe before shimmying into the satin fitted dress.

He didn't take his eyes off me as I did so, and once I pulled it up, he pushed to his feet and moved behind me, pulling up the zipper. His fingers trailed up my skin, and my body heated at the slight touch. He moved back to the bed and turned his attention to the phone.

"Okay, here we go." He cleared his throat. "*Good Morning, Roses. Looks like our scoop this week is public knowledge, so we'll just share what we know. Our latest resident, the wealthy socialite bombshell who moved to town recently, is in a relationship with one of our local favorites. He's the boisterous one, and let's just say he's not only good with the numbers, but he's good with the ladies, too,*" he said with a groan. "My God, they may as well just say our names."

"I love that I'm the socialite bombshell." I waggled my brows as I slipped my feet into the gorgeous red, strappy stilettos I saved for a special occasion. "Please continue."

"*Looks like the rock star ex-boyfriend is sharing his broken heart with the world. But I'm not buying it. The rock star has been seen one too many times with other women to earn any form of sympathy from me. I'd go with the charming local guy we all know and love. The famous rock star may be loved by America, but in Rosewood River, we don't care for all that drama. Time will tell. I think this rose might get prickly with two suitors vying for her heart."*

My head fell back in laughter. "Wow. She just tells us exactly how she feels."

"Without saying actual names, even though everyone knows exactly who she's talking about."

"Who do you think is the author?" I asked him as his eyes perused me from head to toe.

"You look stunning, Wildcat." He cleared his throat. "You know, I'm not sure. Bridger is certain that it's Emilia Taylor. But I just can't picture her writing this."

"She's a florist, and she's so sweet. I don't see that either. Why does he think it's her?"

"Who knows, with Bridger? Once he gets something in his head, he can't get it out. Her family owns the paper. She's young enough to be writing this kind of crap..." he said.

"Hey. She just wrote about us, and she was rooting for us. That was not crap."

Loud laughter bellowed from him, and he pushed to his feet. "Fine. Whatever it is. Gossip. It feels like it's someone young."

"Could it be Laney Waters?" I asked. Her parents owned Rosewood Brew Coffee, and she worked there when she wasn't in school. "Every time I see her at the coffee shop, she brings up the *Taylor Tea*."

"I've heard some people mention her name, but I just don't think the Taylors would print something written by a teenager.

But I guess if she's sending it in anonymously, how would they know?"

"You're exactly right. They wouldn't know. Henley and I would have had so much fun writing an anonymous column back in high school." I grabbed my black velvet Laredo clutch.

"I could see you two getting into a whole lot of trouble together back then." He chuckled. "Come on. We've got a car waiting downstairs, and those two guys I promised a photo to are probably sitting in the valet, waiting to snap a few shots."

"Okay, let's do this, lover boy. I will let everyone know that my man is off-limits tonight."

He smirked. "I'm down with that. And you look... fucking gorgeous."

"Right back at you, handsome. Now, let's go show everyone how ridiculously in love we are."

We made our way through the lobby, and I didn't miss the way all eyes followed us as people walked by.

When we stepped outside, a black car was waiting for us, but two men stood on the side, and Rafe held up a hand to the driver. "Give us two minutes."

He pulled me close and dipped me back, and I burst out in a fit of laughter as he waggled his brows at me. Both men snapped several photos, and he pulled me back up and gave them a nod of thanks.

They continued snapping photos as we slipped into the car, and our driver closed the door before returning to the driver's seat and driving us a block away to the venue.

"Just be prepared, all right?" he said as he rubbed his hands together. "Chloe is a lot. She's spoiled and used to getting her way. Hopefully, she brings a date, but she was determined for us to attend this together, for some unknown reason, and she can be relentless. It's tricky because her father is my boss."

"Maybe that's your sign that you don't need to have a boss anymore," I said, reaching for his hand because he appeared anxious, which was out of character for him. "I know why she wants to date you."

He chuckled. "Because I'm easy to throat punch?"

"Because you're loyal and funny and sinfully handsome. You're the whole package, Rafe Chadwick." I leaned close and whispered against his ear. "And I mean that literally. I've seen it, remember?"

His tongue swiped out along his bottom lip. "It's yours if you want it."

Those six words shot right between my legs. I squeezed my thighs together and tried not to react.

I did want it. But I shouldn't want it.

It would be a terrible idea.

Not for my vagina, obviously, but for me as a person.

He was dangerous. Too good. Too smooth. Too likeable.

Too easy to fall for.

Thankfully we came to a stop, and our driver came around and opened the door for us. Rafe exited the car first, and then he reached for my hand as I placed mine in his and stepped out of the car, grasping my clutch in my free hand.

"Here we go," he whispered against my ear and then kissed my cheek before leading me inside the country club.

17

Rafe

Everyone was dressed to the nines, and my hand rested on Lulu's lower back as I guided her through the space.

My boss, Joseph Chapman, married his bride, Denise, in an elaborate but brief ceremony before we made our way to the reception. He'd been talking about this wedding as if it were the event of the century for the last six months.

Once we stepped inside the grand ballroom, I glanced up at the several chandeliers that hung above.

It was a bit fancy for my taste, but I expected nothing less from him.

There was classical music playing, and round tables and chairs filled the space.

"Wow, the attention to detail is something," Lulu said against my ear.

The smell of pear and vanilla flooded my senses.

There was no doubt I had the most beautiful woman on my arm, as every man in the room turned and followed her with their eyes as we walked toward the bar.

Large floral arrangements packed with red and white flowers sat on every table. The large dance floor in the center was a focal point, and an emblem with a large C in the middle to represent Chapman and a J and a D on each side to represent the bride and groom were painted on the dance floor. The same logo was on the cocktail napkins when we rolled up to the bar.

It was elaborate and very evident that they'd spared no expense.

"A cosmopolitan for the lady, and I'll have an old-fashioned please," I said when the bartender looked up at us.

"There he is." Joseph strolled over to us, his eyes on my date, making no attempt to cover his perusal. His bride was nowhere in sight, also not a shock.

"Joseph, congratulations. This is my girlfriend, Lulu Sonnet." The words rolled off my tongue so easily that I almost believed them myself.

His eyes scanned her from head to toe, and I found myself wrapping an arm around her waist possessively and pulling her back against my chest.

"Lulu, it's a pleasure to meet you. Not surprised that you're beautiful, as I figured it would take a special lady to hold this one's attention," he said.

It was a dick thing to say, but I forced a smile as Lulu extended her free hand to him.

"Ahhh… I've heard so much about you and your beautiful bride. It's a pleasure to finally meet you."

"Where is Denise?" I asked, wanting to remind him that we

were here for his wedding as he continued to eye-fuck my date, and I was losing my patience with it.

"She's probably found a way to spend more of my money from her visit to the restroom." He barked out a husky laugh that made it apparent he'd smoked one too many cigars over the years.

"Daddy, have you told Rafe that he'll be giving the speech with me tonight?" Chloe walked up behind her father, and I tightened my grip on Lulu.

Did she say that I was giving a speech?

Her gaze moved from me to the woman pressed against my body, and the tension was so thick you could cut it with a knife.

"Chloe, this is my girlfriend, Lulu Sonnet. Lulu, this is Joseph's daughter, Chloe."

"Well, I'd say I'm a bit more than *just* Joseph's daughter, aren't I, Rafe?" She quirked a brow.

Actually, no.

We were not friends, outside of her constantly hitting on me at work events, and I'd never so much as flirted back. We'd never had an actual conversation, other than her telling me that she thought we should date.

She was an acquaintance at best.

But this was her father's wedding, and I wouldn't be rude.

"Hi, Chloe, it's nice to meet you," Lulu said, extending her hand and trying to break up an uncomfortable situation. "Did you say that Rafe is giving the speech?"

"Yes. Daddy wants Rafe and me to give speeches on their behalf." She shook Lulu's hand hesitantly before pulling it back abruptly. "Shall we go practice, Rafe?"

"I know nothing about a speech, Joseph. A little heads-up would help." I took a sip of my cocktail, letting the warm liquid roll down my throat.

"It was Chloe's idea. She thought there should be two speakers. Denise agreed, so we thought you'd be the guy to do it. My friends are all old fuckers, and they'll be too liquored up to form a coherent sentence with an open bar tonight." More gruff laughter.

"All right. I can say a few words. I don't think we need to practice, as I'm sure you already have your speech prepared, Chloe. I'll just pull some notes together on my phone."

"I can help you." Lulu smiled up at me, and damn, she was too fucking beautiful for her own good.

"Well, she doesn't really know my father, so I'm not sure how she can help," Chloe growled, and Joseph laughed some more and made a hissing-cat sound in response.

"He talks about your father every night before we get into bed. I feel like I've known you for years, Joseph," Lulu purred, and Chloe glared at her.

No doubt my woman could handle herself just fine, but I still felt protective of her.

Lulu Sonnet was fierce and strong, but I'd seen the vulnerable woman beneath, and I felt lucky that she'd shown me both sides.

"We'll be just fine. We're going to go find our table and put a few thoughts together," I said.

"You're sitting at the head table with us." Chloe winked at me. "After all, Daddy thinks of you as family."

Lucky fucking me.

We excused ourselves as dread filled me.

I couldn't think of a table I'd rather not be sitting at more.

There was a table with a bunch of people from the office, and they were waving me over, and I was bummed we weren't seated with them.

"She's a real piece of work," Lulu said, keeping her voice low as she placed her free hand in mine.

I nodded and led her to where my coworkers were and introduced her to everyone.

"I saw your photos on the internet. You're kind of Instagram-famous now, Chadwick. I'm not even going to tell you off right now for keeping the fact that you're dating *the* Lulu Sonnet a secret from me." Clara was my executive assistant, and she turned to look at Lulu and shook her wrist to show off the three bracelets there before shaking her hand. "I'm Clara. I'm the big guy's assistant, and I'm a huge fan of your jewelry."

"Oh, wow. Thank you so much. That means the world to me. It's so lovely to meet you."

"How did demon Barbie take the news of your relationship?" Clara leaned close so only Lulu and I could hear her as she referenced Joseph's daughter. Chloe had a reputation at the office for her bratty behavior when she'd come to visit her father.

"Exactly as expected." I pulled my glass to my lips.

"Hey, boss," Caleb said. He was new to the team this last year and a cool dude. "Is this your lady?"

I smirked because I kind of loved how nervous everyone was about meeting her.

"Yes. This is Lulu," I said. I went around the table, and they each came over and shook her hand and gushed over her a bit.

"I see you aren't sitting with us," Clara said, glancing at the table in the front.

"Yeah, we just heard we wouldn't be sitting here."

"But we can come sneak over a lot," Lulu said as she took a sip of her drink.

"I like this girl," Caleb said, and then his cheeks flamed when I raised a brow at him. "Not like that. Well, I mean, not that you aren't attractive. Shit, you're fucking gorgeous. I just meant—"

"Okay. We're cutting this young buck off the piña coladas,"

Clara said, and the table erupted in laughter.

"I know what you meant. I like this girl, too," I said, before giving them a nod and letting them know we were going to head to our seats.

We were the only ones at the head table as we found our name tags, and I didn't miss the fact that Chloe had been seated on the other side of me.

Lulu tracked the direction I was looking, and she leaned close to me once we were sitting, her lips grazing my ear, which was a direct shot to my dick. "Well, you've got to give her credit for her tenacity. It's obvious you aren't interested in her that way."

"Yeah. I've made it clear multiple times. And I usually just brush off her behavior, but tonight, it feels disrespectful to you, and that shit pisses me off," I said, pulling my phone out of my coat pocket to type up a few notes for the speech.

"Rafe, it's not like we're together," she whispered. "This is a big night for you. Your boss chose you to speak on his behalf. He sat you at his table. That's a compliment to how much he likes you."

"I don't care if this is real or fake," I said, glancing around to make sure no one was listening. "They don't fucking know that. It was unkind to do that to you, and that does not sit well with me. I'm also quite certain that his daughter demanded I be at this table and that I give a speech alongside her. He and I are not that close."

"Hey," she said, taking my hands in hers. It wasn't for show. It was just to comfort me. "That's not the only reason. He couldn't get over to you quickly enough when we arrived. It's obvious he likes you, which is probably why he wants you to date his daughter. You've got this. Let's type up a few things, and we'll get that out of the way, and then we can have some fun."

We huddled together, and she helped me type up a few thoughts, and it felt damn good that she was here.

I liked Lulu Sonnet.

Hell, I didn't want to admit how much I liked her because I knew it would freak her the fuck out. She was scarred from her past and trusted very few people, but for whatever reason, I wanted to be one of them.

I didn't know what it meant.

But I knew that I felt things that I've never felt before.

I knew that I looked forward to seeing her.

I knew that I wanted to sleep in that bed beside her tonight.

Regardless of what it meant, if we never kissed or touched or did anything moving forward, I wanted this woman close to me.

The DJ interrupted my thoughts, letting us know that dinner would be served soon, and everyone made their way to their tables. The servers came around to fill our glasses with red and white wine, and Lulu and I were having a great time.

Joseph, Denise, and Chloe were at our table, along with Joesph's brother and his wife and Denise's three sisters, who were not only staring at me, but I caught them staring at Lulu just as often.

We had the option of steak or lobster, along with salad, potatoes, and rolls. Lulu and I got one of each entrée and shared. I wasn't even sure if we were acting anymore as the conversation flowed around the table, and we took turns sharing our meals and laughing.

Everyone fucking loved her.

Aside from the diva beside me, who was sulking the entire time Lulu spoke. She had the table completely enraptured, including me.

"Okay, we're just going to tell you," Linda, Denise's younger sister, said. "We've had a couple of cocktails, so we have no shame at the moment."

"I love it when the no-shame feels hit," Lulu said with a laugh.

"We're kind of superfans of yours." Linda shrugged.

"Yes, we follow you on social media. We were so happy you broke up with that tool. And you've clearly upgraded," Mandy, the oldest sister, said, as she waggled her brows at me.

"I couldn't agree more." Lulu bumped her shoulder against my arm.

"It's time to do the toast, isn't it, Daddy?" Chloe interrupted, and everyone turned to look at her.

"Sure, sweetheart. This is perfect timing," Joseph said.

"Come on, Rafe. It's you and me."

I turned to look at Lulu, and she stunned the shit out of me when she put a hand on each side of my face and tugged me close and kissed me.

Her lips were soft and sweet, and I wanted to pull her onto my lap and kiss her all night.

She pulled back and winked. "Break a leg, Rafael."

Denise's sisters were clapping and giggling, and that appeared to enrage Chloe.

The lines were graying for me.

That kiss felt real.

And the fucked-up thing about it—I wanted it to be real.

18

Lulu

Turns out, I'm a hoot at weddings. I got everyone to clap and holler for my boyfriend after he crushed his speech.

Or my fake *boyfriend.*

It didn't really matter at the moment. I was buzzed and having the best time, and maybe I was playing my role a little too well, but so was he.

I'd been dying to kiss him before he left the table, and I knew I could blame Chloe's behavior as my defense. But that hadn't been the reason I kissed him.

I did it because I wanted to feel his lips on mine.

But I certainly couldn't make out with the man at his work function. So, I turned up the charm.

I led the conga line on the dance floor before joining Rafe's coworkers for the Macarena, which we danced to while shouting the lyrics.

Rafe was the best wedding date I'd ever had.

He was hilarious and fun, and he had zero hesitation when it came to dancing with me. I missed dancing so much, and just being out there on the dance floor with him had been a reminder of how much I missed it.

I was used to being in control, but when we slow danced, he didn't hesitate to pull me close and sway to the music, moving his body along with mine.

As he took the lead.

My head fell back in laughter when the song we danced to at my grandfather's party played, and Rafe leaned down and sang the lyrics in my ear.

The rumors really were going around about us now, so it was even more fitting.

"Excuse me," a voice called out, and my head whipped up. "May I cut in?"

Chloe fucking Chapman.

This girl had no shame in her game.

I had the sudden urge to scratch her eyes out.

Rafe looked extremely uncomfortable, and I could tell he was about to turn her down, so I interrupted. "Of course. Rafe, you don't mind, do you? I think Chloe and I could use a moment."

Rafe's eyes widened, and he stepped back with a nod.

"I wasn't talking about you," Chloe hissed, as I swayed from side to side to the beat before meeting her gaze.

"I'm aware of what you wanted. So start dancing because I need to say something to you."

She narrowed her gaze and sighed as she moved with no rhythm at all to the Beyonce song that had just come on. Everyone danced around us, and I tried to think of the best way to handle this.

I've always been a girls' girl.

But this girl was definitely not a member of that club.

But that didn't mean I couldn't help her out. Throw her a bone, so to speak. Although it wouldn't be the bone she was hoping for.

Pun intended.

"Listen, Chloe. It's your dad's wedding. I want you to have a good time. But I want to be straight with you."

"Why would I care what you have to say?"

"Because I can help you. You can take or leave my advice, but I'm going to be honest with you because I don't think most people are," I said, moving close so she could hear me. "Rafe is here with me. We're together. He isn't interested in a relationship with you, and you're being disrespectful to me and to yourself."

Her eyes widened with surprise. Clearly, no one ever spoke up to this woman. "How am I being disrespectful to myself?"

So we were on the same page about her disrespecting me.

"Because you should be with a guy who wants to be with you. Stop chasing my date around and go find yourself a man of your own. Your dad can't make someone date you. Life doesn't work that way. And you aren't going to make any friends by going after other women's dates the way you are going after mine tonight. We're on the same team. Power of the woman."

She was still gaping at me. "I liked him first."

"First of all, you don't know that. Second of all, if he doesn't reciprocate those feelings, it doesn't matter who liked him first. Move the hell on. You're gorgeous, and your speech was fabulous, so you've clearly got a way with words. You're rocking this peach-colored minidress like a badass. Don't settle for someone who doesn't fall at your feet," I said.

Peach was not my favorite color choice for evening attire, but she owned it, and I'd give credit where credit was due. "Never let a man make you feel unworthy. Hold your head high and let them come to you."

She sighed. "I'm sorry. I just really like him."

"I'm sorry. I just really like him, too," I said, and I wasn't lying.

"Dean Sanders was following me around earlier, and he's cute, even if he's a little shy. I could give him a shot." She appeared to be scanning the room. "He's the one in the navy suit with the floral button-up."

"Shut the front door. I saw that guy watching you like you were the only woman in the room when you were giving your speech. He's clearly into you." I had noticed, and he looked to be around her age. "And look at that. He's staring right now."

"He is," she said as her teeth sank into her bottom lip. "What should I do?"

Well, for starters, you could stop following my date around the party.

"Exactly what you're doing. Hold that stare, girl."

Dean started moving in our direction, and relief flooded. I didn't want to hurt her feelings, but I was also done with her hitting on my date.

"Thanks, Lulu." She smirked. "By the way, I have a few rings and a necklace of yours, along with a closet full of Laredo handbags."

"I knew you had good style," I said with a wink as Dean approached. "I'll see you later."

I strode off the dance floor toward Rafe, who was sipping his cocktail, his suit coat slung over his arm, and his dress shirt rolled up to the elbows, exposing his forearms.

His gaze never left mine, and the hunger in his eyes matched the way I was feeling. I took the glass from his hand and brought it to my lips before taking a sip and setting it down on the table. "Come with me somewhere."

"Always," he said as he took my hand in his, and I led him out of the ballroom and down a hallway.

I'd gone to the restroom earlier and opened the wrong door and found a closet, so I knew exactly where I was taking him right now.

"What happened with Chloe?" he asked as he walked beside me just as I came to a stop.

"She's good. I gave her a little girl code chat, and I think she's going to be moving on. At least for tonight."

"So, we aren't running to a getaway car?" His hair was a bit disheveled from all the dancing, and his tie was loosened around his neck, and he looked absolutely delicious.

"Not yet. I never miss an opportunity for cake." I pulled the door open and tugged him into the closet. It was dark aside from the moonlight coming in through the small window in the corner. I pushed the lock on the handle and moved the short distance to the opposite wall.

"What are we doing in here, Wildcat?"

"Well, we've had a few kisses that were all cut short, and I just feel like we should get one good kiss in before we break up tomorrow." I was trying to be light and funny, but my words were breathy and laced with need.

Have I ever wanted anyone the way I want this man?

"Yeah?" His tongue slid slowly along his bottom lip, and I blew out a breath because I couldn't take much more. "Just a kiss?"

"I mean, I'm open to suggestions." I huffed. "We can't have sex, because that would be crossing a line we can't uncross. But everything else is on the table."

Did I just say that?

And why were my words so breathy?

I hated that I was seeping desperation.

His lips turned up the slightest bit in the corners, and he didn't hesitate. Before I could even process what was happening, he had me pushed up against the wall as his mouth crashed into mine. My lips parted in invitation, desperate to feel his tongue against mine.

His body against mine.

One large hand moved to the side of my neck, coaxing my head to tip back so he could take the kiss deeper. The other hand tugged the fabric of my dress up before he squeezed my ass and lifted me off my feet. My legs came around his waist, my fingers tangled in his hair, as his tongue greedily explored my mouth.

It was as if someone had lit a match beneath me.

I was on fire in every way.

Burning for this man in a way I've never experienced.

He groaned into my mouth, his lips strong and commanding, as I rocked my center against his erection, which was now throbbing between my legs.

My God. I couldn't get enough.

He nipped at my bottom lip as both of our panting breaths filled the space around us.

I couldn't get enough friction with all these clothes on, but I bucked wildly against him like a woman desperate for relief.

"Fuck, Lu," he said as he kissed his way down my neck, grinding up against me as if he knew what I wanted.

What I needed.

He slipped the thin spaghetti strap of my dress down my shoulder as my head hit the back of the wall, and I continued dry-humping him shamelessly.

My dress slipped down, exposing my breast, and he tugged at the pasty covering my nipple before he flicked the hard peak with his tongue, and I nearly came right there.

I gasped at the contact, and he covered it with his lips, sucking and flicking and torturing me.

My hips were too high to get any traction now, but the sensation of his mouth on me was so overpowering I couldn't think straight.

As if he read my mind, he kept his lips sealed over my breast as he dropped my feet to the floor.

He pulled back and looked up at me, dark eyes blazing with need, lips swollen from where we attacked one another. He pulled my strap back up over my shoulder, covering me once again, and my heart sank.

Was this too much?

And then he did the sexiest thing I'd ever seen.

He licked his lips and dropped to his knees.

"Spread your legs, Lulu. If you're going to come, it's going to be on my lips."

Yes, please.

I slid my feet further apart as he pushed my dress up, and I grabbed the fabric to let it bunch around my waist.

Thank you, Universe, for convincing me to wear these lacy black panties instead of my Spanx.

I had zero shame in my Spanx game. But if a man is going to head down south to pleasure town, I'd at least like to greet him with some lace or satin, not a fabric that would take real effort or a forklift to move to the side.

His mouth covered the lacy fabric, and he flicked his tongue before sucking my clit, right over my panties.

Holy. Freaking. Hotness.

He pulled back and breathed me in before reaching for the side of my panties. I thought he'd pull them down my legs, but instead, he tore them on each side of my hip and tucked the scrap of fabric into his coat pocket.

"If I get to taste you one time, I'm not waiting. I'll replace the panties," he said, burying his face between my legs.

Licking and tasting and sucking every inch of me.

I bucked wildly just as he lifted my legs, placing them over his shoulders as he gripped my ass to pull me closer and slipped his tongue in. I saw stars.

He worked me over and over, in and out, quicker now, and I was gasping and tugging at his hair.

His thumb moved to my clit, just as bright lights flooded behind my eyelids, and my entire body shook. I squeezed my thighs against his ears and cried out his name as I went over the edge.

He kept rocking me against his lips, making sure I rode out every last bit of pleasure. I'd never experienced such an intense orgasm, and I never wanted it to end.

My breathing slowed as my eyelids opened to look down at the man still buried between my thighs. His head tipped back, his lips glossy with my desire, and his dark gaze met mine.

"Thank you. That was amazing," I whispered. "What a way to end a fake relationship. Best breakup ever."

"You taste as good as I knew you would."

I started to move my legs, suddenly feeling a little vulnerable that I was spread wide open to him.

He helped me to my feet and adjusted my dress. "Sorry about your panties. I'll replace them."

"Don't be ridiculous. That was a sexy move, Rafael." I reached into his pocket where he'd tucked my nip cover and slid it beneath the satin fabric of my dress, unable to miss the giant erection straining against his pants.

"Glad you liked it. So, no sex before the breakup, huh?" His voice was all tease.

"I think that would complicate things. But I would like to return the favor." I cupped his dick with my hand, and he groaned.

"You want me to fuck that sweet mouth of yours?"

"I do," I purred.

He reached for his suit coat that was sitting on the shelf beside us and dropped it to the floor so I wouldn't have to kneel on the cement beneath our feet.

Very chivalrous, considering what we were doing.

I slowly moved to my knees, eager to please him the way he'd pleased me.

Rarely was I this invested in pleasing a man.

I can't remember the last time I cared to do so.

But here I was, on my knees in a maintenance closet at my fake boyfriend's boss's wedding.

I unbuttoned and unzipped his pants. Torturously slow, and he hissed out a breath when I tugged his briefs down.

I'd seen the goods in the shower that day, but being this close was a whole different story.

I could see the thick girth of him. The veins throbbing on his length.

The precum dripping from the tip of his erection.

I swirled my tongue around the top, and he sucked in a breath as his head fell back against the wall.

I opened my mouth, taking him as deep as I could without gagging, and I slowly moved.

Back and forth.

Feeling him grow between my lips.

He gripped my hair as he moaned.

I felt powerful and sexy and desired.

I moved faster, loving the way that I affected him.

I wanted to bring him to the edge, over and over.

And that's exactly what I did.

"Fuck," he groaned, and I swirled my tongue as I took him so deep that I gagged the slightest bit, as he bucked into my mouth.

He fisted my hair in warning, trying to pull me back, but I stayed right there.

I felt it just before it happened.

And I relished in the pleasure that I gave him as he cried out my name and went over the edge.

I stayed right there until I swallowed every last drop.

When I peeked up at him, he was looking down at me like he'd just had the best blow job of his life.

Mission accomplished.

19

Rafe

To say that the wedding had gone better than expected was an epic understatement.

Chloe had backed the fuck off after Lulu had talked to her.

I'd gotten the blow job of the century in a closet during the reception.

And my fake girlfriend was by far the most fun date I'd ever been with.

We laughed. We drank. We ate. We danced. We sang.

We'd both been on our knees and swapped epic orgasms.

I'd call this a win.

We walked hand in hand to the waiting car, and dread filled me because I knew our little game was coming to an end.

There were no more events.

No more people to fool.

We'd remain friends, but I knew that wouldn't involve sharing hotel rooms and naked showers and going down on one another in maintenance closets.

I opened the back door, and she slipped inside. I moved to sit beside her, and our driver took us back to the hotel.

Lulu pulled her phone from her purse and turned it back on, which was followed by a slew of annoying beeps to alert her to all the missed calls and texts.

"What the hell is going on?" she said, staring down at her phone. "I have seventeen missed calls from Henley."

"Fuck," I said, leaning over her shoulder to look at her screen.

"Oh, nooooo. Fucking Beckett can't ever just keep his mouth shut," she hissed.

"What happened?"

"Apparently, he spoke out publicly about our relationship with some big entertainment show," she groaned, leaning against my shoulder as she hit play on the video she'd been sent.

The dude looked haggard. His jeans hung from his slim frame, and his hair was overgrown and hanging in his face. "I've had a lot of messages from fans asking if I'm okay, and I know I posted a little about it, but I agreed to this interview so I could speak out, and you all can stop worrying about me."

"He is such a narcissist," Lulu hissed.

"It's true what Lulu said. She and I haven't been together in a very long time, and I know I messed up. But after seeing the photos that you've all seen, the one of her with her new boyfriend... it did something to me. My eyes are opened. I've been awakened from a very long sleep," he said dramatically, as the woman interviewing him shook her head like she understood what he meant.

Was he a fucking bear? Had he been hibernating?

"We have a break in our tour next week, and I will be jumping on the first plane out of here and heading to Rosewood River. It's time to win my girl back. I hope you all will send me the positive vibes that I can make it happen," he said.

"Of course, he's got to drag the whole world into his drama. It's all about getting attention." Lulu rubbed her temple with her free hand.

And then the douchebag looked right at the camera, moving closer. "Sorry, Rafe Chadwick. I think you took something that belongs to me."

What the actual fuck?

Was this prick for real?

She glanced up at me and sighed. "Welcome to my shit show."

"He also just told all of his fans where he's going to be," I said. "Doesn't he worry about security?"

"No. He'll travel with his security team. He loves the attention," she said, making no attempt to hide her irritation. "I'm sorry. Your name is now out there even more now."

We pulled up in front of the hotel and stepped out of the car. I needed to process the information before I made a decision about what we should do. I paid the driver, and we both thanked him, just as several flashes went off, causing me to startle. I pulled Lulu beside me, taking in the photographers that were lined up near the entrance of the hotel, and hurried her inside.

A man wearing a fancy suit walked toward us, holding his hands up. He explained that he was the hotel manager, and he'd already phoned the police to ask them to clear the paparazzi from the premises.

I informed him that we were checking out in the morning, and he said he'd make sure it was clear when we left the hotel. Lulu hadn't said a word.

We stepped onto the elevator, and she did the most unexpected thing.

Dropping to her knees in the closet had been unexpected in the best way.

But seeing her bottom lip wobble…

Seeing the way she blinked rapidly to stop the tears that were threatening to fall…

It caused a deep pain in the center of my chest. I pulled her close and wrapped my arms around her. "It's going to be fine."

"It's not, Rafe. He's going to come and ruin this place that I'm enjoying. A place where I can work peacefully until I move to Paris. He's toxic and selfish, and he doesn't care about the consequences of his actions. It's like dealing with a toddler all the time."

The last word broke on a sob, and when the elevator doors opened, I moved her quickly down the hall to our hotel room. She dropped to sit on the bed, and she let it all out. I grabbed the box of tissues from the bathroom and bent down in front of her.

"Lulu. It'll pass. Come on, don't let this guy win."

She looked up at me, eyes swollen with a little mascara smeared beneath them. "He has won. We haven't been together in so long, but he comes to town and upsets my family. He drags my name into the press every few months. He makes it so that I don't want to date anyone because I'm so guarded now. And he's going to drag you and your family through the mud. And the craziest part of all of this is that he doesn't even want me back."

I sat beside her on the bed, wrapping my arms around her. "You sure about that?"

I guessed that the dude knew he'd fucked up by letting her go. She was the kind of girl you didn't get a second chance with. The kind of girl you'd never be able to replace.

"Yes." She looked up at me. "He cheated on me several times toward the end of our relationship. He'd been caught on camera, so there was no denying it. But the truth is, it didn't even hurt at that point because I was over him, and I hadn't been physical with him in a very long time. At the end of the day, he likes my name. He likes this volatile picture that he's painted, one that people, especially his fans, are drawn to. This wealthy socialite who came from the best boarding schools and pedigree and the bad-boy rocker. It's become more of a fictional relationship for him, and he likes the attention it garners. But there is nothing there. He loves this. Loves the drama and the attention. And I'm so tired of it. I just want to move on with my life."

I used the pads of my thumbs and swiped the liquid beneath her eyes. "And you are. So he comes to Rosewood River, and we don't waver. We let him see us together. We don't allow him to make a scene. We act ridiculously happy, and we become impenetrable together."

"You don't understand how much we'll be watched now. It's more than sharing a hotel room. This is going to be far more intense."

"So, we play the game. I hate the guesthouse. I'll move into the main house. It'll look like we live together. When I'm not at the office, I'll work at home with you. We'll be seen everywhere in Rosewood River together. Let them photograph us. Let them run with the story. He'll get the hint, and he'll leave."

"We already had our farewell breakup orgasms, though." She sniffed. "This was supposed to be the end of your sentence."

"Hey, hanging out with you is not a hardship. Dropping to my knees for you is not a hardship. I'm not the one who wants to keep saying that this is coming to an end. I'm not the one with all the rules and boundaries. I'm actually having a damn good time."

"Because you have to."

"Do you truly think I ever had to?" I barked out a laugh. "That first day you came to me and said that you needed me to tell your parents we were together, I fucking loved it. You'd just nailed me in the balls with a pool ball the night before, and I couldn't wait to see how you'd torture me next."

She smiled a genuine smile. "I dragged you to meet my crazy family."

"Lulu, look at me," I said, my voice serious now. "I wanted to go. I was happy to spend the weekend there with you. I have never wanted to meet a woman's family, yet I was excited to go with you. And tonight, when you walked into that ballroom with me, I was fucking proud that everyone thought you were mine."

"Rafe," she whispered. "None of this is real."

"When we took a shower that night, trying to fight this attraction we both feel—that was fucking real. When I hold your hand and keep you close, it's because I want you there. And tonight, I had the best time I've ever had with a woman, so I don't know what to tell you, Wildcat, but this shit isn't fake for me anymore."

Her gaze searched mine. "It's because I gave you a gold medal-worthy blow job, isn't it?"

Her voice was all tease, but I could still hear the hesitation.

"It didn't hurt." I chuckled, tucking a piece of hair that had broken free from her elastic behind her ear.

"This wasn't supposed to happen." She covered her face with her hands. "I'm moving. I have big plans. I can't get lost in this, in you, not right now."

"Not asking you to." I pulled her hands away from her face. "I don't know what the fuck this means. All I'm saying is, we like hanging out. Let's just enjoy it. Let's stop calling it fake because nothing about it feels fake to me. Am I wrong?"

She shook her head. "No. But I want it to be."

That was honest.

"Listen, Lulu, I get it. You've been trying to get out of a shitty situation, and the last thing you want to do is complicate it. But no one is going to get hurt here. I know you're leaving. I know you aren't looking for anything serious, and neither am I. So let's stop overthinking it."

She nodded, her bottom lip trembling again. "I've made mistakes in the past that I don't want to repeat. I have things that I need to do for myself, and caring about someone too much will derail that plan."

"So, we hang out, and you can just tell yourself you hate me, even though we both know you don't." I chuckled.

She didn't smile. She didn't laugh. Her eyes welled once again. "I never hated you. But my fear is that you'll end up hating me. And I don't want that."

Damn. This girl was so guarded and strong that seeing her this vulnerable did something to me.

I placed a hand on each side of her face. "I promise, I could never hate you. Let's just continue doing what we've been doing. We're friends with very few benefits. But the ones we have are pretty fucking spectacular."

Her lips quirked up on the sides. And when this woman smiled, it was like the parting of the seas. I finally knew what my dad had been talking about all these years. There was just something about Lulu Sonnet.

Something different.

Something special.

I'd known it pretty early on, yet I wanted to keep my distance because I knew that this couldn't go anywhere. We had very different lives.

But I was grateful that I got to have this short time with her, and I'd take what I could get.

Which wasn't a whole lot at the moment, because she was determined to keep her guard up.

"So, we keep dating, and you move into the house, just so no one will be suspicious." She quirked a brow.

"Right. I can stay in the guest room. No one will know."

"Okay. And what do we tell everyone?"

"What they already think. We say we're having fun. We're enjoying our time together."

"What do I tell Henley now that we're extending things?" she asked.

"Tell her that we wanted to extend things and that we both know that it has an expiration date, and we're fine with that. It's two months. It's not like you're going to fall in love with me if you haven't already," I said, my voice laced with humor.

"Very true. And let's negotiate the terms."

"All right. How about I get to kiss you when I want to, and vice versa? I mean, we aren't dating anyone else, so we should be allowed to enjoy ourselves in the meantime."

"I can live with that." She pulled out her sketch pad and turned to a fresh page and looked up at me. "Okay, so let's just make this official so there won't be any gray area."

"I'm a numbers guy. I love a contract and rules." I barked out a laugh.

"Okay. Number one, you move into the main house, and you stay in the guest room. Number two, we can't see anyone else. We'd be caught immediately because we're going to have eyes on us."

"Done and done. Those are easy."

"Okay…" She tapped the pencil against her lips, and I wanted to tip her back and kiss her senseless again, but I'd need to tread lightly with Lulu. "What else? You can make some demands. I'm turning your life upside down until I leave town."

"So, we've already established that kissing is on the table." I quirked a brow. I'd like to negotiate a blow job, but I didn't want to push my luck.

"Yes. You've got very kissable lips." She wrote everything down on the sketch pad.

"Great. I think orgasm showers are a must."

Her head tipped back in laughter. "I'm not writing that."

"Because you're opposed to it?"

"No." She smirked. "It was the best shower I've had in a very long time. But I think we keep it more general. So I'll write that anything else is on the table, as long as we both agree."

"I can live with that. It appears my cock is slightly hard for you to resist."

She rolled her eyes. "Says the man who tore my panties from my body just to get there quicker."

"Hey, I like to please my woman."

"I guess this is a great plan. We continue hanging out and doing whatever we feel like until I leave. Then we part ways as friends, and there are no hard feelings."

"It's the best relationship I've ever been in," I said, moving my thumb along the line of her jaw.

"No wonder you remain so friendly with all your exes. This is so civil." She finished jotting down the rule about doing whatever we feel like and the fact that there was an expiration date. She underlined that one, as if she wanted us both to remember it. "Sign here, Rafael."

I signed the ridiculous contract, and so did she.

"Feel better now?" I asked.

"I do." Her teeth sank into her bottom lip. "How do you feel about a shower before bed, boyfriend?"

I grabbed her from the bed, tossing her over my shoulder as I hurried her to the bathroom.

"You don't have to ask me twice," I said as I set her on the counter in the bathroom and turned on the shower.

I think this arrangement is going to work out just fine.

20

Lulu

We'd been back in Rosewood River for two weeks with no sign of the annoying rock star, yet this new arrangement was working out really well. Rafe had moved into the guest room, and we spent most of our time together when he wasn't at the office.

We ate meals together.

We watched movies.

We'd make out until our lips ached, amongst other things, aside from sex.

It wasn't an option.

And at the end of the day, I'd kiss him good night and pad down to my room, and he'd go to his.

My best friend was completely confused by the arrangement,

but she supported it, as long as I assured her no one would get hurt. All she asked of both of us was that we parted ways amicably because we'd both be in her and Easton's life forever. So it wasn't an option not to.

I gave her my word, and so did Rafe.

I'd never had such a formal outline for dating someone. Perhaps this would have come in handy in my last relationship, as every possible rule one could break had been broken.

"That design is going to blow the Parisians away," Jared said with a chuckle. We were having our weekly team meeting, which consisted of my three executives, who I trusted immensely. It was much easier for me to trust people on a professional level versus a personal level.

Jared was in charge of operations, and he'd really helped me expand and grow the company over the last eighteen months.

Sarah was in charge of marketing MSL, and she'd branded us well, which had been key to getting large stores to look at us.

Monique was in charge of our creative department, and I ran every design by her. She'd originally worked for my mother at Laredo for many years, but she moved over to work with me last year because my mother thought she could help me grow, as well.

They'd all become close friends, and I knew I had chosen the right people to surround myself with, both professionally and personally.

"Yes. People are a sucker for "Forever," and we should be able to get that piece out on the market by the holidays next year. But sales have been going through the roof with orders for Valentine's Day, so I can only imagine what will happen when we launch this as a set." We were going to do this design in a bracelet, earrings, and a necklace. People loved a set, me included.

"The orders for this launch in Paris are going to be large. I've already got our manufacturers ready to increase our orders, and I'm excited to see how big this expansion is going to be," Jared said.

The front door opened, and Rafe strolled in, wearing a pair of sweatpants and a hoodie after going on his run this morning. Our team meetings were early, as all three of them lived on the East Coast. Rafe usually went for his run first thing in the morning, and he'd been gone before I woke up. He moved around to the screen and smiled.

"There they are. The dream team," he said.

"Look at that tall drink of water," Jared said, waggling his brows, just as his partner, Frankie, walked by and swatted him in the head with a rolled-up magazine.

"Is he already flirting with your boyfriend this early in the morning?" Frankie groaned as he waved at the camera and handed Jared his mug of coffee.

"I just said that he was good-looking. You've even said the man is ridiculously good-looking," Jared reminded his husband.

"Touché." Frankie kissed the top of Jared's head and waved. "I'm off to a meeting. See you all later."

Rafe was still laughing as I shooed him away and wrapped up our meeting.

I studied him as he had his back to me while he scrambled up a few eggs. I had never been one to eat breakfast, but this man had been relentless about how it was the most important meal of the day.

He turned around and caught me staring.

There were moments when I had to force myself not to touch him. To stop myself from kissing him throughout the day, because even though we said we could do it anytime we wanted, I was growing attached to the man.

None of this made sense.

Rafe turned around and set both plates down at the table before snatching my bag of gummy bears sitting beside my coffee mug. He tossed the bag onto the kitchen island and took the seat across from me.

"You can't sustain life on gummy bears, Wildcat," he said. "Eggs first, gummies later."

Coach Jones, my trainer, who I worked with remotely, was always on me about my nutritional struggles, so I knew I needed to eat better, but when it came from Rafe, it felt more impactful. Like he truly cared about my health.

About me.

Why was that so terrifying?

"I mean, if I made eggs as good as you do, I'd probably eat them every day." I shrugged before taking a bite.

Rafe was an amazing cook, and I'd been spoiled now that we were basically roommates, which meant he cooked for both of us.

Roommates who kissed and hugged and touched one another.

The gray area had grown so large that everything was basically gray when it came to my relationship with this man.

"Well, you can eat them every day while you're here. And maybe you'll pick up some new habits that you can take to Paris. Tell me about your meeting."

"The launch in Paris is going to be big for our foreign market, and they are loving the new designs, so they plan to just keep adding to the collection."

One side of his mouth hitched up as if he were oozing with pride. But not for himself, for me. "That's fucking amazing. My girl is such a lady boss."

I chuckled. "Thanks. You've got your big meeting today with the Crawford CEO, right?"

Rafe had been referred by one of his clients to the CEO of a large corporation, who was considering bringing Rafe in as his financial advisor both personally and professionally. It would be a huge win for him, and he'd been preparing for this meeting the last few days.

"Yep. It's this afternoon," he said, as he reached for his juice. "I plan on crushing it."

"No doubt." I took another bite before thinking over my next question. "So, tomorrow is Valentine's Day. And I know this isn't really a normal situation that we're in, but Henley and Easton are going to Booze & Brews after their dinner for country music night, and I thought it might be fun to get out." We'd gone to Booze & Brews together several times. Why was I so awkward?

Am I sweating?

A slow, sexy smile spread across his face. "Are you asking me to be your Valentine, Lulu Sonnet?"

I tossed my napkin at him. "Well, don't make it weird. I didn't know if you knew that it was Valentine's Day, and I just wanted to give you a heads-up."

"I knew. And we've already got plans, but we can finish up at the bar if you want."

"We have plans?"

"Yes. I'm taking you somewhere. It's Valentine's Day. It's what people who are hanging out do." He smirked.

He made plans.

"That was very thoughtful of you. Where are we going?"

"Not telling you that, my little control freak."

"What? I need to know how to dress," I said, although that was only part of the reason I wanted to know.

Being a control freak was the other reason.

"Dress for dinner. It's not fancy, but it'll be fun. And then we can hit up Booze & Brews after."

"That's not helpful at all, but I'll figure it out." I pushed to my feet and cleared our plates, internally chuckling at how domestic I felt lately.

We had a routine. He cooked. I did the dishes. We bantered. We both worked. And we got a little hot and bothered in between.

Or a lot hot and bothered.

"I'm going to go take a shower and then get to work." He came up behind me and wrapped his arms around me from behind.

I wanted to tell him I'd come with him.

I wanted to follow him into the shower and get lost in this man.

My feelings terrified me lately. Every night when I got in bed, I fought the urge to ask him to join me.

"Sounds like a plan. I'm going to go run a few errands, but I'll see you later. Thanks for breakfast."

He stepped away and then called my name, and I turned the water off and turned around. He tossed the bag of gummy bears to me and winked.

What is this man doing to me?

I grabbed my phone and shot a quick text to Henley.

Me: *Any chance you could meet me at Rosewood Brew for a coffee real quick? It's a bit of an emergency.*

Henley: *Of course. Let me wrap up this email. I can be there in fifteen minutes.*

Me: *Thank you. Love you big.*

Henley: *Love you bigger.*

I hurried out the door and was grateful that the snow had melted over a week ago and the sun was out. I walked the short distance to the coffee shop.

I waved at a few locals as I made my way down Main Street.

I loved this little town and the people in it.

Rosewood Brew was an adorable coffee shop with black-and-white-checked floors and three large crystal chandeliers hung above.

"The usual?" Jane Waters asked. She and her husband, John, owned the place, and I stopped in often.

"Yes. Henley's meeting me here in a minute, so we'll both do our usuals." I handed her my card and thought about how impersonal it was for me in the city when I'd grab a coffee. I'd see different baristas every day, and that wasn't a bad thing, but it was just different.

"You got it. I'll bring it over to you as soon as it's ready." She smiled.

"Thank you." I took a seat in the back corner, and Oscar Smith was just leaving the seat at the next table.

"Everyone is anticipating that obnoxious rock star coming to town. You think he'll show?" Oscar grumped, which made me chuckle.

I didn't want Beckett to step foot in Rosewood River, but the fact that Oscar didn't want him to come either comforted me in a weird way. Like he knew I didn't want the bastard to come, so neither did he.

Because most people in town would love the idea of a famous person coming here.

"I hope not, but he does love the attention, and it would make for a good story." I shrugged. "He's unpredictable, so it's hard to say."

"Seems like you've closed the chapter on that story a long time ago. Don't let it get to you, kiddo." He tapped my table before walking out the door.

Even grumpy Oscar had my chest squeezing today. I was clearly off my game. I reached into my bag for a handful of gummy bears, just as Jane set our drinks down, and Henley hurried inside.

She took the seat across from me and studied me. "You okay?"

"Yes. I'm fine. I'm just—I'm a little off today."

"Are you worried about Beckett showing up?"

"I hadn't really thought about it until Oscar asked a few minutes ago. Obviously, I don't want him to make a scene here in this peaceful town, you know? But I'm used to his stunts, so I can handle it."

"So, what's going on?"

"I asked Rafe if he wanted to go to the bar tomorrow. And you know, it's Valentine's Day, so I wanted to give him a heads-up. But he already made plans."

She smiled before taking a sip of her coffee and setting her cup down. "I know. He told me he was doing something fun for you. I think it's sweet. Why does that bother you?"

I could say anything to Henley, and she'd never judge me. She's always been the person I trusted most.

"Because it's sweet, and it's all so confusing, and I don't want to mess anything up. And you know I don't celebrate Valentine's Day."

She took my hands in hers and leaned forward. "It's okay to like him, Lu. I know you've been in this state of anger since your last relationship, and yes, you dated after Beckett, but it was never anything serious. You've put this guard up around yourself, and I've watched you do it. I understand why you have it there because you've been hurt, and it's scary to let someone in again. But Beckett Bane has taken enough of your time and energy. Even his drama can be all-consuming. So, let yourself be happy. It's okay to do that."

A tear ran down my cheek, and I quickly pulled my hand back and swiped it away. "This wasn't supposed to be real. It wasn't supposed to turn into anything. I'm leaving. The timing isn't right. I can't let myself go there right now. My life is just about to take off. I can't get sidetracked by a good-looking man with a pretty penis," I grumped.

Her head tipped back in laughter. "The woman who is all about having a fling and cutting loose has been in a relationship with all these rules she put in place for weeks. Why do you think that is?"

"Because she's smart and cautious and knows trouble when she sees it."

"I don't think so, Lu. I think you care about him much more than you want to admit, and that scares the hell out of you. That's why you haven't had sex with him, and you sleep in separate beds, even though you basically live together. I mean, come on, it's crazy. You've showered with the man. You make out with him every night. And then you go to separate rooms?"

I ended up telling her everything because I needed a voice of reason to tell me that I wasn't crazy for doing this.

And now she was calling this crazy?

"Well, when you say it like that, it sounds insane."

"Because it is." She leaned forward again. "I love you. I know you're scared, and I know you hate feeling that way. Being with Rafe right now does not mean you are going to derail your life. Maybe this is just something you need right now. Maybe you just let go of all of these fears and see where it goes."

"I'll tell you where it goes... I'm leaving for Paris in six weeks. It's going to Paris." I shrugged. "I don't care how magical that man's dick is or how charming or funny he is. I have a plan. I'm not going to let a man distract me ever again."

"He knows you're leaving, yet he's still there. Playing by your rules. He's been dragged into the press pretty much daily since this relationship went public, yet he's stood by your side. He doesn't care if you're crazy-ass ex comes to town; he's got your back. So enjoy it. He's a good one, Lu."

"I don't want to like him this much," I finally said, my voice cracking on the last word. "But I already do. And I'm afraid if I let myself go any deeper, I won't be able to come up for air."

"I was terrified when I let my guard down with Easton. But you can't spend your whole life being afraid. And Rafe knows you're leaving, you've both been upfront about the fact that you aren't looking for anything serious. So enjoy yourself and don't overthink it."

"What is happening? That's normally my speech to you. I'm not the overthinker. I'm not the one who throws caution to the wind. What is it about this man that has me so turned upside down?"

"I think it's because you like him," she said, one brow quirked.

She was right. I liked him. I liked him a lot.

Even though I wished I didn't.

"I think it was the orgasm shower. I'm going with that," I said, and we both fell back in a fit of giggles.

"Just let yourself have this. Even if it's for a short time. You deserve to be happy, Lu. You're always in that fight-or-flight state, and with Rafe, you don't have to be. You can just be you.

So give yourself this. Even if just for a few weeks. And then you'll head to Paris and conquer the world, and he'll be the first one to cheer you on. Along with me, of course."

I sighed. She was always my voice of reason.

At times, I felt like Henley knew me better than I knew myself.

And I knew she was right.

21

Rafe

Easton: *Happy Valentine's Day, dickheads.*

Clark: *Easton is in a relationship this year, and now we get Happy Valentine's texts.*

Easton: *Not my only reason for texting. Tomorrow we start the league again. The Chad-Six are back. Henley will sub when anyone has to miss.*

Archer: *Good. She can cover for me tomorrow. I'm swamped with work.*

Clark: *I have a date tomorrow, so I actually can't make it. Do we have another sub?*

Axel: *You have a date the day after Valentine's Day?*

Clark: *Yes. I don't take a woman out on a holiday if we aren't in a serious relationship. It sends mixed messages. So, we're going out tomorrow.*

Axel: *Smart. I'll be at pickleball.*

Rafe: *I'll be there, but I'm not dealing with your bitchy attitude if you're going to be all competitive and intense.*

Easton: *Fuck you. Bring your A game, and I won't have to be a dick. Ask Lulu if she can sub for Clark.*

Clark: *I bet Lulu is a beast on the court. Watch your balls. You know she likes to take you out when she can. <laughing face emoji>*

Archer: *What's the deal there? You basically live together, and she comes to Sunday dinners and seems like part of the family. Are you finally going to admit it's the real deal?*

Axel: *He's been very quiet about his plans tonight, but he needed to borrow some shit from my barn, so I have a feeling our boy is more invested than he wants to admit.*

Rafe: *I'm an open book. I like her. Pretty sure she feels the same, even if she's cautious as fuck. But she's leaving soon, so I'm just enjoying the time I have with her while she's here.*

Archer: *You going to be all right when she leaves?*

I didn't really like to think about it. I hadn't expected to let things go this far. I've never been this connected to a woman, which was ironic, considering we hadn't slept together. I've had many relationships over the years, mostly casual, a few more serious, but sex had always been involved.

And Lulu and I had been open about our desires, so these rules were definitely unusual.

Yet here I was. Planning a romantic Valentine's dinner for a girl who was clearly one foot out the door.

But there was something about her.

I wasn't going to hold back just because she was afraid of this.

This force.

This pull.

It was impossible to miss.

Me: *I'll be fine. I'm sure she'll be down for pickleball because she's ridiculously competitive, and she will have plenty of opportunity to injure me on the court. <laughing face emoji>*

Bridger: *I hate pickleball.*

Easton: *I don't care. See you all tomorrow.*

"Hey, Pops," I said when I stopped by the house to drop off some flowers for my mom. I always brought her Valentine's flowers. It was just our thing. "Where's Mom?"

"She's getting her nails done." He glanced over his shoulder when I set the vase on the island. "You have time for a quick cup of coffee?"

"Of course."

My dad and I were tight. Always had been.

"How's the renovation going?" he asked.

"I just came from there, and things are moving along. A few more weeks, and I'll be back in my house, which will be great."

So why didn't I sound excited about it?

"That's good news. It's nice that you don't have to live there through the process. That's no fun." He took a sip of his coffee and studied me. "How's it going with Lulu? It seems like it's getting serious."

My parents weren't fully aware of the details of our odd arrangement, nor would they ever push. It wasn't their style. They also didn't know that I wasn't staying in the guesthouse anymore. Not that it mattered, she wasn't in my bed.

"I don't know," I said, scrubbing a hand down my face. "We're good. But she's moving to Paris in a couple of weeks, so it'll be coming to an end."

"Yeah, I know she's moving. But I was asking more about how you feel about her."

I reached for my coffee and took a sip as I thought about how I wanted to answer the question. I couldn't tell him that the whole thing started out as a lie. That I've fallen in love with a woman who wouldn't put her guard down long enough to say she felt the same. Nor could I tell her how I felt, because she'd probably take off running and never look back.

"I like her. She's great."

He narrowed his gaze. "You seem different with her than I've ever seen you with anyone before. You two have a comfort with one another, and it's refreshing."

"Yeah. I'd say she's become a good friend, as well."

"That's an important part of a relationship," he said.

"It can't go anywhere, Dad. If that's what you're asking, this thing has an expiration date, and we're both very aware of that."

He nodded. "Feelings don't expire, son. So if you are as crazy about her as I think you are, don't hold back. It doesn't come around more than once in this lifetime, so my advice would be to make sure you put it all out there while you have the chance."

I scratched the back of my neck. "Not everything is that simple."

He grabbed my hand that rested on the table and covered it with his. His calloused hands were a reminder of how hard this man had worked all of his life. "Things are only complicated if you allow them to be. Love is simple. You either love someone or you don't. And if you do, you figure it the hell out. Life is complicated enough. If you're lucky enough to go through it with your favorite person by your side, everything will always be fine."

I chuckled. "You are one sappy old bastard today."

"Well, it's Valentine's Day, and this is the day that I told your mother that I loved her for the first time. So we celebrate that every single year." He clapped the top of my hand, just as my mother came through the door.

Of course, she gushed over her flowers, even though I brought them year after year.

We visited for a little bit, and I headed out the door.

I worked remotely this morning, and I was still flying high from my meeting yesterday, where I signed a new client.

A client that would make it so breaking off on my own someday, maybe in a year or two, would be possible.

I had just enough time to get home and showered before dinner with Lulu.

When I pushed the door open, I heard the music blasting from her room, and I hurried to my room to catch a shower.

Once I was out and dressed in a pair of dark jeans and a black sweater, I glanced at my watch. We were right on time.

I sent a text to Dolly Rogers to let her know we'd be heading there soon. She replied and told me everything was set, and her son, Jacob, who'd I'd paid very generously to serve dinner, was already there waiting for us.

I came out to the kitchen to find Lulu standing with her back to me. She had a black sweater that hung off one shoulder, exposing that golden skin of hers, along with baggy faded jeans and high-heeled boots. Her wrists were covered in bracelets, and she turned around to find me staring.

"Hey, you look handsome."

"Hey yourself, beautiful. You ready?"

"Yes. You've been very mysterious about tonight, Rafael." She grabbed her red purse off the counter and followed me to the door.

I helped her into the truck and drove the short distance to the dance studio, parking in the back. She glanced out the window, looking for hints, but the lot was on the back side of the building, so she wouldn't figure much out just yet.

I helped her out of the truck, and we walked around the building to the front door, where she paused when she saw the sign.

"We're going to a dance studio?" She quirked a brow.

"Is that what this is?" I asked, my voice teasing, as I pulled the door open and then locked it behind us.

Her hand was tucked in mine, and the place was dark, just as I'd requested.

"Are we supposed to be here?" she whispered.

I didn't answer as I walked her through the front lobby and down the hallway, pushing the door to the studio open. The room had several fake trees covered in twinkle lights, with large floor lanterns and white candles spread throughout the large space to light it up. There was a table in the center, set for two, and I walked her over.

"What is this?" she whispered.

"Happy Valentine's Day, Wildcat. I wanted to do something that I thought would be special for you."

She blinked a few times as she took in the table, which had

several candles lit, along with two tall vases of red roses.

Turns out, I was a romantic dude when I wanted to be.

I just usually didn't feel the need to do it, but I did with her.

I pulled out her chair, and she took her seat, just as Jacob appeared. I barked out a laugh. He was wearing a black tuxedo, which I had not requested. The kid was only sixteen years old, and Lulu and I weren't even dressed up since we'd be heading to Booze & Brews after this.

"Hey, buddy. You didn't need to be so formal. This is Lulu. Lu, this is Jacob. His mom, Dolly, owns the studio."

"Hey, nice to meet you," Jacob said before turning to me. "My mom made me wear this. I was the best man in my uncle's wedding last year, so she insisted I put it on."

"Well, I appreciate the effort," Lulu said with a laugh.

Jacob had two large bags in his hands and set them down beside me, looking up for guidance. I hadn't really planned on him doing more than being here to receive the takeout food I'd ordered, and Dolly had been kind enough to give me a key to lock up after we left.

"I can take it from here. I appreciate you waiting for the food."

"Your champagne is in there, too." He took a step back. "Ya'll have a great night. Leave everything here, and I'll be back first thing in the morning to break it all down before my mom's first class, just like we discussed."

I nodded.

"Thanks. Have a good night," Lulu and I said in unison as the kid hurried out of there.

"Poor guy was forced to wear a tuxedo for all of five minutes," Lulu said with a laugh as I started unloading the to-go boxes.

"Yeah. His mom was Emerson's dance teacher, and she's a

good friend of my mom's, so she wanted it to be nice." I set the containers in the center of the table because we'd always been big on sharing our entrées. I popped the champagne and filled the flutes as Lulu pulled the tops off the containers.

"You thought of everything," she said.

You deserve everything.

We held up our champagne flutes and clinked them together.

"Cheers to a good night," I said.

"It's always a good night with you." She smiled up at me as she scooped some pasta onto her plate, and I did the same. "Thanks for doing all this. And I'm not just talking about tonight. I'm talking about everything."

Her eyes were blinking rapidly again.

"Hey, what's going on?" I asked, reaching for her chair and pulling her closer.

"I'm sorry I've made this all so weird." She shrugged. "It's not because I don't feel this. Because I feel it, Rafe. I'm just—I know I'm leaving. I know you're staying. I know this will end soon, so I'm trying to be cautious."

"I know you are. And that's okay. I'm not pressuring you. I like what we have. Even if just for a short time." I pulled her onto my lap, wrapping my arms around her. "I like you, Lulu Sonnet. Whether you live here or on the other side of the world, that won't change."

She turned to look at me. "I want to have sex with you."

I barked out a laugh. She was quite possibly the most unpredictable woman I'd ever met. "I'm never going to argue with that. But how about we have dinner first, yeah?"

"Yeah." She chuckled before putting one hand on each side of my face. "And I like you, too. A lot. More than I want to admit. But here I am, admitting it."

"See? Was that so hard?"

"It was painfully hard," she said, resting her forehead against mine. "Okay, I'm going back to my chair to eat."

She kept her chair close to mine, and we ate, her legs nestled between mine, as we couldn't seem to sit close enough. We laughed and talked, sharing our plates and having a good time. We polished off the bottle of champagne and half of the bottle of wine that I brought when she reached into her purse.

"I have something for you." She handed me a black box.

I pulled off the lid to find a very cool bracelet that managed to be masculine at the same time.

"I made it for you. I used antique silver and this really cool walnut wood that I intertwined into the design. Walnut is symbolic for intelligence and wisdom. And the silver is representative of healing. I feel like you've healed me in a way. And I didn't even know I was broken." She chuckled.

"You're not broken," I said, running my thumb over the wood and metal that were intertwined together. "And this is the nicest gift I've ever received."

Her lips turned up in the corners, the widest grin spread across her face. "Well, look in the bottom of the box. There's one more thing in there."

I looked inside, and a gruff laugh escaped.

"A condom?"

"Extra large." She waggled her brows. "I was ready to take things to the next level long before you rented out a dance studio and lured me here with delicious pasta."

I clasped the bracelet around my wrist and moved the foil packet between my fingers. "This is the gift that keeps on giving."

I reached down beneath the table where I'd left the gift bag for her earlier today when I stopped by to make sure things were getting set up. "First things first."

She eyed the package before tearing off the red velvet ribbon and lifting the lid to the box.

She didn't speak, which made me a little nervous. I asked Henley what exactly I should order for her, and she told me her favorite brand and gave me her sizes for everything.

Maybe I fucked up.

"Rafael," she whispered as she pulled the pink leotard out of the box and studied it. She reached inside for the ballet shoes and sighed. "You got me a dance outfit."

"I know you miss it. And I was sort of hoping you'd dance for me tonight. It was sort of a gift to myself, too."

Her teeth sank into her bottom lip, and she smiled. "I can do that."

And then she leaned forward and kissed me.

22

Lulu

No man had ever been so thoughtful.

So attuned to my needs.

I left to use the restroom and change clothes as he cleaned up our dinner.

When I returned, I found him sitting in the chair, the table already broken down and leaning against the far wall. His long legs were extended and his feet crossed at the ankles.

Damn, the man was sexy just sitting in a chair.

It was the way he looked at me.

Those dark eyes could see into my soul.

His gaze moved from my head down to my toes as he took in my full dance attire.

"Dance for me, Lu," he said.

It had been a long time since I'd danced for anyone. I danced alone often, but the day I retired the idea of doing this professionally, had been the last time I danced in front of an audience.

I pulled up my playlist on my phone and chose my favorite song, "Giselle," by Adolphe Adam, and set my phone on the floor.

And I danced. I twirled, I spun, I floated, and I did an arabesque in the air. I was lost in the music, lost in his eyes that tracked my every move.

I was lost in this man.

And I wasn't going to fight it anymore.

When the music came to an end, the next song started to play, and I moved across the room toward Rafe. He tugged me onto his lap, one leg falling on each side of him as I straddled him.

Our mouths collided, hands exploring one another eagerly.

We were frantic and needy, as if we both knew that we were going to cross the line tonight.

I couldn't wait one more minute.

"I want you," I said against his lips.

"I want you so fucking bad, I can't see straight."

He tugged the leotard down my shoulders, exposing my bare breasts, as he took my nipple between his lips, and I arched my back to get closer. My fingers fumbled with the hem of his sweater, desperate to feel his skin on mine. He moved from one breast to the next, licking and sucking, and driving me wild. When he pulled back, he looked up at me, and he tugged his sweater over his head, tossing it on the floor.

"I made sure the doors were locked. It's just you and me here." He stroked the hair away from my face.

I pushed off his lap, and he leaned forward. As I raised my foot, he removed my toe shoes, one at a time. He kissed his way down my stomach as he peeled the leotard and then the tights from my body. I tugged him forward, wanting to do the same to him. He kicked his shoes off, and I unbuttoned and unzipped his jeans, pulling them down his legs, along with his briefs. His dick was hard and long and thick, and he leaned down to grab the condom he'd tucked into the pocket of his pants.

"I want to do it," I purred, holding my hand out.

I tore the top off the foil packet and then rolled the latex over his erection.

It was sexy and intimate and emotional all at the same time.

Everything with this man was just so different.

His eyes never left mine as he sat back down on the chair and pulled me closer. I climbed onto his lap, and he tangled his fingers in my hair and pulled my mouth down to his. His hands were on my hips, rolling me against his hardness and taking control just the way I wanted him to.

We kissed until our lips were swollen, and I was so turned on that I couldn't wait one more second. I gripped his shoulders and positioned myself just above the tip of his dick. I stared down at him as a sexy smile spread across his face. And I moved down slowly.

He was large, and I hadn't had sex in a long time, so my body had to adjust to him.

His eyes fell closed, and I could tell he was holding back and letting me set the pace now.

"Fuck, Lu. You're so tight. So wet. So fucking perfect," he groaned.

My breaths were coming hard and fast as I took him in, inch by glorious inch.

My head fell back as I pushed all the way down, and he filled me completely.

Neither of us moved. We stayed completely still.

And then he leaned forward, his lips trailing along my neck.

Along my collarbone.

And I started to move.

Slowly at first.

And when his lips found my breasts, I moved faster.

Needier.

We found our rhythm as if we'd done this a million times.

He tugged my head down and covered my mouth with his, his tongue tasting and exploring.

I was so lost in the moment. Lost in this man.

My entire body started to shake, and he moved his hand between us.

Knowing exactly what I needed.

My head fell back as white lights flashed behind my eyes.

The most powerful orgasm of my life tore through my body.

I felt it everywhere.

He thrust into me one more time until he went right over the edge with me.

And nothing had ever felt better.

We were both panting, and I did my best to slow my breathing.

He pushed the hair away from my face and stared at me with awe.

"You're fucking gorgeous. Everything about you turns me the fuck on."

I smiled, my teeth sinking into my bottom lip. "Even when I'm throat punching you or hitting you in the jewels with a pool ball?"

"Yep. All of it." He tugged me down and kissed me again

before lifting me up and setting me on my feet. He grabbed his clothes and walked to the bathroom, and I followed him. He peeled off the condom and tied it off. I grabbed my clothes and got dressed because I wasn't going to wear my leotard to Booze & Brews. He took the condom and the bags of food out to the trash while I pulled myself back together.

I stared in the mirror at my reflection.

Damn, I hadn't looked this relaxed in… forever.

I was living my best small-town life, and I just had the best romp in the hay with my temporary lover, and it clearly agreed with me.

My cheeks were pink, my lips plump from where he'd just been kissing me, and I used my fingers to fix my freshly fucked hair, which was currently a wild mess.

He came walking back into the bathroom and caught me off guard when he stepped behind me and wrapped an arm around my waist before resting his chin on my shoulder.

I studied us in the mirror. He was beautiful. Dark hair. Dark eyes. Chiseled jawline with a perfectly shaped narrow nose to complement his handsome face. And don't even get me started on those dimples.

My skin was fairer, my hair blonde and my eyes brown. He was a good foot taller than me, yet we looked like we fit together so well.

"I wanted to make sure you weren't freaking out," he said as he nipped at my ear.

"No. I'm too relaxed to freak out."

He smiled as his eyes met mine in the mirror. "Good. Because I plan to do that as many times as I can before you leave for Paris."

"I think I can make that work." I turned around to face him.

"We just need to keep the feelings in check."

"You worry too much, Wildcat. Let's just enjoy it while it lasts." He kissed the tip of my nose. "Let's go meet everyone for a quick drink."

He took my hand in his, and we made our way outside. We agreed to walk to the bar and leave his truck here, and he'd grab it tomorrow.

I turned my phone on so I could text Henley to let her know that we were on our way, and it started beeping repeatedly.

That was never a good sign.

I came to a stop, and Rafe stared down at my phone as I groaned. "Beckett's at the bar. Of course, he came on Valentine's Day."

"All right. Let's go get this over with," he said, as if it was no big deal.

"Rafe, you don't know who you're dealing with. He's not rational. He's going to flip a table and throw a fit and have a slew of paparazzi there to catch it all on film. Let's just go home."

"No." He looked down at me, hands on each of my shoulders so I'd stay put. "Aren't you tired of letting this be a part of your life? You've been done with this dude for a long time. It's enough already," he said.

"I agree. But a big public scene doesn't help anyone."

"Let him flip a table. Let him throw a fit. He doesn't get to have you just because he's back in town and wants to claim you. Fuck him. Let's just go have a good night. If he wants to talk, we'll talk. If he's unhinged, we'll have him escorted out of the place. This is a small town. No one here gives a shit that he's the lead singer in some boy band."

I shook my head with a laugh. "You think it's that simple?"

"It is that simple if you don't allow it to be more. If you don't give him the power to let this be more. Come on, Lu. Think about it. As far as he knows, you've moved on. And I won't stand by and let some rich little asshole come in and attempt to ruin my night with *my woman*." He smirked as he took my hand and started walking.

"Fine. We'll do it your way. Don't say I didn't warn you," I said.

"I'm not worried about it. But when I show you how simple it's going to be to shut this down, I think you could grant me round two of the Valentine's Day romp in the hay." His voice was laced with humor, but I saw the heat in his eyes when he looked over at me.

And damn if I wasn't ready for round two myself.

But I wouldn't give it up that easily.

"Let's see if everyone wants to run me out of Rosewood River after they experience the rant that's about to go down, and then we can see if round two is still on the table."

"Why do you think people will want to run you out of town for the way your ex-boyfriend behaves? That has nothing to do with you," he said as if that should be common sense.

"My father says that you are who you associate with. He has told me on many occasions that I brought this disaster on myself by allowing this man into my life at all." I sighed. "So this is me being accountable."

"If you remained in a relationship with someone who acted this way, sure, they could question your choices. But you ended it, and that's when all this shit started, right?"

"Yes. Once I left him, he became irrational. When I was with him, he was just a selfish asshole." I chuckled.

We stopped about a block from the bar, and he turned to face me. "We've all misjudged people, Lulu. You recognized that he wasn't good for you, and you left. What he's done since then is on him. It has nothing to do with you. So stop acting like you committed a crime. You dated a dude in college, and then he got famous, and his life changed. You walked away, and you should not be punished for that. You should be praised for knowing when to leave someone who is bringing you down. End of story."

"Damn you, Rafe Chadwick." I swallowed hard, trying to push the lump in my throat away. No one aside from Henley had ever not acted like I'd brought this on myself, and I was to blame.

I turned my back to him for a minute while I pulled myself together.

It hit me in this moment that I was exhausted from all of it. From trying to escape a toxic relationship. Trying to build a company that I created on my own. Trying to prove that I wasn't just some rich socialite party girl like the press had made me out to be.

And most importantly, trying to act like none of this bothered me.

"Hey," he said, his arms wrapping around me from behind. "You're okay. I see you, Lulu Sonnet. I see all of you. And I'll take you exactly as you are."

I sighed and pushed the tears back before turning around and smiling at him. "Is that a sexual joke?"

"No joke, Wildcat." He studied me for a long moment. "Come on. Let's go show this dickhead that he's fucking with the wrong girl."

"Let's do this." We turned the corner to find a slew of photographers out front, and Ben Leighton, the owner of the bar, was out there talking to them, along with a few police officers.

"Not your problem," Rafe said, keeping his voice low. "The rules are different here."

"Hey, Rafe. Hey, Lulu," Ben said. "Just letting these guys know that cameras aren't allowed inside, and loitering is not welcome here either."

I waited for him to get annoyed with me for bringing this drama here, but he didn't seem even slightly irritated with me.

"Looks like they need to pack their shit up and head on out of town," Rafe said, as he high-fived and shook hands with the three officers before introducing them to me.

"You guys go on in and enjoy yourselves. The rock star is here, and he's not happy that the photographers aren't allowed in with their gear. I reminded him this is a bar, not a damn reality show. Jazzy's inside, and she'll let us know if there's any trouble," Ben said as we made our way to the door.

Once inside, country music boomed. The dance floor was packed, and I quickly scanned the space. Henley hurried my way, and I spotted Beckett signing a woman's cleavage near the bar. His band members weren't with him, but he had his security team nearby.

Rafe leaned down, his lips grazing the edge of my ear as he spoke. "Do not leave my side. If he wants to talk to you, he does it with me present. We're a team, Lulu. I've got you."

I've been a lone wolf, aside from my best friend, for most of my life, but surprisingly, his words didn't make me panic.

They comforted me.

23

Rafe

I noticed Beckett tracking her the moment we walked through
the door. His eyes found mine quickly, and I didn't look away.
Lulu and I made our way to the back table where Easton, Henley,
Bridger, and Clark were sitting. There were a few women hanging
on my two single brothers, per usual, but they were all watching me.

They knew that a situation was about to go down, and there
was no doubt they'd have my back.

But I wasn't worried at all.

I wasn't intimidated by some Hollywood pop star, nor did I
give a shit if he wasn't happy.

I cared about Lulu.

It was that simple.

Jazzy walked over and handed me a beer and Lulu a glass

of chardonnay, as Easton and Henley had clearly ordered for us, knowing we'd need a drink when we arrived.

"I don't have a good feeling about this guy." Jazzy leaned down when she set my drink down. "I'm pretty good at reading people, and he seems to be itching for a fight."

"I think you're probably right. If he starts anything, I promise you, I'll take him outside."

"Thanks, Rafe. Ben's got a few officers outside on standby. We're sending out some burgers to keep them happy for now." She chuckled.

I nodded, my gaze tracking Beckett and his entourage as he moved in our direction.

"Long time no see, Lulu," the asshole said as he approached our table. "Can we talk for a minute?"

"It's Valentine's Day, and I'm here with my boyfriend, so I don't want any drama. If you want to talk, he comes with me. If you start anything, we're walking out the door," she said.

My girl didn't show any trace of concern, and I was impressed.

"You're going to have some random fucking dude sit in and listen to our conversation?" he said as he gripped the edge of the table as if he were about to flip it. Three large men stood behind him, and if I were reading them correctly, they appeared uncomfortable that their job was to protect some asshole who liked to pick fights with people he didn't stand a chance against.

My chair slid back against the wood floor, making a loud screeching sound, and I stood. My hand found Lulu's shoulder as she remained in her chair. "Don't fucking speak to her that way again. If you want to have a conversation, let's step to the back of the room and have a private conversation. If you raise your voice or flip this fucking table, the conversation ends, and you will be escorted out of here."

"You're going to escort me out of here," he said, a cocky smirk on his face.

I leaned forward, my face just inches from his. "You're in my town, Beckett. You've got your three guys, but I've got three brothers ready to jump in and a bar full of locals who I grew up with, along with several police officers outside, just waiting to kick your ass out of here. So stop acting like a child, say what you need to say, and then move the fuck along. There's no issue here if you don't make one."

He glanced around, thinking it over. He was smaller than I expected. Somewhat sickly looking, if I was being honest.

"Fine. Let's go sit in the back and have a fucking conversation," he hissed before turning to Lulu. "It's the least you owe me."

"I owe you nothing," Lulu's voice was hard. "You have made my life a fucking nightmare just to keep your name in the press when you aren't touring. It's pathetic. But sure, let's go have yet *another* conversation."

I glanced at my brothers as I reached for Lulu's hand. I knew they'd be watching. I guided her toward the back corner, away from the dance floor and the watching crowd. He wasn't being followed in here like he was probably used to because the people here had grown fond of Lulu, and his music sure as hell wasn't the kind of music that played in this bar.

We sat down at a table, Lulu sitting close beside me and Beckett across from us.

"Do you think I should have to hear about your relationship with this fucking guy in the media?" His hands were fisted on the table, and he was seething. I glanced behind him and noticed the security guy closest to him looked irritated as hell, and I got the feeling that he'd watched this guy have a meltdown one too many times.

"We broke up over a year ago. I've dated plenty. I don't owe you an explanation every time I meet someone. And let's just be honest, for once in your life—" She let out a breath. "You like my name. You like the attention it gets you when you drag me into your mess. My family puts out a statement, and everyone is invested. Yet there is no you and me. There hasn't been in a very long time. We don't even speak. I've blocked your number. Why would I possibly reach out to let you know I'm dating someone?"

"It's a respect thing," he said, like the entitled prick that he was.

"A respect thing?" She barked out a laugh. "You cheated on me multiple times during the last year of our relationship. And I don't even care because we weren't even really together. I hardly saw you, and I wanted out of this. It's toxic and miserable, and you are the one who turned this into a living nightmare."

"Because I still love you." He shrugged, and for one split second, I felt bad for the bastard. Because having a girl like Lulu Sonnet was like catching the sun—and losing her, I knew it must suck for him. But it was by design. It was his doing. He had her, and he treated her like shit, so she walked away.

Shit happens, asshole.

"You don't even know what love is. You just want what you can't have because you're an entitled narcissist, and you can't handle that I don't care about your fame or your money. You can't bully me into talking to you, Beckett. It's over. It's been over for a long time, and we both know it. So let's call this done once and for all, and let's move on."

"Do you know how many women I fuck a week?" he said, leaning into the table now, and I placed an arm around Lulu's shoulders protectively.

Don't even think about it, asshole.

I wanted to jump in. Tell him to shut his fucking mouth. But she needed to handle this, and I respected that. Unless he crossed the line and forced my hand.

"Probably a lot, and good for you. I want you to be happy. I wish you well. But the truth is, I don't care. I don't care who you date or who you fuck or what you do." She took a sip of her wine, acting completely unfazed.

Lulu Sonnet was a badass in every way. And I was getting a front-row seat.

"Anastasia is pregnant," he said, and I had no idea who that was.

I glanced at Lulu, wanting to see if there was any sort of reaction to his words. It was what he was hoping for.

"I really hope, for Anastasia's sake and your child's sake, that you pull your shit together, Beckett. You have a woman you've been sleeping with on and off for a very long time. She's been on tour with you from the very beginning, and she deserves better. You should be there with your pregnant girlfriend instead of chasing after your ex-girlfriend who wants nothing to do with you."

"Fuck you. I should lock you in a closet again," he hissed, and my shoulders stiffened at his words.

What the fuck did he just say?

I was about to push to my feet when Lulu's hand found mine beneath the table, and she squeezed it.

I've got this.

"Let me give you a little advice because we do have a history, and because of that, I'll give you this." She set her wine glass down and looked him in the eyes. "That day you're referencing, that's the day that I made a conscious decision to cut you off in every possible way. So thank you for that little lesson where I realized there wasn't even the possibility of a friendship left for us. It's also the day that I decided to start taking self-defense classes. So I promise you this, if you ever put your hands on me again, you won't walk away on two feet. I will snap your little fucking neck because you're a bully and a sad excuse for a man." And then she looked up, over his shoulder. "And the people that work for you, that allow you to behave like an animal, should be ashamed of themselves for looking the other way. You're lucky I didn't go public with what you did, and that wasn't to protect you. That was to save my family any more embarrassment than you'd already caused."

My blood was boiling, and I didn't even know what exactly had happened, but I knew it was bad.

I tugged Lulu closer, and my gaze locked with his. His eyes were bloodshot, pupils dilated, making it clear he was on something. "Did you get your fucking closure? Because this is the last time you bother her. Don't even look in her direction again. Am I being clear? Get your guys together, and get the fuck out of my town. No one wants you here."

He glanced around. No one was paying him any attention, aside from my brothers, who were watching us from a few feet away.

"I just wanted you to know that I'm having a child." He shrugged.

"How about you start focusing on that child? Don't mention my name in the press. Just move the fuck on, Beckett."

He ran a hand down his face. "I fucked up, Lu. That's the truth. I know I'll never find anyone like you, and I know you're never coming back."

"You're right about that." She crossed her arms over her chest and leaned against me. "Goodbye, Beckett."

His gaze moved from me to Lulu, and then he pushed to his feet. "Let's get the fuck out of this shitty little hell hole."

He walked away, his security team falling in place, and I followed them all as they made their way out the door, making sure Lulu stayed tucked behind me.

"You all right?"

"I am. Thanks for sitting beside me and keeping things calm."

"You want to tell me about the closet incident?" I asked, my blood boiling at the thought of him doing something to her.

"Maybe later, okay?" She smiled up at me. "It's still Valentine's Day, and it happens to be the best one I've ever had, so how about we go back to having some fun?"

"You got it. Let's go see what everyone is doing," I said, but I was still on edge about what he'd said to her. What he'd done to her.

We spent the next hour laughing our asses off and putting Beckett Bane in our rearview. There'd been no tables flipped. No photographers. No drama.

Lulu had written the end of their story, and I could tell she felt good about it.

She was sitting on my lap, running her fingers through my hair, as Bridger and Clark asked her questions about Paris.

Easton and Henley had gone home a few minutes ago, and the bar would be closing soon.

"French food gives me the shits," Bridger grumped.

"French fries do not count as French food," Lulu said over a fit of laughter.

"Good one, Lu." Clark held his hand up and high-fived her.

I just watched her. The way she interacted with them. The way she fit so well right here.

In this town.

With my family.

With me.

"It's all the sauces that get me. I've got irritable bowels," Bridger said.

"You've got an irritable personality." Clark slammed the rest of his beer.

"Don't you have practice tomorrow?" I asked my brother, as he was in the middle of his season.

"Yeah. So, Lulu, you think you can cover me in pickleball until you leave for Paris? We've got a ton of games, and I can't play at all until the season ends. Henley is supposed to cover me, but Archer hardly makes it anymore."

She ran her finger over the rim of her wine glass. "Does a bear shit in the woods?"

"What the fuck does that mean? Are you going to shit on the pickleball court?" Bridger asked.

"It means, she can cover for him, dickhead." I barked out a laugh.

"Ah… she's a cocky little one, isn't she?" Clark said. "Buckle up, Sonnet. Easton is no joke about the Chad-six."

"Well, he'll have to amend his rules if he wants me to sub. I won't wear that ridiculous tee. If I'm going to play, I'm going to wear something spectacular."

"Do you actually know how to play?" Bridger groaned. "Because I can't deal with his moping if you suck."

"My best friend has taught me a trick or two. You needn't worry, boys. I can hold my own on any court." She turned to me and waggled her brows.

"I don't doubt that for a minute," I said, tugging her head down and kissing her.

It wasn't for show or for a camera to catch us together.

I kissed her because I wanted to.

I kissed her because I needed to.

"And that's our cue." Clark pushed to his feet. "Come on, big guy. Let's get our asses home. You ran off the two women who actually wanted to go home with us."

"Because Fiona talks too much, and her voice is ridiculously high-pitched, and Wendy spits every time she speaks to me. I'm not going to fake it just to get laid." Bridger pushed to his feet and slapped a few hundred-dollar bills down on the table.

"Well, I was fine faking it," Clark said, clapping me on the shoulder before leaning down and kissing Lulu on the cheek as she pushed off my lap to stand.

Bridger shocked the shit out of me when he wrapped his arms around her. "I'm glad you dumped that jackass and scared him off before I had to put my fist in his face."

"That's the sweetest thing you've ever said to me, Bridger Chadwick," Lulu said, as the corners of her lips turned up, and she pushed up on her tiptoes and kissed his cheek.

"Don't get used to it," he said, slapping me on the shoulder. "See you, brother."

"I like your family," she said as she reached for her purse.

"They're all right." I smirked. "You ready to head home?"

She looked up and smiled. "I'm ready for round two, Rafael."

I hurried her out the door before picking her up and tossing her over my shoulder as I started jogging toward Easton's house.

"What the hell are you doing?" she squealed over her laughter as she smacked me on the ass.

"My woman wants round two, so who am I to deny her?"

Because I don't think I could ever deny this woman anything she wanted.

24

Lulu

Round two had been just as good as round one.

And round three was even better.

This man had the stamina of a professional athlete and the erection of a porn star on Viagra.

But it was more than that.

A part of me wished this was just sex because it had been a long time since I'd enjoyed myself this way with a man.

But it was the conversation and the laughter.

The connection.

And now he was sitting on the floor in the bathroom while I was submerged in the deep soaker tub as we shared a glass of wine.

"Thanks for tonight," I said, my voice quieter now as I handed him the glass back.

"That was all you. You were impressive as hell with the way you handled that guy," he said, setting the glass down on the ledge beside the tub.

I never told anyone what happened the last time I saw Beckett. Not even Henley.

Sure, I was embarrassed that I allowed myself to be in a situation like that. And I didn't press charges because I didn't want my family pulled into it during an election year. And I hadn't told my best friend because I knew she'd be devastated and want to talk about it, and I just didn't want to do that.

Instead, I took action.

I signed up for self-defense classes and cut off every ounce of contact with Beckett on my end.

Rafe was watching me as if he knew what I was thinking about.

It was strange to me that I could feel so close to a person I hadn't known my entire life.

I didn't get close to people often. I kept my inner circle very small, and it was intentional.

I was social and friendly and outgoing, and I had a wide circle of acquaintances.

But deep connections—I could count on one hand the number of people that I truly trusted.

And somehow, this man, who'd stumbled into my life unexpectedly, had become one of them.

I couldn't look at him and tell him. But I knew he wanted to know. And he deserved to hear it. He deserved my vulnerability because he'd shown up for me over and over again, and he had no ulterior motives to do so.

Rafe Chadwick was a really good man. And those didn't come around often.

And I may not have been at a place in my life where I was open to finding a good man, but he'd found a place there anyway.

"Will you take a bath with me?" I asked.

"You want me to sit in warm, dirty water with you?" He smirked.

"It's still hot, and I've bathed twice today, so it's also very clean."

As if he understood what I was asking, he stripped off his briefs and stepped into the tub behind me.

Not because he wanted to, but because he knew that I wanted him to.

I scooted forward, making room for his large body, and chuckled when the water flowed over the rim of the tub.

He reached for the glass of wine, and I took a sip before setting it back down beside me.

"I'm going to tell you something that I've never told anyone," I said, no hesitation in my voice.

"I appreciate that you trust me enough to share it with me."

"I do. And that's saying a lot because I haven't even told Henley. The only people that know are me and Beckett, and one of his bodyguards knows the short version."

He was quiet, and his hands found mine beneath the water.

"A little over a year ago, I had long decided that my relationship with Beckett was over. I told you that he had been unfaithful, and the truth is, it didn't even hurt because I had emotionally made peace with it. Our relationship had run its course. But he was caught in the press with other women, one being the woman who is now carrying his child, Anastasia. My family was angry because the press was painting me as a woman scorned, and it was an election year, so it was an embarrassment for my father."

"It's not like you have any control over that shit. Why is that your problem?" he asked, his fingers intertwined with mine now.

"Great question." I chuckled. "But I was basically told to fix it. I spoke to Beckett on the phone and made it clear that I was done, but he continued to give interviews stating that we were together. He posted old photos of us on his social media, and that would start everything up again. I was traveling a ton, trying to get MSL into some big department stores, and consciously focusing on my business. But his drama was all over the news, which didn't look good for me professionally."

"That is absolute bullshit that he would continue posting photos of you when you weren't together."

"Listen, his band definitely blew up, but his whole persona has been painted as this *bad boy*, and dragging my name into it only added to the allure." I cleared my throat. "I asked him to take the photos down, to stop talking about me publicly in interviews, per my father's request, and he said he would do everything that I requested if we met in person one last time. I was in New York on business, and he was there for a week on his tour. I didn't want to meet him at my hotel because Beckett can be a volatile guy, and after years of trying to help him get clean, I knew that addiction won. I didn't even recognize who he was anymore. So, I didn't tell him where I was staying. I agreed to come to the show and meet him beforehand. It seemed like a wise option because it was a public place, so what could he possibly do? That was my thought process."

"He'd never laid a hand on you, had he?"

"Never. But he had these meltdowns. He'd shatter things and flip tables, that type of irrational behavior. That all started shortly before we ended things, but seeing it a few times was enough to make me cautious about being alone with him."

"So you went to the show?"

"I went an hour before. I figured we could have a short discussion, hash out whatever it was that he felt he needed to say to me, and he'd have to go on stage, and I could sneak right out the back door. That was the plan."

I sighed, and my head tipped back to rest on Rafe's shoulder. His hand came up and stroked my forehead, brushing the loose strands that had fallen free from my scrunchie away from my face.

"It sounds like a good plan." He nuzzled my neck as if he were trying to comfort me. "Tell me what happened."

"He was waiting for me at the back door when I arrived. We went into his dressing room, and we talked." I paused and took a sip of wine. I hated thinking back to that day. Not because it scared me, but because it pissed me off that I hadn't been better prepared. That would never happen again. "I told him I was done and that I wanted to start dating other people. I told him he should do the same, and I asked him to stop posting about me. Stop talking about me in the press. Stop calling and texting incessantly."

"Seems like a fair request for a breakup," Rafe said.

"You would think so." I let out a long breath. "He told me we weren't done. He told me that his manager said that fans liked him in a relationship with me, and that his popularity was declining because I wasn't present in his life. I reminded him that we weren't together, so obviously, I wasn't going to be present. I was done.

"He shoved the table over and smashed his beer bottle against the wall," I said, shaking my head at the memory. "He's such a child when he doesn't get his way. So, I moved to my feet and told him I wasn't going to continue a conversation with someone who behaved that way. I made my way to the door, and he grabbed my arm in a rage and spun me around."

"What the fuck? He put his hands on you? Did he hurt you?"

"No, but he definitely startled me. I shoved him back and obviously told him to go fuck himself. He told me that we weren't done, and I told him that it wasn't up to him, and I would file a restraining order if he didn't stop this madness."

"Yes. That's absolutely what you should have done. He doesn't sound rational."

"He reminded me that if I filed any sort of legal paperwork, it would be public record, and I'd bring more attention to my family. He was holding my arms pretty forcefully and just kept saying that we could work things out. I told him repeatedly that I didn't want to. I was ready to start dating and focusing on my business so I could move forward with my life. His grip tightened, so I tried to shove him back. I kicked him in the shin because he was leaning all of his weight against me as I was pressed against the door, and then I tried to grab the handle to leave."

"This fucking guy," he hissed. "What did he do?"

"Well, that pissed him off. Obviously, he doesn't like being told no. He grabbed my arm again and spun me around so quickly that I lost my footing. I remember falling and hitting my head on the console table near the door."

"Jesus. Did you go all the way down? Did you split your head open?"

I nodded before taking his hand and moving it to my hairline to feel the little scar where I'd gotten several stitches.

"Yes. I was bleeding and a little wobbly as I tried to move to my feet. I thought he'd call for help, but he didn't. He cursed and told me that I had made everything worse. And then when I stumbled to my feet, he grabbed my wrist, and before I knew what was happening, he shoved me into a closet. He locked the fucking door and left me in there." My voice was shaking the slightest bit as I retold the story.

Rafe's arms came around my center now, wrapping me up tight in a hug. "He locked you in the closet. I'll fucking hurt that piece of shit, Lulu. I swear, if I'd known this, I'd have beat him senseless tonight."

"I don't need you to. I made sure that I'd know how to do that if he ever touched me again. That's when I started taking self-defense classes. I have zero fear of him ever trying anything again."

"I'd take pleasure in hurting him," he said, his voice low and hard. "So what did you do? Did you have a phone?"

My hands came over his, and he laced his fingers through mine.

"Well, I had my phone in my pocket, but there was no reception. He's a complete psychopath and turned the music on extra loud when he left the room. I screamed for the first half an hour before I realized no one was going to hear me. No one was coming. They were probably all watching the show. My voice was loud, but not over the blaring music. It was pitch black in the closet and creepy as hell, and I knew my head was throbbing and bleeding pretty badly, so I was trying to keep my wits about me."

"This is fucking outrageous." His voice was angry, yet not loud.

"I was in that closet for over an hour. I tried kicking the door open, but it didn't work because the space was so tight, I couldn't take a step back to put any force behind it." I remembered the feeling of panic that he'd forget I was in there in his drugged-up state and end up going out partying after the concert and leaving me there. "I turned on my flashlight and immediately saw all the blood on my hands, which freaked me out, and I knew I needed to get to a hospital. I guess my survival skills kicked in. I had a bobby pin in my hair, and I took it out and spent a good thirty minutes trying to move the lock on the door. It finally worked, and I didn't know where to go. I had my car parked in back, but I was afraid I couldn't drive with my head hurting so badly."

"What did you do?" His voice was eerily calm, but I could feel his anger as I lay with my back to his chest.

"When I came out of the room and ran toward the back door, I bumped into his head of security at the time, Carlos. He's no longer with Beckett. He just took my hand and hurried me out the back door. I told him I didn't think I could drive, and he said he'd drive me in my car to the hospital. He never asked for the details; he just asked me if Beckett had been responsible, and I said that he had. He stayed with me at the hospital and then drove me in my rental car back to the hotel after. I asked him not to speak to anyone about it, and he said he would never tell a soul, but he was never going back to work for that asshole again. We've kept in touch over the last year. He went on to work for an actress and is much happier now."

"I'm glad he was there to help you. So what happened at the hospital and after?"

"I got seven stitches in my head, and I never told a soul. Henley was finishing up law school, and I knew she'd freak out and want to come make sure that I was okay. And after being shoved into a closet and feeling helpless, I didn't want to feel that way again. I didn't want anyone to help me. I wanted to spend my energy figuring out how to help myself if that ever happened again. I started training with Coach Jones so I would be capable of protecting myself moving forward. I never spoke to Beckett again. I blocked him and ended all communication. But he's shown up a few times when I've been out publicly. This last time was over the holidays at a restaurant in front of my entire family. I think he thought he could pull me back into his disaster of a life. Tonight felt different. Like he saw us together, and he believed it."

"I think he saw your strength and was intimidated by it," Rafe said, hugging me tighter. "I'm so fucking impressed by you. My fierce, strong Wildcat. I knew it the first time I met you."

"That I had a mean right hook?" I chuckled.

"Nope." He barked out a laugh. "I mean obviously, I felt that hit to my throat. But I could tell you were someone who didn't take any shit. Someone who could take care of herself."

"Thank you," I said, looking down at my pruned fingers. "Should we get out?"

"Yeah." He pushed to his feet, taking me with him. He grabbed a towel and wrapped it around his waist before wrapping one around me and then drying off every inch of my skin.

I smiled down at him when he bent down to dry my feet. "You know I can do that myself, right?"

"I don't doubt that for a second. I just want to do it for you." He winked and then stunned me when he scooped me up like a baby and carried me to the bed, setting me down so my head was resting on a pillow. "Thank you for telling me what happened. Thank you for trusting me with it. I promise you, your words are safe with me."

"I believe you," I said as I sat up when he started to step back. "Hey, do you want to sleep in here tonight?"

"Really? Isn't that breaking your rules?"

"I think I broke several tonight, like when I had sex with you in the dance studio and then told you my deepest secret while sitting naked in a bathtub with you. This is hardly one to be concerned about." My teeth sank into my bottom lip. "Unless you prefer sleeping alone?"

He leaned closer, resting his forehead against mine. "I hate sleeping down the hall. It's a really dumb rule."

I laughed and flicked him on the shoulder.

Even though I couldn't agree more.

Sleeping apart was a really dumb rule.

25

Rafe

Easton: *Pickleball tonight, bitches. Bring your A game. Bridger, leave your shitty attitude at home. Literally and figuratively.*

Bridger: *I had the shits from Honey Biscuit Café. That was a valid excuse.*

Me: *Edith puts too much cheese in those potatoes. I need to be near a restroom if I eat them. And we sure as hell didn't want him dropping a steamer on the pickleball court.*

Clark: *You better show up today because I have a late practice and can't be there.*

Easton: *What the fuck is happening to the Chad-Six? Henley and Lulu have subbed for you fuckers the last two weeks. Clark is the only one who gets a pass because he has a valid excuse.*

Archer: *I have to take Melody to speech therapy tonight. That's a valid excuse.*

Axel: *Once again, if you had a normal nanny, you could have her take Melody to speech.*

Clark: *When I stopped by earlier this week to take Melody to arts and crafts class, Mrs. Dowden asked me to rub her feet while she relaxed on your recliner. What the fuck are you paying this woman for?*

Me: *I agree. She asked me to do the same, and you know I have a thing with feet. I don't like them. I barely tolerate my own.*

Archer: *So, what did you say?*

Me: *I had to think quickly. I told her that I used to date a podiatrist, and I had a fear of feet now.*

Easton: *<exploding head emoji>*

Bridger: *I don't fuck with feet either.*

Axel: *You don't have any desire to massage the cracked heels of an elderly woman?*

Clark: *She has bunions, and they are no joke.*

Axel: *You actually did it?*

Clark: *She's a hundred and twenty, dude. I just told her she had to keep her socks on. I did a few squeezes, and she was content.*

Easton: *You're a good man. Anyway, enough of the feet. You better be there tonight, Bridger. We've dominated the first two weeks. Let's just try to rein Lulu in. Her shit-talking almost got us written up.*

Me: *She's got a mouth on her, and I totally dig it.*

Axel: *She called the Wilcox brothers the Cocksuckers.*

Me: *That's because they made some crack about wanting to find a new financial advisor and then saying they would never work with a member of the Chad-Six.*

Axel: *So she got defensive on your behalf. Are you still claiming this isn't serious? She's leaving in a few weeks, right?*

Easton: *I honestly thought you two were faking it in the beginning. But now it seems very fucking real.*

Archer: *If they're faking it, then I'm a neurosurgeon and Bridger didn't shit himself last week at the hockey game.*

Bridger: *It's those fucking cheesy potatoes.*

Clark: *You did not shit yourself in our arena.*

Bridger: *Of course not. I sharted.*

Me: *Shat. Shart. Po-tat-o. Po-tot-o.*

Easton: *<poop emoji>*

Axel: *Dude. You are clearly lactose intolerant.*

Bridger: *You make horse trailers for a living. What do you know about being lactose intolerant?*

Easton: *Well, tell your real, fake, staying, leaving girlfriend that the ref heard her and gave us a warning. But I believe that was after she accused Barry Wilcox of having a small peen. Her words, not mine.*

Me: *It was actually a micropeen. And she only said that because he said he hoped I was better with numbers than I was with a pickleball paddle.*

Clark: *Didn't you smoke them?*

Me: *Yes. He was trying to get into my head.*

Easton: *Well, clearly, he got into Lulu's head. And then she went on to tell Gary Rite that he sucks balls.*

Bridger: *Smart girl. Gary Rite sucks.*

Me: *Agreed. And he threw his paddle on the ground because he couldn't return her spikes.*

Archer: *Damn. The girl has game.*

Me: *We'll be there tonight. And we'll be ready to dominate.*

"According to Easton, the ref said that you need to tone down your shit-talking during pickleball," I said over my laughter as we walked up the walkway to my house. The kitchen remodel was supposed to be done today, and I wanted to check on it.

"What a bunch of babies. If they can't take the heat, then get the hell out of the kitchen, am I wrong?" She paused dramatically in front of my door. "Oh, wait. I'm right… I'm *Gary Rite*."

I barked out a laugh as I pushed open the door. "You're right, Wildcat. I think your skills do all the talking, but you definitely know how to get into their heads when you talk about their manhood."

Now *she* was laughing as she glanced around the space. We'd come several times to check out the progress. We'd been spending a lot of time together since she invited me into her bed two weeks ago. We slept together, we showered together, we played pickleball together, and on the days I didn't go into the office, we worked from home together. She also introduced me to her martial arts training, and I'd taken her to the gym at the club where I worked out.

To say the gray area had taken over our current situation was an understatement. I didn't know what we were, and I didn't fucking care.

I'd always been a guy who lost interest fairly quickly, but that was not the case with Lulu.

I was all in.

Sure, I knew she was leaving, but I wasn't holding back.

I didn't want to.

"Hey, Mack!" I called out.

"I'm in the kitchen. Come check it out."

We came to a stop and took it all in. The large, sleek black island sat in the middle, with white quartz countertops. The rest of the cabinets were a rustic wood and stained walnut.

"Wow. The white countertops really pop against the dark wood and the black, and when you add in the copper, it's so chic." Lulu ran her hand over the copper hood, which had been her suggestion.

"Yeah, this turned out incredible, Rafe. With the wood floors and all the natural light coming from the windows in this great room, it's magnificent." Mack finished washing his hands and then dried them off with a few paper towels. "How are you doing, Lulu? You were the talk of poker night yesterday."

She quirked a brow. "Is that so? What were they saying?"

"I play cards with a few guys from the club, and they were talking about how the Chad-Six brought in two ringers with you and Henley," he said over his laughter. "Apparently, you're dominating at pickleball. But they said you really get into their heads with your smack talk."

"Let me guess. The Cocks brothers and Gary Rite are in this card group?"

"Wilcox," I said, as I barked out a laugh and hooked an arm around her waist to pull her close.

"Whatevs. They are ridiculously whiney. Let me give you a little tip, Mack. All you have to do is reference the size of their package, and they freaking fall apart. It's too easy."

Mack covered his mouth with his hand to contain his laughter. "I'll keep that in mind. They also warned the other guys not to mess with Rafe, or they'd get the wrath of Lulu."

I waggled my brows. "What can I say? My girl is very protective."

Lulu turned around in my arms and pinched my cheeks, making me yelp. "Hey. You're my pickleball partner. You have to have your partner's back."

"You sure that's all it is?" I nipped at her ear.

"Yep. Come on, Rafael. Let's check out these appliances."

We spent the next thirty minutes looking at everything in the kitchen. The floors were also down throughout most of the house. The bathrooms were next, and the new slider would open up the entire wall to the river in the backyard.

When we were done checking out the house, we said our goodbyes to Mack and made our way over to the club to get ready for pickleball.

"The house is really coming along. Sounds like you'll be back in right around the time I'm leaving," she said, as she grabbed her duffle bag from the back seat when we pulled up to the club.

"Yep. Mack thinks it'll be right around then."

"That's exciting," she said, bumping me with her shoulder.

"Yeah," I said, but there was no real passion behind the word. Yes, I was looking forward to finishing my home. No, I wasn't looking forward to Lulu leaving.

"Hey, Rafe," Jolie said as she walked toward us. I'd gone out with her a few times more than a year ago, and she played a lot of tennis up here. I'd introduced her to Lulu more than once, and she continued to act as if she didn't see her standing there.

"Hi. How are you doing? You remember Lulu, right?"

"You must. We've met multiple times, and I'm not that forgettable," Lulu said, not hiding her irritation, and her smile looked forced.

"I wouldn't say you're forgettable either." Jolie smirked and then moved her hand in front of her as if she were drawing an invisible line around Lulu. "There's a lot going on here."

"Oh, I see. You're *that girl*." Lulu crossed her arms over her chest, her lips turning up the slightest bit.

"And what girl would that be?"

"The kind of girl that cuts others down to feel better about herself." Lulu quirked a brow. "Next time, just say hi. You can put the claws away. I'm leaving in a few weeks, so I'm not a threat to you. It's not that deep. But the way you've treated me, I'd say you've shot yourself in the foot. Rafael is a very loyal guy. He won't forget."

Jolie's eyes widened. "I, er, I should have said hello. Sorry about that."

"Thank you." Lulu sighed and then left me standing there as she walked toward the locker room to change.

The woman was so bold and fierce, and I was in awe of her most days. She lived the way we all should.

No bullshit.

"So it's not that serious between you two, then?" Jolie asked, and I forgot she was still standing there.

"What?" I asked.

"You and Lulu. She said she's leaving soon. So I'm guessing it's not that serious between you two. And, I'm not sure if you heard, but Josh and I broke up. I'm back on the market," she said, waving her hands in the air. "Single and ready to mingle, Rafe Chadwick."

"She was right about me being a loyal guy, Jolie. You've been really rude to my girl, and I've noticed." I shrugged. "And for the record, Lulu might not think it's serious, but seeing as I'm all in, I'd call it about as serious as you get. Have a good night."

I changed into my gear and tried to shake off the fact that her words had pissed me off.

What about this wasn't serious?

It was fucking offensive.

I tossed my bag over my shoulder and walked out to the courts, where Lulu was bent over stretching. We were the first ones here, and I stalked in her direction.

"Hey, why'd you say that back there?" I asked, not hiding my irritation.

"Seriously? Because she's rude. If you want to date her after I'm gone, go for it. Hell, if you want to date her now, just tell me and go back to the guesthouse. No one is watching us anymore, so you don't need to stay in the house with me for appearances."

The fuck?

"I'm not staying there for appearances. And I'm not talking about dating Jolie. I have zero interest in her. I'm talking about the fact that you said what we have isn't serious. Or that it isn't that deep. Whatever the fuck you said, it's fucking offensive," I hissed.

She narrowed her gaze, hands on her hips as she tipped her chin up to look at me. "That was a lot of fucks. You're offended by that comment?"

"Well, it's offensive, so yes. I am."

Her lips turned up in the corners, and she flashed me those white teeth. "Sorry, Rafael. I just meant that I'm leaving, so things can't get too deep when we both know that there's an expiration date."

I groaned. "I've never met someone that talks more about an expiration date. So fucking what? Most relationships have expiration dates; they just don't know it at the beginning. I think that we're lucky because there won't be any surprises. What we have right now is great. And I don't appreciate you demeaning it."

She wrapped her arms around me. "I'm sorry. I'm very happy with what we have right now. It's been the best surprise about coming to Rosewood River. It's been my silver lining."

"Thank you. It has been for me, too."

She stepped back. "But it is going to end because I have plans, Rafe Chadwick."

"For fuck's sake. I am more than aware. And I want you to go chase your dreams. But you're here now, and I've got plans for you these last few weeks. Because..." I let out a breath. "I like you, Lulu Sonnet."

I like you way more than I ever thought possible.

"I like you, too, Rafe Chadwick. So, what are these plans?"

"Pickleball. Sex. River rafting. A few new Netflix series. And of course, we've got my sister's wedding, which will be several days of activities. So we've got lots to do before you leave. Don't be running for the hills just yet. And stop reminding me that you're leaving."

She smiled, her eyes looking a little wet with emotion before she slipped her sunglasses back onto her face.

"I'm all yours for a couple more weeks," she said, before pushing up on her tiptoes and kissing my cheek.

I intended to enjoy every last damn minute I had with her.

26

Lulu

I sent a few designs off to the team I'd be working with in Paris and remembered that I had a missed call from my father when I was in the meeting.

Rafe had worked at the office today, and I was surprised at how much I missed him.

It was actually a little terrifying how much I missed him, if I were being honest.

Henley told me not to overthink it, but my brain couldn't shut off these feelings lately.

This was not part of the plan.

And now I was missing a man that I wasn't supposed to miss.

I tried to push the panic away as I dialed my father back.

"Hey, sweetheart," he said, but there was an edge there.

"Hi, Dad. How are you doing?"

"I just saw that your ex-boyfriend has gotten a woman pregnant, and it's all over the news."

For once, I wasn't part of Beckett's story, yet my father still sounded irritated.

"Yes. I heard about it. I think it's great. Hopefully, he's moved on."

"Your name was mentioned in the article. People suspect he isn't marrying her because he still has feelings for you." He sighed. "I don't know what the public's fascination is with this young man. He's nothing but trouble. It bothers me that people think of you every time his name is mentioned."

"It's not really my problem, Dad. I'm not sure what you want from me regarding Beckett. I dated him in college while he was studying jazz and I was studying dance. We had a lot in common back then. And he turned into a big, famous rock star, and we grew apart. He changed, and if I'm being honest, I probably changed, too. It happens all the time." My tone was much harsher than I intended, but I made no attempt to tone it down. "But it's been over for a very long time, and I'm tired of constantly worrying about him being in the press. Not because I care if my name is mentioned. I don't. I'm worried about getting an angry call from you after you hear about it. I can't control what Beckett says or does. All I can control is what I do. So you don't need to tell me every time he's interviewed. And you don't need to remind me that you're disappointed that I dated a guy you didn't approve of when I was younger. I'm more than aware. But I've moved on, and I would appreciate it if you would do the same."

It feels good to get this off my chest.

"You think I'm disappointed in you?" He sounded wounded, and it made my chest squeeze.

"I know you are. And I understand it to an extent. I should have left the relationship much sooner than I did. I embarrassed the entire family. But young people make mistakes, Dad. I'm not sure if you've noticed, but I haven't made all that many if you take a look at my track record."

"Lulubelle," he said, his voice softening now. "It was never about being disappointed in you. It was about being scared for you. Wanting more for you. Do you have any idea how proud I am of the business that you've built?"

No, I can't say I do.

"I don't know, Dad. We don't really talk about my business. You've been pretty focused on my ex-boyfriend and the media this past year. I've been doing everything I can to make it go away, and I'm just ready to move on to new things."

He was quiet for a few beats, and I knew my father well enough to know that he was processing what I said. He would normally bark at me and defend himself, so he clearly knew that there was truth to my words.

"I'm sorry, sweetheart. I am so proud of you, and I've failed you if I haven't shown that. You're correct. You have been doing all that you can to separate yourself from a bad situation, and I should have praised you for it and not made you feel like you'd disappointed me. And as far as the media goes, it's out of your control. I know that better than anyone. I've lived in that light most of my life in this family." He sighed. "Let's talk about Paris. Mom showed me the products that you're going to be launching, and we were both blown away."

"That means a lot to me. They believe in the MSL line, and I think it's going to do big things in that market."

"You'll stay for at least six months to start?" he asked.

"The Paris apartment is in the city, so that will make things very convenient for you."

My parents owned a gorgeous flat in Paris, and that's where I'd be calling home for the next several months. I loved it there. I spent summers and holidays in Paris growing up, and it felt like my second home.

"Yes. I need to polish up on my French over the next few weeks."

One month.

I was leaving at the end of March, and my time here was winding down.

"You'll pick it up fairly easy." He chuckled. "So what happens with Rafe? Mom and I really liked him. And obviously, Francois thinks he's the real deal."

I cleared my throat. I was tired of lying. Of pretending I was someone that I wasn't just to please my father. My family. To not feel like the black sheep. The screwup.

I was kicking ass professionally. It was time to hold my head up high and own it.

"He's great. I'm lucky to have had this time with him. He's made me realize that I can trust again, you know? I thought I'd never get there, but Rafe has really changed my perspective." I took a beat to swallow the lump in my throat. "But Rafe lives here, Dad. He loves this town, and his whole family is here. I'm moving to Paris, and I may never come back. I just don't know what my future holds, so I think we're going to just enjoy this time we have together and then wish each other well when it's time for me to leave."

"You're really making MSI your priority, and I respect it. But life isn't only about work, Lulu. Your mom and I have expanded Laredo's growth together. We're a team. You can have both. You know that, right?"

"You can if you're both on the same page. We have very different plans for our lives, and Rafe is the one who has taught me that that's okay. We can enjoy the time we have together, and then we'll go off and chase our dreams on our own. When I was with Beckett, I lost sight of my dreams, and I won't do that again. I worked hard for this partnership in Paris. So freaking hard. I chased it and didn't give up the first four times they rejected the line. This is my priority right now because, in a way, I'm finally focusing on my own dreams, and I'm proud of that."

After all I've been through in the last year, I was ready to spread my wings and fly.

"I'm proud of you for building something from the ground up and believing in it. But most of all, I'm proud that you are so focused and determined to accomplish the goals you set for yourself. I'm sorry I didn't notice sooner."

I swiped at the single tear rolling down my cheek. It had been a long time since I not only heard my father say he was proud of me but actually felt it.

"Thank you, Dad."

"Well, give our best to Rafe. Hopefully, we can FaceTime with you both this weekend again."

We'd started doing these calls together, and my parents loved him.

"Yeah, he told me he's going to keep the weekly calls going with you even after I leave," I said with a laugh.

My chest squeezed at my words.

At the thought of saying goodbye.

I had a hunch we'd keep in touch for a while. And then he'd probably meet someone, and it would be awkward to continue talking on the phone at that point, so things would eventually change.

It was part of life.

I hated the thought of Rafe with another woman.

The irony was not lost on me that I'd dated Beckett for years, and I felt nothing but relief about him having a child with another woman. I'd been desperate for him to move on for a long time.

But Rafe, a man I'd known for just a few months, a man who'd started out dating me on a lie to help me out—he was the one that I couldn't stand to think of with another woman.

It made no sense.

I shook it off, pushing it out of my mind when the doorbell rang.

I hurried over and pulled the door open to find Henley on the other side.

"Hey," she said, as she stepped inside. "I got off work early and thought we could go look for some outfits for all the events this weekend."

It was Emerson's wedding, and there was a bridal shower, a rehearsal dinner, and then the actual wedding.

"Yes! I need three outfits, and shopping is always a good idea," I said. "I also wouldn't mind a burger from the Honey Biscuit Café."

"I'm starving. Food first. Clothes after."

"Perfect," I said, grabbing my purse as we made our way out to her car. We could have walked, as the sun was out and we weren't too far from downtown. But we knew we'd have a ton of bags to carry, and this was just an easier plan.

We parked at the café and would leave the car there while we shopped.

"Well, well, well," Oscar said. "My two favorite gals are here."

"Who's the one flirting now?" Edith said, her voice all tease.

"Woman! Are you out of your mind? I'm old enough to be their grandfather. It's your mind that's always in the trash when it comes to those Chadwick boys."

Edith rolled her eyes as Henley and I laughed.

I loved this town.

This place.

These people.

"Hey, I'm just a woman with good eyesight. I can't help it if they're pretty to look at." Edith led us to the booth in the back and took our drink orders before leaving us alone.

"I wish you weren't leaving in a few weeks. It's been so fun living close to one another," Henley said, and we paused to place our lunch order when Edith set our drinks down.

"I know. But you're coming to Paris once I get settled, right?"

"Yep. I can't wait," she said as she took a sip of her soda. "Do you think you'll miss it here?"

I thought it over, even though I already knew the answer. "I mean, of course, I'll miss you."

She quirked a brow. "Come on, Lu. It's me. You can tell me that you're going to miss Rafe. He's being as tight-lipped as you are about it. You're both acting like it's no big deal, yet you basically live together."

"That is only because we were faking it at first," I whisper-hissed. "And then it seemed silly to have him move out, seeing as we spend so much time together. But we both knew what we were getting into. It'll be fine."

"I've just never seen you like this with anyone. You and Beckett were always so volatile, you know? You never seemed all that happy. You seemed like you were—" She tapped her chin as she thought it over.

"I was what?" I pressed as our plates were set down in front of us, and I bit off the top of a french fry.

"Stuck. You seemed like you were stuck. Long before you ended things with him, I didn't think you were happy. I just thought you didn't know how to get out of the relationship."

"That's because you know me. And in a way, I was stuck for a long time. I'm not proud of it because I don't believe in allowing someone to have that much control over your life. But it happened slowly. So, you're spot on, bestie. I was stuck. And now, I'm proud to say that I'm officially unstuck. I have been for quite a while." I chuckled. "Even my father finally believes me. He apologized for how hard he's been on me about it."

"That's because he can tell you're happy now. And I think a lot of that has to do with Rafe. I like seeing you so relaxed with someone. And he's so adorable with you, the way he's so protective and proud of you."

I rolled my eyes. "You just want me to date your boyfriend's brother."

"Not going to lie, I don't mind the sound of that. But that's not it. I didn't think much of it when it first started, but I've been watching the way you interact. Like you've known one another your entire lives. Like you speak your own language. And don't even get me started about the way he put you up on his shoulders last night at pickleball because you nailed the game-winning point. It was kind of adorable." She shrugged before cutting her burger in half and taking a bite.

"Those Golden Girls are no joke on the court. And they were flirting their asses off with Rafe, so I just had to distract them with my pickleball moves."

"I just wanted to say that sometimes you find what you're looking for when you're not expecting it." She put her hands up to stop me from jumping in. "I know you were derailed once in your life. I know this Paris opportunity is a big one. I know that Rafe has a life here, and he's happy. I'm just saying, sometimes we find something worth changing course for."

And sometimes when you put all your eggs in one basket, it blows up in your face.

Fool me once, shame on you.

Fool me twice…

I wouldn't be a fool twice.

I had a plan, and I was sticking to it.

27

Rafe

Emerson had always been the only girl in the family when we were growing up. The only female sibling and the only female cousin.

She had a huge wedding planned with her ex-fiancé, who cheated on her and slept with her maid of honor shortly before the big day.

We'd all hurt for my sister. She finished her pediatric residency at a big-city hospital, training under the top physicians in the country, and she changed course.

Her life had been turned upside down, and she moved to a small town, Magnolia Falls, where she found Nash Heart. He and his son, Cutler, were not what she was looking for, yet she'd written a new ending to her story.

A much better ending.

The ending she deserved.

And now we were all going to celebrate her wedding to the man of her dreams. This weekend was full of events, as my mom had planned most of it, and she'd gone all out.

There was a bridal shower yesterday, just for local family and friends, and her girls from Magnolia Falls had come into town early to celebrate with her, as well.

Lulu had been included like she was part of the family. She and my mom had grown close, and Emerson had FaceTimed with Lulu several times about fashion advice.

She fit in with my family like she'd always been there.

Of course, the girl that finally fits and feels right is the one I can't have.

The one I can't keep.

Maybe that was why it felt safe, because I knew it couldn't go anywhere.

I wanted to believe that I was only in this deep because I knew she was leaving.

I wanted that to be true.

But in my gut, I knew differently.

And somehow, my sister seemed suspicious, as well. She and I had walked over to pick up some parsley from the Green Basket that my mother needed for the rehearsal dinner tonight.

Emerson had asked me to come with her, but I had a feeling she had an agenda because as soon as we left the store with the parsley, she suggested we take the long way home and walk along the river.

"Are you ready for tomorrow?" I asked.

She smiled up at me. "I've been ready since the day he asked me to marry him."

"I'm so glad you held out and found what you deserve, Em."

"Me, too. It's funny, you know? I moved to Magnolia Falls after I called off the wedding to Collin, and the last thing I was looking for was love. But maybe that's how it's supposed to happen."

"What do you mean?" I asked.

"You know how Dad said he just felt different with Mom? Their connection was different from anything they'd ever experienced. I never had that with Collin, but I didn't think it meant anything because we'd known one another most of our lives. I had nothing to compare it to until I met Nash. And everything was just different, you know?"

"That makes sense. It all turned out as it should. I'm so happy for you. You deserve the fairytale. The happily ever after. All that romantic bullshit." I barked out a laugh.

"What about you? Don't you deserve that, too?"

I quirked a brow. "I don't think everyone is looking for the same thing. I'm a pretty happy dude, no need to worry."

"I know you are, Rafe. I've never worried about you. But I've also never seen you like this." She shrugged as we paused to sit on the bench along the trail, staring out at the water.

"Like what? I thought this was your wedding weekend. Did you lure me out here to psychoanalyze me?" I asked, my voice laced with humor.

"No. I'm being honest with you. You've always been a happy guy, but you're different with Lulu. I didn't know you could be happier than you already were." She chuckled. "But there's a comfort there that surprised me. It's like you two have known one another forever."

"We just get along really well. And I told you that we started off faking it, so maybe we're just really good actors."

She turned to look at me. "Come on, Rafe. There is nothing fake going on there. And your reasons for putting on a show when you first met her are gone. Yet you're still basically shacked up together. You freaked out when Sherry Carlton wanted to take a two-week vacation with you after you'd been dating for three months. Yet you are happily living with Lulu Sonnet. Clearly, there is something deeper there. We all see it."

"Sherry Carlton wanted to move things along much quicker than I did. I never liked staying at her place because she had three cats, and you know I don't do well with sneaky pussies." I waggled my brows at her as her head tipped back in laughter. "And I've always been cautious having a woman stay at my place because if you don't want to spend the night, you can't just make up an excuse and go home. Because you're already home."

"Yet you live at Easton's house with Lulu. Word on the street is, you aren't staying in separate bedrooms. You spend all your free time together, and I see the way you look at her, Rafe. I see the way she looks at you, too. Stop trying to make it like it's not a big deal. What are you so afraid of?"

Damn. Leave it to my sister to ask the big questions.

I blew out a breath. "Listen, Em, I'm not going to lie. I didn't anticipate it turning into this. And once it did, I just rolled with it. She reminds me at least once a day that she's leaving. We've got three weeks left, and she'll be moving to Paris for at least six months, if not a year. I live here. We agreed that we'll call this done when she leaves."

"And how do you feel about that?"

"Honestly, I don't think about it. We've always known there was an expiration date."

"But you didn't know you'd feel this way about her. Or am I misreading it? Is it not serious?" she pressed. She already knew the goddamn answer. I was basically living with her, all while knowing that she was not staying.

Who would agree to this deal?

Only a guy who was madly in love with a girl and wants to keep her as long as he can.

"It doesn't really matter, does it? She has these big dreams, and I love that about her. She's going to go launch her business in Paris, and my life is here. So analyzing our feelings won't do anyone any good."

"Well, you're only talking to me. I'm not suggesting you have to dissect it with her or anyone else. But you could tell me what you're feeling. I'm sure it's hard to always be the guy that plays it cool. The guy who pretends nothing bothers him. The guy that will always be okay." She squeezed my hand. "I tried to be that girl for a long time, Rafe. And after my life blew up, I wasn't okay. And what I learned is that you don't have to always be okay. If you feel the way that I think you do, it's going to hurt like hell when she leaves. I just want you to know that you can talk to me."

Fuck. Am I that easy to read now?

"I agreed to this deal. I knew what I was getting into, and I did it with both eyes open."

"So you deserve to suffer alone in that? When you agreed to this deal, you didn't know that your feelings would be what they are now. So it's okay to be upset that she's leaving. It's okay to say that you want her to stay."

"I'd never fucking say that," I said, surprised at how harsh my words were.

Her eyes widened. "Why not?"

"Because she dated a dude who held her back for a long time. She was born into a family that has put a lot of pressure on her to present herself a certain way. But she has dreams and things she wants to accomplish, and those won't happen here in Rosewood River. I'd rather be heartbroken and alone than hold her back. I'd never be the one to put her in a box. She deserves to spread her wings and fly."

My sister's eyes watered, and she squeezed my hands. "You're in love with her."

I didn't answer. I didn't need to. She already knew it.

"Listen, it's your big weekend. We've got to get this parsley home before Mom has a panic attack, and I don't want to dive any deeper into this. I don't have blinders on, and there are no surprises coming. She and I have been very open and honest with one another about our future, and I agreed to it. And I'll respect it."

"Have you told her that you love her?"

I pushed to my feet, irritation moving through me. I did not want to talk about this anymore. "No, Em. That would make things more complicated."

"For who? Her or you?"

"Both of us. Some things don't need to be said. Now let's go celebrate your big day. Mom's probably losing her mind waiting for the damn parsley." I chuckled, desperately trying to distract myself from my thoughts.

Emerson wrapped her arms around me. "I love you, Rafe. You're such a good man."

"Love you, too, sis." I smiled down at her, and we started walking home.

She dropped the subject, and I was grateful.

When we got home, a slew of people who worked for the wedding planner were in the backyard getting things set up for tomorrow. This was what Emerson wanted. A wedding at the childhood home where we'd grown up.

Henley and Easton were sitting on the couch, drinking a glass of wine with Nash, while Lulu and Cutler were playing cards in the same place they'd been when we left.

I handed my mom the bag of parsley and suddenly wondered what the urgency was. "The rehearsal dinner isn't even here, and the wedding tomorrow is catered. What did you need the parsley for?"

"Oh, turns out I don't need parsley," she said with a chuckle. "But wasn't it nice to have a little time with Em?"

"You are a devious woman." I wrapped her in a hug and kissed the top of her head.

"All right, we need to get home and change if we want to make it to the restaurant on time," Easton said, with Henley on his heels.

"Beefcake, you're a shark!" Lulu said over a fit of laughter and tossed the cards onto the table.

"I don't know, Lulu. You had me worried for a minute." Cutler pretended to swipe his brow. "Uncle Rafe, your girl is a shark, too."

Your girl.

"Hey, I thought you said that I was *your* girl." Lulu ruffled his hair and smiled down at him.

"Oh, you're my girl, too, Lulu. But I just didn't want to hurt Uncle Rafe's feels," he said.

"You mean Uncle Rafe's feelings." Nash quirked a brow.

"Nope. I mean feels, because Mama told me that Uncle Rafe is all in his feels for Lulu."

Everyone erupted in laughter, and I rolled my eyes, acting unfazed.

But they were right.

Uncle Rafe was definitely up in all his feels for this girl.

28

Lulu

When we arrived at the house for the wedding, I couldn't get over how stunning it looked. I've only attended weddings in banquet halls and country clubs. I've never been to a wedding that was so detailed and warm and everything a wedding should be.

Beefcake had introduced me to all the friends that had come from Magnolia Falls. Romeo and Demi had the cutest little baby boy named Hayes. I fangirled a little bit because I learned that Romeo was a professional boxer, now retired, but I remembered that fight he won as the underdog. It had been all over the news for months. River and Ruby were hilarious, and Rafe, Henley, and I sat in the middle of them during the ceremony.

Emerson and Nash had decided not to do a big wedding party as they thought it would be too many people, so Keaton walked his daughter down the aisle, sweet little Melody dropped flower petals and delivered the ring, and Cutler stood up there with them. Easton had officiated the nuptials, since he went through the process a few months ago so he could marry them.

They only wanted close friends and family to attend the ceremony, and I felt honored to be included. Apparently, the whole town would be coming out for the reception. The chairs were lined in rows, and there was a huge floral gazebo with the river in the distance. Peach and cream flowers were draped along the aisle.

They said their vows, and I've never experienced a more heartfelt wedding before. There wasn't a dry eye out here. Hell, I didn't know them that well, and I couldn't stop the tears from falling. Once they were announced husband and wife, we moved to a gorgeous area under these giant trees for photographs.

The sun was shining, and the sound of the water moving down the river was so soothing.

Hayes and Savannah introduced me to their twin baby girls, Piper and Penelope. They were passed around the group and everyone took turns holding them while we stood together as different groups were called for photos. Kingston and Saylor had just come back from using the restroom for the third time in an hour because she was very pregnant and apparently couldn't go very long without peeing, and everyone teased her endlessly about it.

"I wonder what they put in the water in Magnolia Falls," Henley whispered as we watched different groups pose for photos.

Emerson and all her brothers and cousins took a slew of

photos. My eyes tracked Rafe like it was my day job. The man wore a tan suit and cowboy boots, and it somehow managed to be the hottest thing I've ever seen.

"Trust me, I don't drink the water. I'm not risking getting knocked up before I'm ready," Ruby said, and Henley and I both laughed.

"Oh, we're blaming the water, huh?" Savannah said, cradling one of her sweet little girls in her arms.

"Listen, we got a two-for-one. There is definitely something in the water," Hayes said, and I couldn't help but smile at this big, burly man cradling his little baby girl like she was made of porcelain.

The way that man looked at the little bundle of joy in his arms, followed by Rafe rubbing his finger along her little forehead when he moved beside me, had my ovaries sparking to life.

And that had never happened.

Me and kids were not one.

Well, aside from Melody and Beefcake. If I were guaranteed to have clones of either one of those kids, I'd probably be open to the idea.

"Lulus, will you take a picture with me and Uncle Rafe?" Melody came up and took my hand, and my chest nearly exploded.

"Oh, my sweet little bug, these photos are for family members, but we could take one on my phone if you want," I said.

"You are absolutely going to be in these photos, Lulu Sonnet," Emerson called out like she had some sort of superpower hearing, catching me off guard. "We're doing couples next, but let's get one of Rafe, Lulu, and Melody first."

Rafe winked at me and scooped Melody into his arms, settling her on his hip before reaching for my hand. He leaned down near my ear and whispered, "I was in Gramps' eightieth birthday pictures when you barely even knew me. You are not getting out of here without taking a whole lot more."

I nodded before looking at the photographer as Melody's little hand moved to my shoulder and Rafe's free hand found my waist.

The Chadwicks were such a warm family, and they had a way of making you feel like you belonged.

Hell, I'd spent most of my adult life feeling like an outcast in my own family, so this was definitely not what I was used to.

But I wasn't complaining. I was soaking it in.

I had a few more weeks before my life changed drastically, so I'd just enjoy it while it lasted.

After a ton of photos, which I argued about partaking in, we were off to the reception. The Chadwicks knew how to throw a party.

Most everyone in Rosewood River had come out to celebrate Emerson and Nash, not to mention the out-of-towners from Magnolia Falls who'd shown up.

The DJ rallied everyone to the dance floor more times than I could count, and we had too much food and too many drinks and endless laughs.

"Damn, I've never been a fan of weddings, but I have to say, this one is next level," I said, as I took another bite of cake.

"Same, girl. I mean, I tied the knot wearing a T-shirt and jeans, so I'm clearly not the most traditional about this stuff. But the last few weddings I've been to have been fabulous." Ruby took a sip of her champagne as she sat on one side of me.

"I think you're becoming a little sappy, Rubes," Saylor said, her voice teasing.

"I'm so glad to finally meet you all. I've heard so much about you from Emerson, and of course, Beefcake has told me all about his girls back in Magnolia Falls," Henley said as she forked another bite of my cake since we agreed to share a piece.

And now we've devoured three pieces between the two of us.

"Hey, I thought I was Beefcake's girl," I said with a laugh.

"He's been collecting us like baseball cards." Demi chuckled.

"But look who his most special girl is," Savannah said, tilting her head toward the dance floor, eyes wet with emotion, as everyone cleared the space, and Emerson and Cutler made their way out there together.

"All right, we're going to take a moment for this special mother-son dance. Let's give it up for Cutler "Beefcake" Heart and his mama, Emerson Heart. Our beautiful bride chose this song especially for her son."

"Beautiful Boy" by John Lennon started playing, and there wasn't a dry eye in the place.

My God, what was it with these people? They were like an overflowing emotional tidal wave. I've never experienced so many feelings at one event.

"Oh my gosh, this is too much," Ruby said. Saylor handed her a tissue, and she dabbed at her eyes.

"It's okay to be in your feelings, Rubes," Demi said.

"They found their way to one another. That's why today is so special." Saylor sniffed several times.

"My hormones are still out of whack, and I can't handle much more." Savannah's words broke on a sob, and Demi wrapped an arm around her. We all started laughing at what a weepy mess everyone was and the fact that these two dancing together had wreaked havoc on our makeup.

We agreed it was fine, seeing as Emerson had this plan that at the end of the reception, we were all going to jump into the river together. Apparently, she and Nash had made a pact months ago that they'd end the ceremony with a celebratory wedding party swim, even though the weather was still chilly. We all agreed to take a quick dip with them. So, we figured our makeup wasn't going to last anyway.

I glanced around the room to see Rafe and Easton standing on each side of Nash as he watched his wife and son together with so much adoration.

Rafe must have felt my eyes on his because he turned right at that moment. His dark gaze locked with mine. His lips turned up in the corners, and he held my stare.

"Holy hotness." Ruby leaned her shoulder against mine. "That man just undressed you with his eyes right here in front of all of us."

A loud laugh escaped Henley's lips. "Yep, thank you. It's impossible to miss, right? But my stubborn bestie likes to say it's nothing serious."

"Listen, I own a romance bookstore, and I am here to say that the way that man is looking at you right now, that's what sells books right there." Saylor waggled her brows. "That is definitely not nothing."

The song ended, and the next thing I knew, Kingston and Rafe were dragging all the guys out to the dance floor as the DJ played "Sexy and I Know It," and everyone cheered and laughed as they made fools of themselves dancing.

"It appears she looks at him the same way," Savannah said.

"Yep. We've all seen that look before, Lulu." Demi stroked her little boy's hair away from his face as he slept in her arms.

"I'm not claiming he isn't hot. I'm just saying that it's temporary," I said with a shrug.

All of the women around me laughed in unison as if I'd just said the funniest thing they'd ever heard, and I gaped at them.

"Sorry. We've heard that before. I was the queen of temporary, my friend." Ruby patted me on the back. "And then I went to Vegas and got hitched."

"She really fought it," Saylor said. "But you can't fight love, or at least I hope you can't, because then my bookstore would probably go out of business."

"You guys are all really sweet with your hubbies. I admire it. I'm not against the whole fairytale concept…" I paused to take a sip of my bubbly. "It's just not for me. We're having fun until I move to Paris in a few weeks. I've got big plans for myself."

Saylor's gaze softened. "A man who loves you will never stop you from achieving your dreams."

I coughed over the sip I'd just taken. "We're not in love."

"You sure about that?" Savannah asked as she arched a brow.

"Yes. We agreed on all of these terms before any of this even started," I said proudly. "We put some rules in place, and we've stuck to them."

Now it was Henley's turn to cover her laugh with a cough as everyone turned to look at her.

"I'm sorry. I just—" She shook her head and looked at me. "Lu, your rules are ridiculous. You live with the man. You are in a full-blown relationship, and you're the only one who doesn't know it."

"Shacking up for the last few months was just part of the arrangement," I said, but I wasn't sure who I was trying to convince anymore.

Them or me.

"Listen, I'm a girl who has always had a plan. I get it. You like to fly solo, and you've got big things to do, and you should absolutely do them," Ruby said, holding her champagne flute up and clinking it with mine. "But just remember, if plans change along the way, that's okay, too. It's the most valuable lesson I've learned over the years. It's okay to change course."

"That was very philosophical, Rubes," Demi said with a laugh. "And I couldn't agree more."

"And remember this—you can't make the mile-high club if you're always flying solo, girl." Ruby winked, and everyone laughed again.

I looked up to see Rafe striding my way. Long legs closed the distance between us, and dark eyes held me hostage, as everything and everyone around me went silent.

He held out a hand. "Dance with me, Wildcat."

I glanced over at the women around me and smirked. "Dancing solo isn't any fun either."

As he led me out to the dance floor, I heard them whistling and hollering behind me.

Rafe pulled me close as "Thank God" by Kane and Katelyn Brown played through the speakers.

The dance floor was packed with couples dancing, and I looked over to see Easton and Henley beside me. I couldn't remember a moment that I'd ever felt such contentment.

Just out here on the dance floor with this beautiful man, surrounded by all these amazing people, and I was genuinely happy.

Rafe twirled me and then pulled me close as I slammed against his body.

My chest to his.

His hands moved to each side of my face.

And he leaned down and kissed me. Right in front of everyone.

And I surprised myself when I didn't pull back.

Instead, I tangled my fingers in his hair and kissed him right back.

29

Rafe

I've never been a man who worried about time. I've been too busy living my best life.

But time was suddenly my worst enemy. A brutal reminder that everything good comes to an end.

Not everything was meant to last forever.

Lulu was leaving in a week. We'd prepared for it. We'd talked about it too many times to count. How we'd remain friends after she left. How we'd go our separate ways as we'd be living across the world from one another.

"Do you think you'll want to get into a more serious relationship after I leave?" she asked, as if we were discussing the weather.

We were sitting on the couch, looking for a new TV series to binge.

We couldn't pick a series with too many seasons, because we only had a week to finish it.

I glanced at her wearing her cute white flowy crop top and jeans. We just had dinner with Henley and Easton, which ended down by the water. Henley had insisted on snapping a few photos of us as we splashed around in ankle-deep water, almost as if she knew it was all we'd have left to hold onto.

"I wasn't looking for anything serious before you arrived in Rosewood River, so I don't know why that would change when you leave." I shrugged as I moved to thrillers and mysteries and continued scrolling.

"I think you'd be a great long-term boyfriend, Rafael. You know, for someone looking for that."

I chuckled and looked over at her. "Thanks. You, too."

I tried not to let my irritation show. She was always inquiring about what I'd do after she left. For someone who wanted to make sure I knew she was leaving, she was awfully concerned about what I would do after she was gone.

"Do you think you'll be sad when I leave?" she asked.

I set the remote down on the couch and pulled Lulu onto my lap. "Something on your mind, Wildcat?"

"You know I'm an inquisitive person. I'm just wondering how you're feeling about everything. We obviously had this plan, and I just want to make sure you're still okay with everything."

"I'm okay. I mean, I wish you were staying longer, but I knew it was coming, and I know that going to Paris is important to you."

Her gaze narrowed, and she ran her fingers through my hair. "It's important that I stay focused, you know? It's a big opportunity for MSL. For me."

"I know that. I'm excited for you." I cleared my throat. "Not going to lie, I wish Paris and Rosewood River weren't so far away from one another."

She smiled. "Yeah, I know. But I did a long-distance thing before, and it was a disaster. I won't make that mistake again."

"I agree. I don't think relationships work if you can't spend time together. They're hard enough as is. And we knew what this was when we started."

"Exactly. It was always the plan to call it done when I left."

I could see the relief on her face that I was agreeing with her, and it felt like a kick to the gut.

A reminder that she was leaving, and she was happy about it.

I've never been in this position before, so it was foreign to me. Loving someone so fiercely but knowing that I shouldn't tell her. It would only complicate things.

So instead, I'd show her.

Sometimes, when you loved someone enough, you had to let them go.

So, I'd let her go and love her from afar.

Because that's what she wanted.

"So, we'll call it done, Lulu," I said, reassuring her. I tugged her head down and kissed her.

Our nights together were always intense.

The sex. The intimacy. The conversation.

Even sleeping with this woman was a mind-fuck because she'd always sleep curled into me, fitting beside me like she was made for me, like she couldn't stand to be even a few inches apart.

I tipped her back on the couch, hovering above her now.

"I need to taste you right now." I smiled down at her as her chest rose and fell.

The truth was, I wanted to memorize everything about her.

Every curve and feature on her gorgeous face.

Every inch of her beautiful body.

"You won't get an argument here," she whispered, her lips parted and eyes heated.

I kneeled between her legs and peeled her leggings down her body, taking her lacy panties with them.

"Arms up," I said, and she knew exactly what I wanted.

I wanted her bare for me.

I tugged her shirt over her head and tossed it to the floor, pleased to find she wasn't wearing a bra beneath. I ran my thumbs over her hard peaks before leaning down and kissing her.

Slowly at first.

Her lips. Her neck. Her collarbone. Her tits.

I moved down her stomach, to the apex of her thighs.

And then I buried my face between her legs and licked her from one end to the other.

She groaned as she bucked against me.

And I fucking loved it. Loved the way she responded to me.

"I want you to come with me," she said as I continued licking her. I raised my head, eyeing her curiously. "Touch yourself while your head is buried between my thighs."

Fuck me.

I tugged my joggers down, my dick throbbing as I wrapped my hand around it.

And I stroked myself as my tongue slipped inside her.

She tangled her fingers in my hair, grinding up against me as my tongue slid in and out.

She fell back onto the couch, and I watched as she arched her back, her tits bouncing just slightly, nipples hard enough to cut glass.

Her thighs squeezed the sides of my head, and I knew she was close.

I moved faster.

My tongue.

My hand.

Everything a blur.

I was so lost in this woman that I couldn't see straight.

She bucked against me before crying out my name as she went over the edge. I continued moving between her legs as she rode out every last bit of pleasure.

I was so turned on, it didn't take much.

One more stroke. "Fuck," I hissed.

I leaned forward, unloading myself onto her stomach as she watched, her honey-brown gaze sated and sexy.

We were both panting, and I let my head fall back as I caught my breath.

Once our breathing slowed and my eyes found hers, she smiled up at me. "That was much better than Netflix."

I barked out a laugh before moving to my feet, pulling up my joggers, and going to the bathroom to get a towel and cover it in warm water. I made my way back to the couch and cleaned her up before pulling her onto my lap and wrapping my arms around her.

"Hey, Rafe," she whispered as we sat in silence in the dark.

"Yeah."

"I don't think you should date Jolie. You're way too good for her."

I chuckled because this was Lulu's way of dealing with what was about to happen.

"You got it." I intertwined my fingers with hers. "And I'd like you to stay away from rock stars."

"That's not going to be a problem."

"It's our last weekend together," I said, reminding her that tomorrow was Saturday. "Is there anything you want to do?"

She pulled back to look at me. "You're keeping your horses out at Axel's stable, right?"

"Yep. I've got three, and they're gorgeous."

"I'd love to go riding. I don't think I'll be horseback riding in Paris." She chuckled. "How about you? Do you have anything you want to do?"

"I'd love to fuck you on a horse."

Her head fell back in laughter. Lulu Sonnet's laugh could end wars. It could cure diseases. It was that damn good.

"I'm a fairly adventurous girl, but that sounds a little challenging."

"I'd settle for the stables," I said.

"Done. We'll ride the horses, and then I'll ride you, Rafael."

"Sounds like a perfect Saturday to me."

I carried her down the hall and made our way into the bathroom off the primary bedroom. I brushed my teeth and pulled on some pajama bottoms before kissing her forehead and heading for the bedroom. Lulu took a lot longer to get ready for bed than I did. She used a ton of creams and oils, from what I could tell.

I grabbed my laptop and sat down on the bed to work on the numbers for my new client. Some possible investments that I was hoping he'd consider. He told me he had a few friends who were looking for a new advisor, so I was hoping to impress the hell out of him.

My phone vibrated with a text from my boss.

Joseph: *Hey. I know it's the weekend, but Denise booked us a last-minute trip to Cabo, and I'm flying out in the morning. I've got three meetings scheduled tomorrow that I'll need you to lead. I sent the files to your email for you to review tonight.*

This was classic Joseph. He didn't do the prep work for anything. He was the king of delegating. I glanced at my email and noticed he'd just sent the files now. At 9:00 p.m. for an 8:00 a.m. meeting tomorrow, followed by one at 10:30 a.m. and another at noon.

I'd be up all night if I even wanted to attempt to prepare.

I'd never treat my clients the way he treated his.

He did this often, and even though it pissed me off, I always came through for him.

He was my boss, after all.

Lulu strutted out to the bedroom, her hair tied up in that blue thing she called a scrunchie. She was wearing lingerie, a lacy, white one-piece contraption that didn't cover much.

Holy shit.

She had on a pair of black high heels, and she leaned against the doorway, taking

me in. Her eyes scanned my laptop and phone.

"Do you need to work tonight?" she purred, and my dick sprung to life eagerly.

It was my last weekend with Lulu, and I wasn't going to spend it working.

I closed my laptop and typed out a quick response to Joseph.

Me: *Not around this weekend. You'll need to find someone else to cover for you.*

I didn't apologize because I wasn't the selfish asshole who passed off my clients at the last minute.

I realized in that moment that Joseph Chapman was never going to help me break off on my own. He needed me too much. And if I kept doing my job and his, I'd never break off on my own either.

I silenced my phone and set it on my laptop as I placed them both on my nightstand.

"Hell no. I'm all yours, Wildcat."

• • •

I saddled up the horses and helped Lulu up. She hadn't been on a horse in years, but she was stubborn when it came to accepting help. She liked to prove that she could do everything on her own.

"Hey," I said, wrapping my hand around her boot that she'd just slipped into the stirrup. "This is my area of expertise. So stop fighting me on it and let me lead, all right?"

"Oh, there's nothing sexier than an alpha cowboy," she said.

Axel barked out a laugh as he grabbed a bale of hay off the back of his truck and dropped it on the ground. "That's going in the group chat. We're all going to start calling you Alpha Cowboy."

"If the boots fit," Lulu said over her laughter.

"Thanks for that." I shook my head and climbed onto Hank. I've had him for about four years, and he was a stunning stallion. Lulu was riding his brother, Bucky, because he was much easier to keep in check. "You ready?"

"I'm ready, Cowboy," she sang out excitedly, and I could hear my cousin laughing as we took off.

The mountains were gorgeous out here, and she hadn't gotten to explore this side of Rosewood River a whole lot.

I took her down my favorite trail that very few people knew about, and she surprised me when she stayed right behind me through the narrow passes. We'd been out for over an hour, and I used my hand to motion for her to come up beside me as I came to a stop. "This is my favorite spot out here. You've got the perfect view of the river and the mountains, and the smell of pine makes it even better."

"Wow. It's stunning. It feels good to be outside today. I missed riding. Henley and I used to ride all the time at boarding school."

She told me about her high school experience, and we laughed at how different ours had been. She went to boarding school, and I was here in Rosewood River, attending a school that all my siblings and cousins attended, as well.

"I try to ride as often as I can. It clears my mind," I said. "Haven't been riding much with keeping the horses out at Axel's ranch."

"You seem a little distracted this morning. What's on your mind, Cowboy?" she said, her voice laced with humor, but when I looked up, I saw the concern in her eyes.

Obviously, I was more than aware that this was our last weekend together, and that was weighing on me more than I thought it would. We still had several days until she left. I was being a pussy, and I wasn't proud of it.

But I sure as hell wasn't going to tell her that I was struggling with our brutal reality.

"I'm starting to think that Joseph is never going to support me leaving him. In fact, I would bet all the money I have in the bank that he's doing all he can to keep me right where I am."

"Yep. He's a professional cockblock," she said with a shrug.

I leaned forward on a laugh. "What the hell does that mean?"

"You know what a cockblock is. He's just doing it professionally. He's interfering with you breaking off on your own." She shrugged. "And there's only one reason that he would do that."

"And what is that, ole wise one?"

"It's because he knows how good you are. He needs you because if you leave him, people will follow. Employees and clients. So, in reality, he wants to hold you back because he fears you."

"Damn. You appear to know a lot about this."

"People have been trying to hold me back most of my life. I just see it more clearly now." She shrugged. "And you know what?"

"What?" I chuckled.

"Fuck Joseph Chapman. He's shown you who he is. The big question is, are you going to believe him?"

"It's not that simple, Lu. It's not the perfect time to jump. I need to get a few more clients to commit to me first," I said. I've been crunching the numbers and saving for this day, but I kept changing the number I'd need to pull this off the closer I got.

"A very wise man once said, if you know what you're worth, then go out and get what you're worth."

"Did you just quote Rocky Balboa?" I barked out a laugh.

"Damn straight. That man has helped me through half the decisions I've made in my life."

"I'll keep that in mind." I stared out at the water.

"I have a better idea. How about I take your mind off of things and race you to your stables? Then I'll let you have your way with me."

"Now you're speaking my language, Lulu Sonnet."

And she took off on Bucky, in the direction of my house.

This was definitely better than covering Joseph's ass for the millionth time.

And this was definitely my favorite way to spend a day off.

30

Lulu

I woke up feeling like the world was ending.

Yet it was the most exciting day of my life.

Was I sick?

I even tried playing the "Rocky" theme song on my phone while I showered in hopes that it would get me pumped up for my big day—that was a hard no.

I was in a slump.

I stared at my reflection in the bathroom mirror.

You're not sick. You're moving to Paris. You're living your best life.

Maybe it was the lack of sleep that had stolen the excitement from me. Rafe and I had stayed up most of the night having sex.

As if we were given a few hours to live, and we took advantage of every last second.

But neither of us were dying. We were just saying goodbye.

I never minded goodbyes in the past. I had always loved moving on to new things. I've always been the first one to leave family functions.

But leaving Rosewood River. Leaving Rafe Chadwick.

It didn't feel right.

Rafe came around the corner, holding my favorite periwinkle velvet scrunchie in his hand before setting it on the bathroom counter in front of me. "I don't want you to forget this."

He seemed perfectly fine this morning.

I was the one who was struggling.

Maybe he was happy to get back to his regular life. After all, this had started as a game.

Maybe he played along until the end.

I wasn't thinking clearly. Last night, when we were having sex, I swear he was about to tell me that he loved me. It was the way that he looked at me. The way his fingers had intertwined with mine, and he held my stare. The way he started to speak and then stopped himself.

Maybe I was misreading everything.

"Oh, thanks. Are you packed up?" I asked, my tone quieter than usual.

"Yep," he said, as he leaned in the doorway. "I'll head home after I drop you at the airport."

We agreed that he'd drop me at the airport, and we wouldn't make it a big deal.

But it suddenly felt like a really big deal.

We were both packing up and going back to our regular lives.

And that's what I asked for. What I wanted.

But come on, throw a girl a bone.

He could at least fake being a little sad. He probably already had a date for tonight.

Now, I was fuming as I applied my mascara and stormed past him. I slapped the scrunchie into his hand. "Keep it. It'll be something to remember me by."

He chuckled like this was a big freaking joke. "It's your favorite, Lu."

No. You're my favorite, you dumb, clueless boy.

"I have more than one, Rafe. It's not going to kill you to keep one thing of mine, is it?"

He wrapped his fingers around my wrist and tugged me against his chest as his arms came around me. "I know what you're doing."

"What am I doing?" I grumped, feeling the lump in my throat grow thicker.

"You're trying to pick a fight right before we leave for the airport. Of course, I'd love to keep your scrunchie. Hell, I'll keep anything you want to leave because I'm going to miss the hell out of you."

I sighed. That was better. "Thank you. I'm just feeling a little anxious."

"Yeah, it's a big move. But you're going to kick ass, and we both know it."

"That was really nice of your parents to have that going away dinner for me last night," I said, sniffing a few times as my head rested on his shoulder.

"It was nice. Everyone is going to miss you," he said, clearing his throat. "Henley was pretty quiet."

"She and I always hate saying goodbye." I shrugged, stepping back and swiping beneath my eyes as a single tear broke free.

"But she's coming to visit me as soon as I'm settled."

"That's what she said. That'll be fun." He stared out the bedroom window as if he were a million miles away.

I tried to shake off my funk as I followed him out to the kitchen, and he poured us each a cup of coffee. The framed photo of him and me out by the river that Henley had taken just days before was sitting on the counter. She gave each of us a copy. I already packed mine, and I stared down at his: my back to his chest as I tipped my head back and kissed him. We were both wearing white tops and jeans, the water splashing at our ankles, as if we were in our own world. We hadn't even realized she'd snapped the photo.

We looked happy.

Ridiculously happy.

My phone rang, and it was a FaceTime call from Jared. He, Clara, and Monique all came into view just as Rafe moved to stand behind me so we could both say hello.

"*Bonjour*, bitches!" they all shouted at the same time.

"Hey," Rafe and I said with a sliver of their enthusiasm.

"Oh, my, we're in a mood this morning," Jared said.

"No, we're fine. We just didn't get a ton of sleep." I shrugged.

"I'll bet you didn't, with that handsome devil keeping you up all night," Monique said as she waggled her brows.

Rafe and I stared at the screen with zero expression.

I had zero sense of humor at the moment.

"All right, girl, we're going to let you guys have your time together," Clara said, shooting a look at the two people beside her. "Call us when you land in Paris."

"Yes. We want to see you with a baguette in hand, and not Rafe's baguette," Jared said as he barked out a laugh and winked and then gaped into the camera. "Nothing? Really? Rafe's baguette gets me crickets? Very disappointed in you two this morning."

"It was funny," Rafe said, forcing a smile, as it was clear that he was now in an equally bad mood, too.

Grumpiness was contagious, and I was a super spreader.

I tried to rally. I dug deep. I forced a smile. One of those awkward smiles where you force your lips apart to show your teeth, but there's no joy there. That was the smile I was giving. "*Au revoir.*"

"All righty then. Talk soon." They ended the call, and Rafe dropped to sit, my scrunchie now on his wrist. And that earned the first smile of the day. I glanced at his other wrist, where he wore the bracelet I made him. He never took it off, and I was flattered because I knew it meant something to him.

I pushed to my feet and walked over to where my purse sat on the counter, bringing over my most recent creation that I made for Rafe this week. I was hesitant to give it to him now, as I'd planned to give it to him when I said goodbye at the airport.

"I was playing around with some new designs, and I made you one more." I handed it to him. "We're thinking of doing a men's line, and I thought I'd try this out and see what you think. It's a stainless steel-linked chain with a super rare brown ion stone. We'll make engraving an optional addition."

He studied the links and then the plate where I'd carefully engraved the name *Rafael*. "This is gorgeous. You used your new engraver."

"I did. You were my first."

So many firsts with this man. I always thought that my first love was a bust because I'd wasted it on someone unworthy. But the truth was, that epic kind of love that you read about in books, I experienced it for the first time with a man I never saw coming.

It was the first time that I've ever experienced anything like this.

Right place. Wrong time.

He clasped it around his wrist and stared down at both of them resting there together before pushing to his feet.

"I got you a little something, too. It's nothing big because I don't know how to make anything, so I can't compete with this," he said, pointing at his wrist as he handed me a pink gift bag.

I looked inside and pulled out a pair of periwinkle fuzzy socks.

A large bag of gummy bears.

A desk sign that read *Boss Lady*.

"You are speaking my love language right now," I said with a laugh.

"I know you hate it when your feet are cold, so you'll have these for the plane. And I don't think gummy bears are very popular in France, so you have these for the plane, and I stuck a ten-pound bag in your luggage already."

"Wow. You've thought of everything. And the desk sign is a nice touch."

"You need to let them know who's boss," he said.

"So do you. I know Joseph was pissed off about this past weekend, but you were born to lead, Rafe Chadwick. He knows it, too, and I think it terrifies him." I tucked the items in my carry-on bag as I spoke.

"We're not worrying about me today. Today is about you." He carried our coffee mugs to the sink and glanced down at his watch. "And we need to get you to the airport."

It was time to go.

I glanced around Easton's house and remembered that first day that I arrived. The way he startled the hell out of me, and I punched him in the throat.

It was the start of something beautiful.

And today was the start of a new chapter.

So, I pushed away the lump in my throat and tipped my chin up. "Let's do this."

We were both quiet on the drive, and I glanced down to see a slew of texts from Henley telling me that she missed me already.

I stared out the window, watching the mountains move by in a blur.

"Thank you for everything," I said, as he pulled up to the small airport and put the truck in park.

"You have nothing to thank me for. I'm the lucky one in this deal." He unbuckled my seat belt and tugged me onto his lap. "Thanks for the best three months I've ever had, Wildcat."

Don't cry.

Do not freaking cry.

You are not that hysterical airport girl.

You own your own business, and you're moving to Paris.

I wrapped my arms around him, just as someone pounded on the window. "You can't park here."

I jumped off his lap, and Rafe opened his door and came around to get mine before growling at the asshole who'd banged on our window for no reason.

"You do realize that no one is here, right, Burt?" Rafe hissed, as the man wearing an airport security outfit stood there with his arms folded over his chest.

"It's the rules, Rafe. Doesn't matter if I like you, I can't break them just for you."

Rafe glanced around. We were literally the only car in passenger drop-off.

He moved to the back of the truck and pulled out my luggage, and I slipped my backpack over my shoulders.

Rafe wrapped his arms around me and hugged me, not saying a word.

There was nothing left to say.

Burt decided that was a perfect time to blow a whistle right behind me, and we both startled.

"For fuck's sake, Burt!" Rafe shouted.

"I'm going to have to ticket you. My supervisor is watching," the older man said.

"It's fine. I'm going." I shook my head a few times as I looked at Rafe, blinking rapidly so that I didn't cry. "Thanks for the ride."

Thanks for the ride?

Those were my parting words.

He just stood there, watching me. "Yeah. Of course. Safe travels, Lu."

"It's about time," Burt grumped as I walked past him, and I flipped him the bird.

He ruined my airport moment.

I hadn't said anything that I wanted to say.

And I might not see Rafe for a very long time.

Who knew what would happen?

He'd probably be married to a beautiful woman, and they'd have equally gorgeous children the next time I saw him.

The tears were streaming down my face, and panic set in. I turned around as he was rounding the truck. I dropped my backpack on the ground and left my suitcase beside it, and I started sprinting.

"Wait!" I called out, and he turned around just as I lunged my body into his arms.

But he wasn't prepared, and he stumbled back, slamming into his truck as he went all the way down to the ground, with me on top of him.

He just lay there at the back of his truck, laughing. He pushed the hair away from my face. "Did you forget something, Wildcat?"

"I forgot to tell you that I'll miss you. That it's been the best three months of my life, too. And that's all because of you."

He pushed forward, sitting up before moving to his feet and taking me with him.

"It's fitting that you would pummel me when you said goodbye because it's kind of your thing." He smiled down at me.

Tears were running down my face now, and I didn't even care. Burt blew his whistle, and I turned around and shouted at him. "Zip it, Burt. Let me say goodbye properly, or I'll be taking you out next."

He held his hands up and shook his head. "Fine. You've got two minutes, Blondie."

"Oh, I see how you are. You only bend the rules for a pretty girl."

Burt held his hands up in the air and turned his back to us.

"Thanks for coming back," he said, swiping at the tears that were running down my cheeks with the pads of his thumbs. "Don't cry, beautiful."

I wanted to say it.

It was on the tip of my tongue.

I love you. I can't stay, but I love you.

"I'm sorry for the back pain that you'll wake up with tomorrow," I said, as my voice wobbled.

"It'll be worth it. Any pain I feel tomorrow, Lulu, it was all worth it." There was so much more behind that statement, and we both knew it. The pain in his back would be nothing compared to the pain we'd both feel waking up alone.

He leaned down and kissed me.

A security car pulled up with flashing lights, and Rafe rolled his eyes. "I'm going."

"I've got to get to my flight anyway. I'll miss you, Rafael."

"I'll miss you, too," he said, glancing down at his watch. "Go chase those dreams, Wildcat."

I nodded. And then I turned on my heels, grabbed my bags, and started running toward my gate.

Running toward my future.

But I knew in that moment that I'd just left my heart behind.

31

Rafe

One month and three days without her.

Too many drunken nights out with the boys where I moped like a pussy.

One disastrous pickleball game where I walked off the court.

This was my life now.

Nothing was going right. I moved back into my house, and though it was newly renovated and everything I wanted it to be, it didn't feel like home.

Nothing was the same without her.

Lulu Sonnet had turned my world upside down, and now I didn't know how to get back to where I was.

My job sucked. My boss was an asshole. And everyone around me was losing their shit that I was in a perpetual bad mood.

Clark: *Is the dark cloud still amongst us?*

Easton: *Yep. He stormed off the pickleball court yesterday because one of the Golden Girls asked about Lulu.*

Me: *That is not why I stormed off the court.*

Bridger: *It was because his necklace broke.*

Archer: *He's wearing a necklace now? Like a locket?*

Axel: *Damn. The dude is definitely losing it. Does he keep a lock of her hair in there?*

Me: *Ummm… newsflash. "The dude," a.k.a. the dark cloud, is on this text chain, assholes. And it isn't a necklace.*

Easton: *Toe ring?*

Clark: *Promise ring?*

Me: *Fuck off. Bridger's paddle hit me in the wrist, probably fracturing the bone, which is still wrapped in an Ace bandage, by the way. But he also clipped the link on my bracelet.*

Axel: *Who wears a bracelet to pickleball? I thought we were kidding about the jewelry.*

Me: *They're both sentimental, you clueless wankers.*

Clark: *Both? As in, there are two bracelets?*

Me: *Yes, one plus one equals two, numbnuts. And I like to call them wrist ice.*

Bridger: *For the record, I didn't hit you. Your wrist hit my paddle.*

Me: *You probably broke my wrist, and you snapped the clasp on my bracelet, and you have the audacity to blame me?*

Bridger: *Yep. You heard me.*

Easton: *He said that you were flailing your arms around like a little bitch, and you slammed into the paddle.*

Me: *This is insanity.*

Archer: *Agreed. Wrist ice is not normal.*

Me: *I'm talking about injuring someone and then blaming them and following that up with not apologizing.*

Bridger: *I'm sorry that you broke your man jewelry when you hit my paddle during your meltdown, you big baby. Happy?*

Axel: *That was very heartfelt.*

Archer: *Agreed. It felt very genuine.*

Me: *It was fucking lame.*

Easton: *The dark cloud is still clearly present.*

Clark: *Just call the girl and tell her that you miss her.*

Me: *<middle finger emoji>*

I've dealt with these moody bastards most of my life, so the fact that they couldn't handle me having an off day pissed me off.

"Hey, Rafe." My assistant, Clara, poked her head in my office. "Mr. Chapman wants to see you."

I internally groaned. The man had been relentless since I

declined to help him a month ago. It had been the first time in all the years I've worked here that I'd ever turned him down. Now, it felt like he was testing me daily with ridiculous tasks.

"You got it. Let him know that I'll be right in."

"Is your hand okay?" she asked, as she took in the Ace bandage I wrapped around it this morning because it hurt like a bitch.

"Yes. Bridger hit with me a paddle." I held it up, and she looked horrified.

"On purpose?" she asked.

"Probably," I grumped. "Well, he claims it was my fault."

"Were you guys boxing?"

"Nope. We were playing pickleball."

Her head tipped back in a laugh, and once she realized I wasn't joking, she straightened. "Oh, I didn't know that was such a rough sport."

"Yes. It's highly competitive." I arched a brow. "Hey, didn't you tell me your brother is a jeweler?"

"Yes. Are we looking for a ring for Lulu?" she asked.

Everyone at the office still thought that Lulu and I were together. I made it sound like she was just in Paris for a short time. There was no need for a formal announcement. It's not like I was dating anyone else.

Nothing about that appealed to me.

"Nope. Not quite there yet. But she made me a special bracelet, and the clasp snapped during the pickleball accident last night. I don't want to tell Lulu while she's away, and I was hoping to get it fixed."

"Of course, he'll be happy to fix it. Do you have it here?"

I reached into my pants pocket and pulled it out because I brought it with me, hoping to find a jeweler in the city. I handed it to her and told her to just let me know what it costs, and I'd take care of it.

I made my way to Joseph's office, where he was tipping back a glass of scotch.

It was ten o'clock in the morning.

"Hey, Joseph. You wanted to see me?"

"Yes, come in. Take a seat." He set his glass down. "Would you like a drink?"

"I'm all right. Thank you."

"So, I wanted to talk to you about Jordan Waters," he said, moving to the bar to refill his glass.

"What about him?" I asked, my voice coming out harsher than I meant it to. But he knew all that he needed to know about Jordan, as we'd already discussed it, so my guard was up.

"I don't know if you're ready to handle him on your own." He returned to his seat and swirled the ice in his glass. "I'm thinking that we should have him listed as my client, and you can assist where needed."

You've got to be fucking kidding me.

"Why would we do that? He's my client."

"Relax," Joseph said, holding his hands up like I was acting outrageously. "I'm not taking anything from you, Rafe. I'm doing this for your protection."

I barked out a laugh. I couldn't help myself. Nothing about this was for my protection. It was for his.

I just signed the largest client this firm has ever had, outside of my brother, Bridger, who also owned a billion-dollar company.

With both of these clients together, I could easily break off on my own.

Hell, I could do it just based on the family members I managed.

But signing Jordan Waters more than doubled my portfolio, and Joseph knew it.

He hadn't signed on any new clients in a long time. He counted on his reps to bring the big names while he was out on his yacht vacationing.

And there was no judgment coming from me. He built a business that allowed him to do what he wanted at this stage in life.

But trying to steal my client was something I had a problem with.

I'd heard that he did this kind of bullshit with other reps, but he hadn't tried it on me. My brother had been the most financially lucrative client up until I signed Jordan, and obviously, Joseph knew my brother would never agree to be moved from me to him.

Obviously, I had other clients that I worked with outside of my family, and there were many, but they didn't have the same amount of wealth as Bridger or Jordan, so he'd never bothered to get involved.

"Joseph, you're pushing your luck. He's my client. He and I have a relationship, and I don't need protection. Thank you for the concern." I didn't make any effort to hide my irritation.

"I gave you your break when you came here looking for a job right out of college. You had no experience. You owe me." He tipped his head back and polished off another drink.

"I owe you what? I've made you and this company millions of dollars. I appreciate you for taking a shot on me back then, but I assumed I'd thanked you by bringing on the most clients this firm has brought on since I started. Year after year, I've increased my client list more than any other associate here."

"And you are able to continue growing under the safety of my name. I carry the risk. I think it's in the best interest of this company if both you and I work directly with Jordan Waters."

Yes, Joseph had taken a chance on me all those years ago. And I'd repaid him tenfold by bringing in new clients and revenue.

But I knew without a shadow of a doubt that he was trying to either steal my client or find a way to keep me here, working for him.

Either way, my best interests were not part of this equation.

However, picking a fight with Joseph before preparing to make a move wouldn't be in my best interest either.

"I understand. How about you give me the weekend to figure out the best way to move forward, and I can speak to Jordan and come up with a plan?" I said, keeping my voice light and easy, as if I wasn't aware of what he was up to.

I needed time to figure it out.

"That's my boy. I knew you'd come around." Joseph moved to his feet, and I thought he was coming over to shake my hand, but instead, he made his way to the bar for yet another refill. The man was clearly not on his game, so I said my goodbyes and excused myself.

I stared down at my phone when I got back to my office, disappointed there wasn't a text from Lulu this morning. She and I texted a couple of times a week, but we kept it casual. She seemed to be busy and thriving in her new role. She was the first person I thought of every day when I woke up in the morning and the last person I thought of before I went to sleep.

I picked up my phone because she was the person I wanted to talk to right now.

Me: *What are you doing?*

Lulu: *Eating a baguette and some gummy bears for dinner.*

Me: *Well, you've got your fruit and carbs covered.*

I glanced at my desk, where her velvet scrunchie rested beside my keyboard, and I picked it up and rolled it between my fingers. The photo of her and me sat on my desk, like some sick fuck who was still in a relationship with her. I liked seeing her every day, and it comforted me.

Lulu: *What are you up to? Let me guess, you're on a hot date, and you're bored because she hasn't assaulted you once yet.*

She brought up dating every time we texted. I wasn't sure if she was just trying to plant a seed because maybe she was already getting out there, and she worried that I wasn't. But I tried not to overthink it.

Me: *Well, it's ten o'clock in the morning here, so I'm actually at the office. But I haven't been on a date yet, and I haven't been assaulted since you tackled me at the airport.*

Lulu: *Are you okay? Is something on your mind?*

Me: *I'm fairly certain that Joseph is trying to fuck me over. He wants me to hand over Jordan Waters. I think he's just trying to keep me here as long as he can.*

Lulu: *If I were there right now, I'd happily assault your boss on your behalf.*

Me: *Airport tackle? Pool ball to the groin?*

Lulu: *You know me so well. I think I'd knee him in the balls, followed by a chop to the throat, and then I'd tell him to stop trying to stifle you.*

Me: *I miss you, Wildcat.*

Lulu: *Miss you, too.*

Lulu: *But I wasn't done yet.*

Me: *Let's hear it.*

Lulu: *The reason he's trying to keep you is because he sees your potential. And so do I. That means you have the power to make demands of him. He doesn't want to lose you, so you can call the shots. Get yourself that corner office and ask for a promotion if you aren't ready to leave yet.*

Me: *That's not a bad idea. I'll take the weekend and think about it. Get back to your healthy dinner. Thanks for your help.*

I wanted to pick up the phone and call her, but we were supposed to be putting distance there. So we both just randomly texted the other, knowing that it would lead nowhere.

Lulu: *Always.*

And then I missed her even more.

32

Lulu

Paris in the springtime was everything I thought it would be. The people were all dressed to the nines, cigarettes in hand, as they enjoyed their evening glass of wine.

I came to the same café every night after work, and I sat alone, enjoying a glass of wine and wishing I was embracing my new life more.

I glanced at the couple beside me. They were laughing as they sat on the same side of the table, which seemed weird to those of us not from here, but they don't call it the most romantic city in the world for nothing.

The man was admiring her bracelet as he fiddled with her wrist.

My eyes nearly popped out of my head when I realized it was an MSL design she was wearing.

It was always exciting to see my designs out in the world.

But watching them reminded me how lonely I felt most days. It wasn't because I didn't have opportunities to be with other people. I worked in an office with several employees who worked in the French division of Laredo. My mother had made sure I had a gorgeous space to work, and there were several people my age working here, so it would be fairly easy to make friends.

I've been asked out by three men since I arrived in Paris.

First, there was Pierre, a buyer for Laredo. He was a few years older than me and very handsome by most standards, but unfortunately, most standards didn't work for me.

I found his chiseled jaw, ocean-blue eyes, and French accent to be subpar compared to my ex-fake boyfriend.

Apparently, I preferred small-town alpha cowboys now.

Then we had Jacque. He was the guy in my building who lived one floor down from me, and he liked to check his mail on the way back from his morning workout. I've never seen him in anything other than a pair of gray low-slung joggers with his chiseled chest glistening. He had long, wavy hair that was effortlessly sexy and had the confidence of a man who left women heartbroken in his wake.

Again. He did nothing for me. And it wasn't for lack of effort. I've been here for over a month, and he's asked me out no less than a dozen times.

I found creative ways to turn him down each time, and I felt absolutely nothing when I did.

My last offer had come from a man named Charles, who owned the deli on the corner. He was seventy-two years old and a lifelong bachelor who smelled like salami and cheese, but he claimed he'd be willing to change his ways for me. I told him I was focused on my career and sadly still hung up on a man back home.

Rosewood River.

He said he understood before handing me the Croque Monsieur that I ordered.

My phone rang, and I was thrilled to see Henley's name light up the screen.

With the time change, we hadn't been able to talk as often as we were used to, which meant we now only spoke once a day instead of many times throughout the day.

"Bonjour, Lulubelle," she sang from the other end of the phone, and I groaned in irritation.

"If I had a nickel for everyone who calls me from the States and says Bonjour, I'd be a very wealthy woman," I grumped.

"You already are a wealthy woman, so you'd be a wealthy woman with an extra quarter?" She chuckled.

"Jared is using some French language app and thinks he's fluent now. He only wants to speak French to me on the phone. The calls take twice as long because I have no idea what the hell he's trying to say."

"I see you're still a ray of sunshine."

"I've just been busy with work." I sighed. I've been in a foul mood for a few weeks now. "I mean, I love living here. It's the dream, right? I've just been in a bad mood since I got here."

She chuckled. "I was just there a few days ago, and I have to say, your moodiness seems to bode well for you in Paris. If someone gave you a cigarette, you'd look like you've lived there your whole life."

"I miss you," I said, reaching for my wine glass as I scanned the people walking by. "I loved having you here."

"Yeah, me, too. So what happened with the half-naked mailroom guy? Has he asked you out again?"

"Yes. This morning. I think the fact that I'm rejecting him is making him like me more. But he smells like patchouli oil and lemons, and the combination is offensive."

"You've always got the butcher, and you said he smells like salami and cheese."

I laughed for the first time since she left. Work was kicking my ass, and I was putting in long hours. I didn't even want to have a day off because it would be too much time to think.

To think about what I was missing.

"How's everyone doing there? Did you dominate at pickleball this week?" I asked, chewing on my thumbnail as I tried to figure out how to ask about Rafe without making it obvious.

"We won by the skin of our teeth because Rafe forfeited his game when he stormed off the court because Bridger's paddle hit him in the wrist and broke the bracelet you made him and possibly fractured his wrist."

"What? He broke his wrist?"

"We don't know. He refuses to go to the doctor because he's going to Magnolia Falls tomorrow for Beefcake's baseball game, and he said he'd have Emerson check it. Have you talked to him?"

"I mean, we send the occasional text messages. We just check in. We haven't spoken on the phone because what's the point? We both know we need to move on," I said, and my chest squeezed as the words left my mouth.

"You guys are both so stubborn. He's been a mopey bastard since you left, and you don't seem any better. So just pick up the damn phone."

"And say what? Hey, Rafael, I live in Paris, and this is the best thing I've ever done for my business. And you live on the other side of the world in Rosewood River, which is your favorite place to be. But maybe we can spend hours on the phone until you meet some local girl who can give you what you deserve."

"Wow. Okay, then. Sorry for the suggestion. I'm sure you'll both eventually stop moping and move on," she said.

"What does that mean? Is that your way of telling me that he's dating? Is it serious? I hope he's not with that biotch, Jolie. That will infuriate me," I hissed, and the dude sitting at the table beside me glared at me for ruining his romantic moment with his lover, and I scowled at him until he looked away.

"I don't think he's dating. Easton hasn't said a word other than telling me that Rafe is in a bad mood. He skipped Sunday dinner, which had everyone worried."

"Maybe he was on a date," I said because I couldn't not think about it.

Henley laughed. "You're insane. I think he just sits home alone, and we both know he's a social guy, so that's not really his style. But I think he's moping, too."

"Will you just find out how his wrist is and let me know please?"

"Yes, of course. I've got to get back to work. Love you big, Lu."

"Love you bigger."

. . .

The next few days were spent working long hours. We'd selected the fall line for the next season, and our first Paris launch would be in two weeks. We just wrapped up our meeting, so now we'd get to work on placing the orders.

I sat in my office, taking a moment to process the silver lining of my choice to move here.

Things were happening professionally. Everything I'd hoped for was underway.

But it didn't feel the way that I thought it would.

"You are a natural at this, you know that, right?" Camille asked as she stood in my doorway.

She was the head of marketing at Laredo and had helped me with a marketing plan for MSL. She and my mother had grown up together, so I've known her my entire life.

"Thank you. I'm learning a lot as I go."

"Life lessons are the best." She made her way inside my office and took the seat across from me. "Your mother is worried about you."

I sighed. "I think she and Dad might just like being worried about me. Because I've done everything that they wanted me to do."

I broke all ties to my loser ex, who had finally stopped trying to contact me, nor had he spoken about me in the press. I moved to Paris to make a name for myself and my company.

And they were still worried.

"Oh, darling, don't think for a moment that just because they're worried about you means they aren't proud of you. I speak to your mother daily, and you are her absolute joy." She leaned forward and used a hand to cover one side of her mouth. "I actually think she's a little jealous."

"Of what?" I said with a laugh.

"You have built your company from the ground up. Your mom never had that luxury. She was handed Laredo, and she never had a lot of options outside of taking over the family business," Camille said.

I never thought about that. I didn't want to take over the family business when I first graduated. I wanted to create something on my own. My mother never had a choice because her father got sick shortly after she finished university.

"Well, she's grown that business so much, along with Dad's help, too."

"Yep. I don't think she'd have been able to devote her life to something she wasn't as passionate about if she hadn't done it with your father."

"What do you mean?"

"Darling, life isn't about putting all your eggs in one Chanel bag." She chuckled. "It's about collecting lots of eggs so your life is balanced."

"I feel like I was a little lost right out of school and focused on the wrong things. I've really worked hard to find my niche, my calling, and prove that I could do something with it. But now I feel like I could easily drown in this. There aren't enough hours in the day, so I could just spend my life building my company, you know?"

"Balance is the great mystery of life. If you look at the people who spend their entire lives in an office, dedicating themselves to growing their career, you'll find they don't live very long. Because when they can't keep working those hours, they just wake up and find themselves all alone."

This is quite possibly the worst pep talk I've ever received, if that's what she's here for.

"Great. So now I'm going to die alone if I don't go on a date soon," I huffed.

She chuckled as she sat in the pink velvet chair across from me, wearing her chic black pantsuit.

"That's not what I'm saying." She came around my desk, taking my hands in hers. "You're young, Lulubelle. Your life is not going to give you everything you want if you spend all your time in this office. Your success won't mean as much if you don't have anyone to share it with. So now that you've figured out the business side of things, it's time to figure out who you want to share these moments with." She smiled down at me. "You're in the city of love, my darling. I have no doubt that you'll find it."

What if I already found it but left it behind to chase my dreams?

She kissed me on the forehead and walked toward the door.

"Camille," I called out just as she was about to leave.

"Yes, darling?"

"How did you know Louie was the one?" I asked. They've been married as long as my parents had. I always loved him because he was an artist, a painter. He was passionate and funny and full of life. He balanced out her serious demeanor, and they always seemed so crazy about one another every time I saw them.

Her red lips turned up in the corners. "I dated quite a few men before I met Louie when I first graduated university. Did you know I even dated a prince?"

"What? No. I never knew that."

"Yes. He wanted to marry me when we were still in school, but it never felt right." She shook her head and smiled. "I called it off, and then I met Louie, and everything was different. I just knew he was the one for me."

"How did you know?" I asked because I genuinely wanted to know.

"I knew pretty quickly, and there were a few signs that sealed the deal," she said, one brow arched as she crossed her arms over her chest, her gaze locked with mine. "First, he was the only man I ever missed when I wasn't with him. I'd think about him all the time when he wasn't around or if one of us was traveling."

"That's sweet." I gulped down the lump in my throat.

"Secondly, the man could make me laugh. No matter what was going on, he knew just what to say to get me going. He balanced me in a way I'd never felt before. And the older you get, the more you realize how important it is to laugh as often as possible. It keeps you young." She sighed before continuing. "And last, but certainly not least. He just got me, you know? When other people thought I was being outrageous or dramatic or I worked too much—whatever the hell they thought—he was the one person who understood me from the very beginning. And when you find someone who gets you, someone you connect with, you realize what a rarity it is, and you hold on tight."

"What if the timing isn't right?" I asked, my voice just above a whisper.

"Oh, darling, you worry too much. When you find it, you won't let anything get in the way."

But here we were.

Living on opposite sides of the world from one another.

And I hadn't even had the courage to tell him how I felt.

33

Rafe

B ridger stopped by to give me a ride to the hangar, as I was taking his helicopter to Magnolia Falls today. We all took turns going to Cutler's games, and I was looking forward to seeing him play.

I was ready to get away. I had a lot on my mind, and I didn't have a clue what I should do.

"You doing all right?" my brother asked, glancing over at my hand still wrapped in the bandage. It was pretty swollen and bruised, so I figured keeping it covered was a wise choice.

"I'm good," I lied.

"Don't bullshit me, brother. Tell me what the fuck is going on." He turned down Main Street, heading toward the hangar.

"I'm just off my game lately. I don't know what it is, but I'll figure it out."

He pulled into the parking lot and put the truck in park.

"How about you just tell me what's bothering you?" he said, surprising me because Bridger wasn't big on talking things out.

"Dude, this is not your thing." I unbuckled my seat belt.

"The helicopter isn't leaving until you start fucking talking, Rafe."

I turned to face him. "My boss is a dick. He's trying to steal my clients because he's afraid I'll leave him."

"Didn't you bring on more new clients than any other advisor this year? And don't you bring in the most revenue?"

"Yes."

"Well, then, this isn't much of a shock. He's holding on to his prize horse. Losing you will hurt him and his company." He shrugged.

"So I'm just supposed to let him shit on me?"

Bridger rolled his eyes, not hiding his irritation. "Of fucking course not."

"Bridger, I've got a raging headache, my hand is throbbing, and I'm not in the mood to try to read between the lines," I hissed.

"It's time, brother. Time to jump fucking ship. You've been ready for a while. He needs you. You don't need him."

"It's a big move."

"One you've been talking about and planning for the last eighteen months. You've saved a ton of money. Come on, brother. I've known you my whole life; this isn't you."

"This isn't me? What the hell does that mean?"

"You're the guy who doesn't overthink things. You're the guy who trusts his gut. You are not the dude who lets fear rule you." His gaze was hard, and I wanted to be offended, but I knew he was coming from a good place.

"Fuck you," I growled and reached for the door handle. "This is not fear. This is me trying to be smart. Making sure I have a plan."

"Rafe," he hissed. "Sit the fuck down and listen to me."

I shook my head, irritation coursing through my veins. I turned to look at him, arching a brow. "You wanted the floor. Go ahead and kick me when I'm down."

"I'm not kicking you when you're down, brother. I hate this shit. But I see what you're doing—hell, everyone sees it, and no one wants to say it. The whole family is worried about you. So I'm here trying to get you to pull your head out of your ass." He glanced out the front windshield and then back at me. "You were living with Lulu, and I've never seen you happier. But you let her pack her shit and move to Paris without so much as a fight. And now you're pissed off about your pussy-ass boss trying to steal your accounts from you, and you're doing nothing about it. You're afraid. For whatever fucking reason, you're fucking afraid."

I blew out a breath and ran a hand down my face. "What was I going to do with Lulu, huh? Ask her not to go? No one has supported her dreams before now, and I won't be that guy. This opportunity meant everything to her. I was trying to be a good guy."

"I'm not suggesting you ask her to stay. I'm suggesting you figure out another way to make it work. I think you're afraid she won't take you up on it, so you aren't even going to try. Instead, you're going to be a miserable fuck because you know you should have fought for her."

His words stung, and I glared at him before I let his theory sink in.

"I don't know if she feels the same way I do," I finally said.

"I'm not big on feelings, but even I couldn't ignore what was going on. She feels the same way, dipshit. So stop sitting on your ass and just fucking ask her because when it's too late, you're going to regret it."

"Thank you for the advice, Dr. Phil. I'll think it over." I smirked. "And as far as work goes, I just need to get my ducks in a row. Make sure the timing is right."

"The timing will never be right, Rafe. Let me ask you something." He reached for his bottle of water and took a sip before continuing. "Do you think I'm a smart businessman?"

"You started a tech company out of your garage, and you cleared a billion dollars last year. Yeah, I think you're a smart businessman." I chuckled because the question was ridiculous.

"I would not hand over my books and bank accounts to anyone I didn't think was brilliant. I don't give a shit if you're my brother or not. If you weren't really fucking good at what you do, I would not let you manage my finances," he said. "You are cheating yourself by working for someone else at this point. So make the move. He's shown you his hand. He has nothing left to offer you. Stop being fucking afraid, or I'll break your other wrist."

"At least you own that you broke the first one." I barked out a laugh. "Listen, I appreciate everything you said. And as much as I hate to admit it, I think you're right."

"Can I get that in writing, asshole?"

"Give me this weekend to work this shit out and get my head on straight. Thanks for talking this through."

He shocked the shit out of me when he grabbed my shoulder and pulled me into a hug. My older brother had never been an emotional guy, so I hugged him back, holding it a little too long because I knew it would freak him out.

He shoved me back with a laugh. "All right. Stop being a pussy and figure out your shit."

"Ah… ever the philosopher." I reached for the door handle and grabbed my duffle bag. "See you in two days."

I climbed onto the helicopter and thought about his words all the way to Magnolia Falls. I didn't doubt that he was right; I just wasn't sure how I'd handle it.

Once the helicopter was on the ground, I thanked Lars, the pilot.

Emerson was standing against the hood of her car as Cutler ran toward me.

"Uncle Rafe, I knew you'd come!" he shouted, as he launched himself into my arms. I tried to keep my wounded hand out of the way and held him with my good hand.

"Of course, I came, buddy. Wouldn't miss it for the world."

"Cutler, you need to be careful of Uncle Rafe's sore hand," Emerson said as she chuckled.

I knew Nash was working this morning, but he'd meet us at the game in a few hours.

"Oh, man. I totally forgot because I was so excited to see you," he said, looking at me with concern as he slid down to the ground.

"It's fine. I'll have your mama check it out."

"My mama is the best doctor in the whole wide world, and that's a big ole world," he said.

Emerson rumpled the top of his hair and hugged me. When she pulled back, she held her hand out to inspect my wrist. Her eyes widened as she took it in. "We're not going to even unwrap that here. Let's stop by the office. It's closed today, but I can use the portable X-ray machine to see how bad it is."

"We'll look at the pictures and see how bad it is, Uncle Rafe," Cutler mimicked his mother.

"Thanks, Dr. Beefcake."

"Dr. Beefcake!" He fell back in a fit of laughter as we drove the short distance to Emerson's office. She was the local pediatrician in Magnolia Falls, and my sister was one of the most brilliant people I'd ever known.

I sat down on the chair in one of her patient rooms, and Emerson sat on the little rolling chair and moved in front of me. Cutler stood beside her, acting like he was the chief of surgery, looking all concerned.

"Let's get it unwrapped first and see how bad it is," she said as she unwound the cloth carefully.

Her eyes widened, and Cutler gasped once the bandage was removed. It was a deep purple color and twice the size of my other wrist.

"Can we get a priest up in here? This is not good," Cutler said, as he rubbed his temples and sucked in a breath. I barked out a laugh and then winced when my sister pressed slightly on my hand.

"He's going to be just fine, my love." She winked at her son. "I'm hoping it's a bad sprain and not broken because surgery is no fun."

She carefully turned it over to inspect both sides.

"How will we know?" Cutler asked.

"I'm going to get the portable X-ray machine and take some photos. You stay here and keep Uncle Rafe company, and I'll be right back."

He reached for my good hand, his eyes filled with empathy. "How bad is it? You can tell me."

"Scale of one to ten, I'd say it's a six." If I was being honest, it wasn't what was bothering me the most right now. I had other things on my mind.

"A six isn't too bad. Did someone call Lulu and tell her that you're hurt?"

"Nah. She's living in Paris now. I don't want to bother her with something silly."

He narrowed his gaze. "Something silly? If Lulu was hurt, wouldn't you want to know?"

Fair enough. "Of course."

"Man, all my uncles are not very good with the ladies." He chuckled and shook his head. "I feel like I always have to tell everyone what to do."

"Lulu's not really my girl. We don't even live in the same country," I said. But I kept hearing Bridger's words in my head. Maybe I was afraid. I didn't want to pull her away from her life and her plans, so where could this go?

"Do you love her, Uncle Rafe?"

Damn. Beefcake was such a straight shooter.

"I do." He was the first person, outside of myself, that I'd admitted it to.

"So why don't you just live in the same country?"

"It's not that simple, buddy." I shrugged. "She really needs to be in Paris right now. It's a big opportunity for her. I can't ask her to give that up."

"Well, my mama said that you've lived in Rosewood River your whole life. If you can't ask your girl to move by you, how come you don't just move by her?" His little hand was holding my good hand as if he were trying to comfort me, and I just looked down at him with my jaw hanging open.

Great fucking question.

"Well, for starters, my house is in Rosewood River."

His head tipped back with a laugh. "Uncle Easton's house is in Rosewood River, too. That's where Lulu punched you in the throat that first day, remember?"

I chuckled. "Yep. I remember."

"Well, Uncle Easton moved out of his house so he could live with Henley. I remember he told me it doesn't matter what house they live in as long as they're together. I'm sure there are houses in Paris, Uncle Rafe."

Fair point.

"Right. But then there's my job to think about."

"Oh, man. They don't do the numbers in Paris?" he asked, his gaze searching mine with genuine concern.

"They do the numbers in Paris," I said, lifting one shoulder as if I were conceding.

"Or maybe you don't want to move cause you're afraid to leave your home. I remember Pops was worried when Mama was going to move away before he asked her to marry him." He looked up at the ceiling with a big grin on his face. "Man, I had to give Pops a talking-to about that."

"What did you say?"

"I said we could move wherever Mama went because we were a family, and we should be together. Doesn't matter where, right?"

"How'd you get to be so smart?" I asked.

"Well, my mama is a doctor, and she's real smart." He shrugged, and I laughed, just as Emerson wheeled the machine into the room.

"What's going on in here?" she asked.

"Just getting some life lessons from Beefcake."

"He gives it to you straight," she said proudly and set up the machine.

"He sure does." I winked at him.

And then I thought about everything he said. Everything Bridger said.

Everyone was right. I was miserable without her.

It was time to make some moves, and I was ready to make them.

34

Lulu

I'd just hung up the phone with Leonard, the CEO of Luxe, the largest department store in France. He informed me that the launch was beyond successful, and they wanted to double their original order.

I sent a message to Jared and the team, letting them know the good news.

They sent all sorts of emojis and celebratory memes, but it still felt a little empty.

I'd been burning the candle at both ends, and I was tired.

I stared down at the photo on my phone. The one that Henley took of Rafe and me. The one that also sat in a frame on my nightstand. My chest ached. I've never missed anyone in my life the way that I missed him. I physically ached for this man.

Rafe and I had continued texting, but we still hadn't spoken on the phone. He claimed he wasn't dating and sent me a selfie of him and Beefcake in Magnolia Falls last week.

He'd gone there for Cutler's baseball game, and the photo actually made me miss him more. I ran my finger over the phone screen as if I could touch his face.

I was been stunned to see how bad his hand looked. He held up the splint that Emerson had put it in. He told me he hadn't broken any bones; he just sprained it pretty badly.

We'd been texting even more since he returned home to Rosewood River, and he seemed to be putting in long hours at work. We both were. But I looked forward to our texts every day, like a desperate schoolgirl with a crush.

It was the highlight of my day.

And today, MSL had just had the biggest win since the day we opened the doors all those years ago, and none of it felt like a celebration because I couldn't talk to the person I wanted to share it with.

So, I sent him a text. I made the rule, and it was a dumb rule.

Me: *Hey, do you have time to talk?*

I waited.

And waited some more.

I picked up the phone and dialed. My stomach fluttered with excitement about hearing his voice.

It didn't even ring. It went straight to voicemail.

It was early in the States; maybe he was working.

Maybe he didn't want to get on the phone. That wasn't part of the deal.

I closed my eyes as I listened to his voice message. It

comforted me in the strangest way. It beeped, asking the caller to leave a message.

"Hey, it's me. Lulu. I know we don't usually call, but I just had something that I wanted to tell you," I said, and for whatever reason, a sob left my throat. Why did the Universe choose to turn on me at the worst times?

What the actual fuck?

I desperately tried to pull myself together and push the lump away. "I, um, I don't know what that was. I'm fine. Really good. I have good news. It's nothing bad. Oh my gosh, you probably think I'm calling to tell you I'm pregnant or something now." I cried some more because this was quite possibly the worst voice message of all time. "Oh my gosh. No one is pregnant. I mean, someone probably is, but it's not me. I was just calling to tell you that I had a great day—"

The phone beeped, and I waited for an option to delete the message, but it just said that the message had been sent.

This just went from bad to worse.

I sighed and sent another text message.

Me: *Hey. I accidentally butt-dialed you, so just go ahead and delete that message, please.*

Me: *Everything is good.*

Me: *I'm fine. Everything is fine.*

I let my head fall against the desk, my forehead resting against my notepad.

I pushed to my feet. It was still light outside, and I could go for a celebratory glass of wine and some dinner.

A few people from the office had invited me to join them, but that was over two hours ago, and I'd still been in meetings.

I waved goodbye to Marissa and Harvey, who were cleaning at the other end of the hallway.

And then I waved to Walt, the security guard who worked nights, as I walked outside, heading for the café beneath my apartment.

I sat at the table where I sat most nights and ordered a glass of chardonnay and a small charcuterie board. I set my phone on the table and willed it to ring.

The sky was just starting to darken, and I broke off a piece of bread and popped it into my mouth. I reached for my glass of wine when my phone vibrated.

Rafael: *Hey. Yes. I always have time to talk. Are you home?*

Relief flooded. This man always seemed to know what I needed.

Me: *I will be soon. I'm just at the café downstairs, having a glass of wine.*

Rafael: *Are you alone or on a date?*

Me: *I'm alone. I don't really want to date.*

There. I said it. That was a step.

Rafael: *You don't want to date anyone? Too busy at work?*

Me: *I can't really explain it. How about I tell you when I get upstairs, and we can FaceTime?*

I chewed on my thumbnail as I waited for a response.
Three little dots swirled and then disappeared.
Nada. Nothing. Zilch. Crickets.
Was he seriously going to ghost me in the middle of a serious conversation?

Was the idea of FaceTiming me that horrible?

"How about you explain it to me now? I'm starving," Rafe's voice called out as he strode toward me, long legs closing the distance between us. He had a duffle bag slung over his shoulder, looking sexy and confident.

I nearly knocked the table over as I pushed to my feet and lunged at him.

"What are you doing here?" I said as tears leaked from my eyes again.

Apparently, I was a big, fat crybaby now.

My inner feminist was appalled.

But my heart was too busy crying all the happy tears.

I buried my face in his neck, and he pulled back to look at me.

"You sounded upset on your voice message. Are you disappointed that you aren't with child?" He smirked.

"I just left that message," I said with a half-laugh, half-cry, shaking voice. "You were clearly already here. And not to worry, there are no little Chadwicks in the oven. That was just me being me."

"I know." He stroked the hair away from my face and led me back to my table.

I sat down and patted the empty seat beside me. "They sit on the same side of the table here."

He sat down and studied me for a few beats. "I already love it here. I get to sit on the same side of the table as you."

"What are you doing here?" I asked as I held my hand up and waved at our server, requesting another glass of wine for Rafe.

"Well, here's the thing, Lulu. I told you my bracelet broke during pickleball, and I had it fixed. But when I got it returned to me, I had a hard time getting it clasped with my damn wrist being out of commission. So, I was trying everything to clasp it, and it kept falling on my desk."

"Did you come here to tell me to change the way I make the clasp?" I said, my voice teasing.

He pointed at it on his wrist, showing me his name that I engraved on the rare stone. And then he slowly turned it over and looked up at me.

I love you.

I engraved it on there the day before I left. I wondered if he'd ever notice it, or if he did, whether he'd acknowledge it.

"I came to ask you if you wrote this," he said, arching a brow in question.

"You flew to Paris to ask if I engraved that on the back?" I chuckled. "Do you think it just came with the stone?"

"I flew to Paris because I was too much of a pussy to tell you that I loved you before you left. So I was hoping you weren't going to tell me that all the bracelets had this sentiment on them and that you feel the same way that I do." He smirked, and I smiled up at him because I was the happiest I'd been since I arrived here.

Because everything was better with Rafe Chadwick by my side.

"I wrote it because I love you." I shrugged.

He put a hand on each side of my face. "I'm fucking miserable without you."

"Really?" I shouted as our server set down another glass of wine.

"Well, you don't have to be so excited about it." He chuckled.

"I'm miserable, too," I said, swiping at the tears that continued to fall. "I mean, I love it here. The MSL launch was more successful than anyone had expected. But I can't enjoy it because I miss you."

I said it. I put myself out there. My heart was his to break.

"I'm so proud of you, Wildcat. You're exactly where you need to be." His thumb stroked along my jaw. "But I miss the hell out of you, too."

"Maybe we can make the long-distance thing work. Maybe I'll only be here for six months," I said, desperate to find a solution. "We could FaceTime every day."

"You shouldn't rush home in six months if things are going well."

"So, we just talk on the phone for the next year and try to visit every few months?" I asked, shaking my head because we both knew that that would never work.

"Here's the thing. I want to see you chase your dreams, and I can chase mine at the same time."

"I don't see how it works." I sniffed.

"Well, I'm currently self-employed, so I can work from anywhere, I mean, if you know of any good rentals in the neighborhood. This seems like a nice place to settle down for a few months or a year." He turned and took a sip of his wine as if he hadn't just dropped a bomb.

"Rafael." My voice was shaking.

"Yes?"

"What are you saying?"

"I'm saying that I can crunch numbers from anywhere. I was thinking of renting out my house and spending some time in Paris. It's the most romantic city in the world, right?"

"You're moving here?" I whispered, my heart racing.

"If this is where you're going to be, this is where I want to be."

"You would move here for me?"

"Lulu," he said, wrapping a hand around the back of my head and pulling me close. "I would move to the fucking moon to be with you."

My teeth sank into my bottom lip. "Did you really just say that in the most romantic city in the world?"

"I did. And I meant it. I can do what I'm passionate about while watching you do what you're passionate about, all while being with the woman I love. It's an easy decision for me."

"But you've always been in Rosewood River," I said, not even attempting to swipe the tears away anymore as they clouded my vision. "You love it there."

"I love you. And I want to be where you are."

"I want to be where you are," I whispered. "I love you so much, Rafe Chadwick."

"Then we're doing this?" he asked.

"We're doing this."

"How about I kiss the girl first?" And he tugged my chair closer, leaned down, and kissed me.

My hands tangled in his hair as I kissed him back.

I kissed him like it was our first kiss.

I kissed him like it was our last kiss.

I kissed him like it was a forever kiss.

Because this felt like forever.

And I was all in.

Epilogue

Rafe

I've been in Paris for the last four weeks, and time had flown. I kept several of my clients, giving them all the option to come with me or stay with Joseph, who owned a larger company than mine.

At least for now.

Most of my clients had chosen to go with me, including Jordan Waters.

I'd already let Joseph know that I was leaving the week before I came here to see Lulu. He'd been angry and tried to manipulate me, but in the end, he wished me well, and things had ended amicably.

I thanked him for the opportunity, but it was time to break off on my own. Bridger had been right. I'd let fear almost rob me of the woman I loved and the opportunity to grow a business that I owned.

This allowed me to work from wherever I wanted, and right now, I wanted to be in Paris with my girl. My assistant, Clara, had agreed to come with me, and she was thrilled about working remotely. I'd eventually hire more people, but right now, this would work.

My family was beyond supportive, and Lulu and I had decided not to rent out my house so we would have a place to stay when we visited, and we could play it by ear once we had a better idea of how long we'd be in Paris.

"I love starting my day like this," Lulu said as she straddled me, my fingers interlaced with hers.

The morning sun came through the sheer curtains in our room, creating a halo of light around her.

"Well, you do like riding stallions, right?" I gripped her hips as she slid down my erection.

She smiled, teeth sinking into that juicy bottom lip as she leaned down and kissed me.

We'd been making up for lost time since the day I arrived here.

She pulled back, looking down at me as we found our rhythm. Her perky tits bounced with every movement, and there wasn't a more beautiful woman in the world.

I never loved anyone the way I loved Lulu, and I never been more sure about my decision to move here since the second her eyes had found mine that night at that café when I surprised her.

"I could bury myself between your thighs every day for the rest of our lives," I said as she moved faster.

"Don't stop, Rafe," she said as her head fell back.

"Never."

We moved faster.

Our breaths were the only audible sound in the room, as the city had yet to wake.

My hand moved between us, knowing she was close. Knowing just what she needed.

Her back arched, and I could feel her tighten around me as my name left her lips on a cry, and she went over the edge.

I loved watching my girl fall apart around me.

I loved the sound of my name on her lips.

I bucked into her again.

And again.

And I followed her into oblivion.

"Fuck!" I shouted as she continued to move, both of us riding out every last bit of pleasure.

She fell forward, her wild mess of hair sprawled all around me as we both struggled to catch our breath.

I lifted her head and kissed her before rolling her onto her side and sliding out of her. I made my way to the bathroom to dispose of the condom before coming back over to lie beside her.

"Sex is even better in Paris." I chuckled.

"It was pretty impressive in Rosewood River, too."

"Agreed." I stroked her hair away from her face, grateful to finally be out of the sling as my wrist had healed a lot since I arrived. "I booked our flights home next week."

"I can't believe they made it to the Stanley Cup. Henley said everyone in Rosewood River is freaking out."

"Yeah. Clark has made a name for himself this season. He's playing the best he's ever played. I can't fucking believe my brother is a starter on a team playing for the Stanley Cup."

"He seems pretty calm about it, too," she said.

We FaceTimed with him several times over the last few days,

and we were looking forward to being there to support him.

"He does. I'm sure he feels the pressure, but he's pretty chill with that stuff. He's got the right temperament. But he's been a standout this season, which puts a target on his back with the opposing team. They'll be all over him."

We been able to stream his games here, so I been keeping track of his stats, and I was proud as hell.

"Well, you certainly aren't chill when he's playing," she said as a wide grin spread across her face.

"I can get a little intense, but weren't you the one that broke the remote when he got a bad call?" I teased.

"That call was bullshit."

"It was. But it's all part of the game." I pulled her head down and kissed her before she settled her cheek against my chest. "You've got a busy day today, right?"

"Yep. We've got some new designs to present, and then I've got a meeting with another large department store this afternoon. How about you?"

"I've got a packed day, but that's a good problem to have. And then I'm meeting my girlfriend at the café downstairs for dinner," I said.

"It's a good life, Rafe Chadwick."

"It's the best life," I said, scooping her up and heading to the shower.

We had fallen into a routine of showering together before work. Dinner out at different restaurants. She'd taken me all over Paris the last few weekends, and I'd gotten to know a few locals.

I didn't know what I'd done to deserve this woman, but I wasn't questioning it.

I loved her.

She loved me.

And I knew—just like my father had known about my mother all those years ago—that I'd found my forever.

She was a fierce, strong, sexy, kind, beautiful woman.

And she was all mine.

. . .

"I'm so happy you're both here for this," my mother said, squeezing my hand as we watched my brother skate out onto the ice for the last period.

It was a tie game.

You could feel the tension in the arena. This was game seven. Whoever won tonight would be the Stanley Cup Champions.

Lulu and I had returned to Rosewood River, and then we'd gone to all seven games, moving from San Francisco to Denver, where the Lions and Wolves battled it out.

They each had three wins under their belts, and heading into the last period, the score was five to five.

I'd say these two teams were equally matched.

My brother had scored two of the five goals tonight.

I never been more proud watching him do his thing on the ice.

We were playing at home, so the crowd had gone wild.

Cutler was sitting on Lulu's lap, acting like he was too nervous to sit on his own, but he winked at me a couple of times when she wasn't looking.

The kid was a huge flirt.

My sister was a nervous wreck, on her feet shouting most of the time and then pacing in between periods.

Nash was trying to keep her calm.

Melody sat on my lap, shouting every time the buzzer rang.

Archer and Bridger were quiet, and you could feel their nerves radiating off them. Easton and Henley were sitting beside us. Easton had already called out the ref for a bad call, and the crowd had agreed. My parents were just taking it all in, proudly wearing their Clark Chadwick jerseys, as we all were.

When the team walked out of the tunnel and skated onto the ice, the crowd roared. I had my arms around Melody, and my heart raced.

Clark glanced up at us and gave a fist pump, which caused all of us to scream wildly. I glanced over at Lulu. Her hair was up in her favorite scrunchie with one arm around Beefcake and her other hand in mine. She and Henley were leaning against one another, and I fucking loved how close she was with my family.

How much they adored her.

I missed them, missed my life here, but I was enjoying this adventure I was on with my girl more than I thought I would. I knew we'd be back eventually, and Paris was not a bad place to spend a couple of months or a year.

I turned my attention back to my brother as the buzzer rang. The puck was hard to follow as it switched from one player to the next.

Tensions were high as they ran the clock down.

Battling over and over to take the lead.

The crowd grew more anxious as players jumped from the bench to the ice every time they switched out their teams.

Players were sent to the penalty box.

Tensions were growing as time wound down.

No one had scored, and there were only twenty-three seconds left on the clock.

"Let's go!" Lulu and Cutler shouted at the same time.

The Lions had the puck.

Weston passed to Smith.

Smith passed to Jones.

Jones passed to Chadwick.

And before we could process what was happening, my brother was skating down the ice with a pack of Wolves behind him.

He was faster, but they were on him. He moved right unexpectedly, a play he told me they'd practiced. Everyone thought he'd pass the puck back to Jones, so the other team moved, and as a small opening appeared down the center, Clark took his shot. Two members of the opposing team were right behind him, doing what they could to stop the shot. Another player moved quickly on his left. Clark saw the opening, but they were too late to do anything to stop him.

The world seemed to stand still as we followed the black puck down the center of the ice in a blur. Right into the net.

The cheers were deafening. Everyone in the arena was on their feet.

My parents had tears streaming down their faces. Lulu was jumping up and down with Henley and Cutler.

Emerson had flung herself into Nash and then Bridger.

Archer and Easton were both bent over their knees as if they were unable to catch their breath. Axel was losing his shit with Aunt Isabelle and Uncle Carlisle.

And I had Melody on my hip as she pumped her little fist in the air.

The Lions had just won the Stanley Cup.

"I think he's hurt." I heard Bridger's voice as we all turned to see my brother down on the ice with his teammates around him. "That dude checked him low right after he took the shot."

The celebration continued as a medic came out and moved

everyone out of the way. I noticed my brother standing awkwardly on his leg as they helped him to his feet, and he held his arms up to let everyone know that he was okay.

The crowd roared in celebration, and we continued cheering, though I saw the concern on everyone's faces around me.

He hadn't walked off that ice on his own.

"Is he okay?" my mother asked.

"He'll be fine. He just scored the winning point to win the Stanley Cup," my father said proudly.

But Bridger and I shared a knowing look. Clark didn't skate off the ice; he was assisted by his teammates, with a medic staying close by.

We were hugging, and the girls were all crying as we continued celebrating all the way down to meet Clark, where friends and family were invited to wait.

"That was amazing," Lulu said, her hand in mine as we walked through the tunnel. "Do you think he's okay?"

"Hockey's rough. He's been hurt many times, and I'm sure he'll be fine. He'll have some time off now, so that'll help. I'm so glad you were able to come with me to support him," I said, leaning down and kissing her hard.

"I go where you go, Chadwick."

"I like the sound of that, baby."

We waited for a while outside the locker room with other family and friends who were gathered to wait for the players. The team started coming out, one at a time, hands in the air as we all cheered. There were media and photographers there, and from what we heard, everyone was going crazy out in the street.

I wouldn't have missed this for the world.

When Clark came out, holding himself up on a set of crutches, a deafening cheer left the crowd. He held his hand up and searched for us before the crowd made room for him to make his way over. My mother hugged him and then asked if he was okay. It wasn't the first time we've seen Clark in crutches, but I could tell by the look on his face that he was in pain, even if he was doing a good job of acting like it wasn't a big deal.

"Yeah. Just tweaked my knee, and I don't want to make it worse, so I'll keep the pressure off for the next few days."

"You did it, brother," I said. "Congratulations."

"Yeah, glad you were here, man. This is a once-in-a-lifetime," he said as he leaned down and kissed Lulu's cheek. "Glad both of you are here."

"You're a stubborn ass, Chadwick," a woman with long, wavy blonde hair said, and my brother narrowed his gaze.

"How about we just enjoy the moment?" Clark hissed, not hiding his irritation.

"A wheelchair was advised until we know what's going on, and you blatantly ignored me." She crossed her arms over her chest and glared at him. "It's your career, so you have no one to blame but yourself."

She stormed away, and we all gaped at him.

"Who is that?" Lulu asked.

"Coach's daughter, Eloise. She just joined the team as our official trainer and physical therapist, and she's making a big deal out of a knee injury I've sustained more than once."

"Dude, you weren't able to skate off the ice. Perhaps a wheelchair isn't a bad idea," Easton said, keeping his voice low.

"She's been here for all of two weeks, and we just won the fucking Stanley Cup!" Clark shouted, as the crowd started cheering again. He was handed a bottle of champagne, and he tipped his head back and chugged it as Easton and I both moved closer to make sure he was stable on those crutches.

Everyone was caught up in the moment, but I didn't miss the way Clark's gaze moved to his coach's daughter when he passed the bottle to his teammate. She glared at him, and he winked before turning his attention back to a reporter who was shouting questions at him.

He assured Easton and me that he could stand just fine with his crutches, and he fielded questions for the next twenty minutes.

I wrapped my arms around Lulu, her back to my chest, as we stood and watched the guys continue to pop champagne and shoot it at the crowd.

I glanced around to see everyone that I loved standing here, watching him with pride.

And then Lulu tipped her head back and looked at me. "Paris is great. But I can't wait to be back home this time next year to cheer them on again."

"Home is wherever you are, Wildcat."

She turned in my arms and pressed up on her tiptoes and kissed me. "Love you, Rafael."

"Love you more."

Acknowledgments

Greg, Chase & Hannah, I love you endlessly!

Willow, thank you for being such an amazing friend! I am so happy to be on this journey with you! Love you!

Catherine, thank you for knowing when I need you to call me and for giving me a mug that reminds me daily just how much you love me! LOL! Love you!

Kandi, I am so grateful for our daily chats and for your friendship! Thank you for always listening and encouraging me when I need it most! Thank you for being such a bright light in my life! Love you!

Meghan, forever grateful for YOU! Thank you for ALWAYS being there for me and for being such an amazing friend! I took my phone off of Do Not Disturb for you! Traveling without checking a bag is going to be more challenging! LOL! Love you!

Elizabeth O'Roark, so thankful for your friendship. Thank you for always making me laugh when I need it most! Love you my sweet friend!

Pathi, endlessly thankful for you! Love you so much!

Nat, I am so incredibly grateful for you! I love being on this journey with you! I would truly be lost without you! Love you!

Nina, I'm so grateful for you! Thank you for believing in me and being such a support to me! Love you so much!

Jessica Turner, I'm so grateful for you! Thank you for believing in my books! Seeing them in bookstores is a dream coming true, and I'm so thankful for you! Xo

Kim Cermak, so thankful for you! Thank you for having a thick skin on my behalf and for the Bravo chats and the endless support! Love you!

Christine Miller, Kelley Beckham, Tiffany Bullard, Sarah Norris, Valentine Grinstead, Meagan Reynoso, Amy Dindia, Josette Ochoa, Ratula Roy, Jill McManamon, Jaime Guidry, Megan Cermak, and Emma Walczak, I am endlessly thankful for YOU!

Tatyana (Bookish Banter), thank you for being such a support, and teaching me your savvy tricks! Love you!

Abi, thank you for beta reading and for going back through each series to help me create new bonus material! Love you so much!

Janelle (Lyla June Co.), thank you for your support and friendship! I'm so grateful for you!

Paige, you make mother proud. I love you so much and I'm so grateful for your friendship!

Stephanie Hubenak, thank you for always reading my words early and cheering me on. Our daily chats are my favorite.

Kelly Yates, so thankful for your friendship! I love our chats and I'm so thankful for the endless laughs!!

Logan Chisolm, thank you for being the best booth babe at the signings, and for creating the most gorgeous videos for me! I'm so grateful for you!

Kayla Compton, I am so happy to be working with you and so thankful for YOU!

To all the talented, amazing people who turn my words into a polished final book, I am endlessly grateful for you! Sue Grimshaw (Edits by Sue), Hang Le Design, Sarah Sentz (Enchanted Romance Design), Christine Estevez, Ellie McLove (My Brothers Editor), Jaime Ryter (The Ryters Proof), Julie Deaton (Deaton Author Services), Kim and Katie at Lyric Audio Books, thank you for being so encouraging and supportive!

Crystal Eacker, thank you for your audio beta listening/reading skills and for always coming through for me when I'm in a state of panic! So grateful for you my sweet friend!

Erika Plum, thank you for the adorable bookmarks! You nail it every time!

Jennifer, thank you for being an endless support system. For running the Facebook group, posting, reviewing and doing whatever is needed for each release. Your friendship means the world to me! Love you!

Rachel Parker, so incredibly thankful for you and so happy to be on this journey with you! My forever release day good luck charm! Love you so much!

Natasha, Corinne and Lauren, thank you for pushing me every day and being the best support system! STFU! Love you!

Amy & Rebecca, I love sprinting with you so much! So grateful for your friendship! Love you!

Monica, my Bravo sister...our chats are a highlight in my day! Love you!

Sammi Sylvis, always thankful for you! Love you!

Gianna Rose, Diana Daniels, Rachel Baldwin, Sarah Sentz, Ashley Anastasio, Kayla Compton, Tiara Cobillas, Tori Ann Harris and Erin O'Donnell, thank you for your friendship and your support. It means the world to me!

Mom, thank you for being my biggest cheerleader and reading everything that I write! Ride or Die! Love you!

Dad, you really are the reason that I keep chasing my dreams!! Thank you for teaching me to never give up. Love you!

Sandy, thank you for reading and supporting me throughout this journey! Love you!

To the JKL WILLOWS... I am forever grateful to you for your support and encouragement, my sweet friends!! Love you!

To all the bloggers, bookstagrammers and ARC readers who have posted, shared, and supported me—I can't begin to tell you how much it means to me. I love seeing the graphics that you make and the gorgeous posts that you share. I am forever grateful for your support!

To all the readers who take the time to pick up my books and take a chance on my words...THANK YOU for helping to make my dreams come true!!

*Don't miss the exciting new books
Entangled has to offer.*

Follow us!

 @EntangledPublishing

 @Entangled_Publishing

 @EntangledPub